I could not put *Summer on the Black Suwanee* down! The words flowed as if I was standing right there beside the old black river itself. All the characters were well defined and the setting was so well described that I could almost hear the flow of the river and see the faces of each person, whether they portrayed good, bad or evil itself. I hardly ever make time to read a book in one day. *Summer on the Black Suwanee* was an exception!

Cheryl Cannon
elementary education teacher, retired
multi-year recipient of Teacher of the Year

This jaw dropping, emotional roller coaster will surely touch your heart. Not only does it teach you the value of friendship and family, *Summer on the Black Suwannee* radiates the awareness of God and His presence, as well as exemplifying that no matter what circumstances you may face He will always be with you through the trials of life.

Abigail Lonadier
Reader
15 years old

Summer on the Black Suwanee is not only a thrill ride of a story for young people, but it also addresses very real issues of spiritual warfare, occult practices, demonic activity, and the power of prayer. It is at once enlightening and encouraging without skirting around the issues of consequences of making ill-advised decisions.

Dr. Ricky Roberts
Senior Pastor, True Light Ministries

Jennifer Odom has hit the jack pot again. *Stranger with a Black Case* offers young adults (and older ones) tantalizing mysteries, gripping suspense, and a heartwarming story of friendship and community. At the same time it acquaints them with faith, forgiveness, prayer, purity, and redeeming love—all essential keys for triumphing over the pain of parental absence or abuse, as well as the dangers and disappointments of their everyday lives. What a difference in our world if teens everywhere could absorb and apply these truths!

Elsie Bowman, MSW, LCSW
Owner and lead psychotherapist
Common Sense Counseling

In *Stranger with a Black Case*, Jennifer Odom has written a worthy successor to *Summer on the Black Suwannee*.

Earlene Carte
Principal
First Assembly Christian Schoo

Not fair! Where's Book 3? Tears and cheers caught me up in the book's home town family drama where I wasn't quite sure what would happen next. *Stranger with a Black Case* kept me guessing. With so many books and movies that end badly or sad this is a joy to read and become involved in. The life lessons are well taught and the prayerful depictions had me reevaluating how I personally pray. I have a feeling the adventure has just begun.

Sylvia Swain
Educator

STRANGER WITH A BLACK CASE

Published by WordCrafts Press
Cody, Wyoming 82414
www.wordcrafts.net

STRANGER
WITH A
BLACK CASE

a novel of suspense

JENNIFER ODOM

WordCrafts

Dedication

To a great encourager, Mickey Cruey, a great man who despite all odds fights the good fight of faith.

1996—Paradise Trailer Park, Gaskille, Florida

Twin demons, Callous and Tyrant, drifted along the train tracks near Paradise Trailer Park. Invisible to Vinnie the teen, they followed his big sneakers over the gravelly cross-ties that lay underneath the rusty rails. In fact, they'd clung to his entire family and kept them company for at least six generations.

Callous gave Vinnie a shove and snickered when the kid tripped over a cross-tie. *C'mon, get a move on.*

Behind Vinnie followed the girls, age ten and nine, and the boy, barely six—all followed by their own imps.

Callous's tongue flicked out and he licked his beady golden eyeballs in anticipation of this assignment.

The demons slipped along like toads, blending well with the growth of hickories, the gloom of the trailer park, and the shady orange groves beyond.

Callous snorted. People rarely discerned the demons. The few who saw them mostly belonged to *Him*. Mostly. But not all.

A discerner might glimpse a shadow or a fleeting presence. Or actually smell the demons. They might hear a noise—or feel creeped out—but hardly ever witnessed their form.

And *others—how naive...*

Callous laughed and glided on. *Others* just thought of demons as fairy tales. He flicked out his tongue and licked an eye.

Tyrant, as warty and hideous as Callous, leaped along beside him. He raised his fist and slammed it down on Callous's head like a sledgehammer. Then like nothing had happened, he went right back to the obnoxious habit of drumming his padded fingertips together. A long string of drool drained from one side of his wide smile.

Callous hissed. "You're ugly, bub."

"Shut up, squirt. Keep movin'," Tyrant said, as nasty as usual. Yet he, too, seemed eager to get started on the long-term assignment.

The demons shared broken-toothed grins. Sulfurous breath rolled out between the amber crags.

"Here come the inferiors," Callous said and tipped his head in the other demons' direction.

There they slunk, behind the three kids, Subjugation and his pale pack of friends. Not *friends*. They all hated each other. Callous let out a hiss.

Tyrant yelled out, "Keep to the rear, you scum-bodies. Don't even think about coming up here with the likes of us."

Subjugation, as pale and milky as a glob of glue, hung his head. He thrust out his belly and bottom lip.

Callous cackled. "Pasty-faced albinos. Feel unwelcome," he hollered, and wiped more drool from his neck.

Tyrant slammed his fist down on Callous's head and laughed.

Callous growled, but returned his attention to the teen. *Just wait.*

Those trailer park mothers had no idea about Vinnie, the one to whom they'd entrusted their kids to walk them across the highway.

He licked his eye again and laughed.

Three ducklings with a fox.

2

Nine-year-old Freckles stepped over the train tracks. Pony Tail, her big sister, and Dougie, their six-year-old neighbor, clung to her heels.

They slid down the embankment behind Vinnie. At the bottom he crawled under a clump of wisteria vines beside the electric pole. Freckles peeked through the vines as he twisted a large tin can out of the dirt. She'd seen him jam it there, upside down, the day before, his secret smokes and matches hidden underneath, as dry as a gopher.

She shuddered. Vinnie wasn't supposed to be smoking, but those strong hands could hurt her if she tattled.

"Keep ya mouth shut," he'd warned. A bunch of times.

Now Vinnie laughed and pointed to a patch of grass, "Sit down in a line. Right here." Only his order sounded more like, "Siddowninaline. Right. Here."

The rails behind him curved sharply to the south, away from town. He squatted. "You pipsqueaks ever hear of dragons? This here's what dragons do," he said, drawing on the cigarette and letting the smoke flow out his nose.

Freckles glanced at the sweaty underarms of Vinnie's t-shirt. *Nasty old high-schooler.* Other teenagers talked about showering after gym class. She'd heard them. They sprayed on Right-Guard and smelled pretty nice at the end of the day. But not Vinnie.

Tobacco smoke billowed around his head and across their faces. It mixed with the strong perfume of wisterias he had stirred up. Freckles coughed and so did Pony Tail and Dougie.

"Now listen here," Vinnie said, cutting through their noisy

3

chorus. "You guys can't be goin' home with no tobacco breath. So just sit there. Watch and learn."

He knelt in the grass, flicked an ash, and grabbed a fat stick. Raising it up, he leaned toward Freckles and Pony Tail, and whacked it against the ground. His eyes were wide and scary.

She edged backwards. So did the other two.

Vinnie could do that; change into a wild-man. All it took was a wrong word from one of them.

"Don't go gettin' smart on me and tellin' no grownups about this here. It's our little secret."

She and Pony Tail shook their heads. No, they wouldn't tell. Vinnie stared at Dougie who finally caught on and shook his head, too.

Vinnie leaned closer and squinted his eyes. He waved the stick in front of his face. "And you, Miss Big-Mouth. I'll get your mama with this if you go tattlin'."

Would he stab Mama? Hit her in the head? Mama was little enough. Vinnie could do all those things.

He tipped her chin up with the stick until she had to stare down her nose at him. "Then I'll hurt your sister. And your little pee-pants friend here—Dougie." He snorted. "Dougie! What a baby-name."

Freckles gritted her teeth. "He's just a first-grader."

He glared and went on. "Uh-huh. And first graders shouldn't be wettin' their pants anymore." Vinnie pointed an accusing finger at Dougie. "It fits you, don't it, runt?"

Vinnie leaned in to Freckles' face. His moist breath stunk like tobacco. "And ain't you nine? Nine-year-olds don't tattle, neither."

Unable to open her mouth, Freckles spoke through her teeth. "I won't tell."

Her eyes turned toward a lone figure passing over the tracks where they had just crossed. Vinnie let go of her chin and twisted around to see too. A shaggy-haired boy of about 12 approached through the grass with a notebook under his arm.

It was Robert, Freckles' friend.

Her arm shot up and she waved.

Last Sunday he, Freckles, and Pony Tail had built a fort in the orange grove behind the park. Robert's mother, cooking supper over at the migrant tents, had hollered for him to come eat. He'd run off and left his father's pocket knife under the trees.

Freckles kept it, guarding it in her dresser drawer. Her secret. She'd return it on the weekend when they played in the groves again. Hopefully he hadn't gotten in trouble for it.

She had another secret stuck to her mirror—one she kept from her nosy older sister, Pony Tail. It was a heart-shaped piece of notebook paper taped behind a card that said FE + RC. RC for Robert Cavasos, her friend who had just crossed the tracks.

The train's whistle blew as it drew near. Beside her, Pony Tail and Dougie waved at Robert, too.

The ground rumbled under Freckles' legs.

Vinnie stood, and like a hawk watching a rabbit, he eyed the approaching brown-haired boy.

He stepped toward Robert, his words barely audible over the train's increasing clamor. "Well, lookee there, if it ain't little *Roberto,* that trashy migrant boy." Vinnie turned back to the kids. His next words, to Dougie, came across loud and clear. "Come on, Pee Pants, let's see if this big old fifth grader can give you a ride."

Dougie scooted backward in the grass.

Freckles elbowed her sister. "We shouldn't have waved. Not with Vinnie around."

In one long stride, Vinnie jerked Dougie up by the arm and dragged him, kicking, squirming, and squalling, in Robert's direction. Freckles and her sister huddled together, their hands over their mouths.

She should have hollered at Robert to run away.

"Shuddup, Dougie," Vinnie said as the train swung around the curve and totally drowned out the first grader's complaints. Vinnie twirled Dougie around and poked a finger in his face. Freckles could only read his lips. "Stand right here and don't move."

Vinnie planted himself in Robert's path with his feet apart. The stick whopped against his leg.

Two demons attached themselves to Vinnie's back. Tyrant slid his warty hand along Vinnie's arm and guided his hand. *"Put that little migrant in his place,"* he whispered. *"Migrants don't deserve to be here in your trailer park. This is your place. You show him."* On and on Tyrant whispered.

Callous reached inside Vinnie's chest and covered his heart with a hard hand. *"No pity. Show no pity. Who cares about those pipsqueak kids behind you. It's time they learn about life, learn to suck it up."*

Robert, the migrant, hesitated, then stopped. His eyes flitted from the stick to the girls, then dropped to the grass by his feet. He dipped his head.

In one swift move, Vinnie dropped the stick and wrenched the migrant boy around by his wrist. Robert's notebook fell to the ground. His chin flew up. Vinnie had yanked Robert's hand behind his back and shoved it up between the migrant's shoulder blades.

Robert grunted but said nothing. The notebook's carefully inscribed pages twisted in the sand beneath the bigger boy's foot.

Vinnie's cigarette bobbed between his grinning teeth, as he thrust the boy's wrist down against his side.

The migrant cradled his tender arm, but Vinnie's hand, as fast as lightening, had already clamped like a vice over the top of the boy's straight hair. Vinnie wrenched the boy's head around like a faucet.

Robert's eyes widened.

Vinnie let go and shoved a finger in Robert's face. "Let our little friend get up on your back." Before Robert could move, Vinnie grabbed Dougie by the seat of his now wet pants and swung him up on the migrant's back like a sack of potatoes.

Vinnie seized his stick again. "Giddy up! March, donkey!" He swatted Robert's tan shorts and marched him back and forth next to the hurtling train cars. And each time he stumbled in the gravel Vinnie smacked the migrant's legs.

"Stop it! You're hurting him!" Freckles screamed. Pony Tail wailed beside her. But the roar of the train swallowed it up. Dougie, bucking and kicking for Robert to step away from the moving train, bawled to be let down, but Vinnie kept them inches from the barreling cars.

His voice disappeared in the rumble, but Freckles could read Robert's lips as he begged Vinnie, "Let him get off, he's scared."

Vinnie responded by whopping him harder on the back side. Robert winced, his knees nearly buckling. Then Vinnie took the cigarette out of his mouth. When Robert turned his back, Vinnie leaned down and touched the red embers against the boy's calf.

7

The migrant's leg jerked away. It flew against the rusty iron wheels of the train.

Robert's bloody scream curled up for a brief second, pierced the thunder, then snuffed out as the wheels gobbled up his feet, flipping his body two, then three times.

Dougie, unhurt, rolled into the grass where he lay bawling.

Freckles screamed. "Robert!"

Their friend lay face-down and twisted on the broken granite, the shadows of empty freight cars flickering over and over across his motionless body. The racket and metal-on-metal scrape and grind of the wheels faded to distant echoes. Robert's lower legs and feet lay mangled between the rusty rails.

He had to be dead.

Paralyzed, Freckled clutched her sister. What had just happened? She sobbed silently, burying her face in her sister's hair.

Pony Tail squirmed away and Freckles glanced toward Vinnie. He stumbled through the grass with a face as white as his rolled up tee shirt sleeves. Dougie scrambled toward them on all fours then stood.

Vinnie ran one hand over his wide-eyed face. "W-we all s-saw him s-stick his leg under the train, right, kids?" He rubbed the back of his hand under his nose, and teetered there, his eyes flitting to the trees, the sky, but not the body. "You s-saw that, right?"

The girls nodded, leaning their heads together. Dougie, at Vinnie's elbow, whimpered and wiped his nose and cheeks across his arm.

"Y'all go on home now. But lookee here," he said, retrieving the stick and holding it, all trembly now, against his trousers, "We saw what we saw, right?" Again they nodded. "So get on home. I-I'll call the cops and get him some—some help."

Then, as if on second thought, he lowered himself beside the entwined girls. His eyes bugged out like a crazy man's. Even worse than before.

He squared his jaw and snatched Dougie's to his side. His white-knuckled fist stabbed the end of the stick into the ground.

Dark words seeped through his clenched teeth.

"I said I would get help. So. Don't. You. Say. Nothin'."

Vinnie jerked the stick from the dirt. Sand rained over them as he waved it in their faces.

"Remember, I can kill all your mamas."

And he would. Vinnie would.

Tyrant and Callous clapped for glee and slithered up against the trembling teen. They clung tight. *We're right here with you,* Tyrant mocked. But the kid couldn't hear him.

Tyrant reached around the front of Vinnie and gave Callous a high five. *I'll take it from here.*

Subjugation and two ugly buddies slipped in behind the three little kids and followed close as they high-tailed it back to their trailers. They'd keep the kids' mouths shut up for a long long time.

Chapter 1

Tony reached for the back door knob but froze in place. The muffled conversation filtering down the hall from Mom and Dad's bedroom had stopped him on the way out. Neither parent nor Maria the maid had noticed him slip back in the house to grab his forgotten phone. And this conversation was clearly none of Tony's business. He tilted his head to hear more.

Dad's distraught words were clear. "'I'm comin' after ya,' the guy tells me. Then he hangs up the phone."

Mom responded to Dad in her usual calm voice, but Tony couldn't make out a single word of it.

Tony rubbed his hand across his neck. He both loved and hated his dad, Vinnie Vinetti. And right now, it wasn't so much Dad's words, but the outright fear in his voice that gave Tony that prickly sensation. Tony bit his lip. Dad had never sounded this way before. He was always tough—he never backed down. And now to hear him scared—scared out of his wits...

Dad's words echoed down the hall again. "What am I supposed to do, Nancy woman? When some guy says 'I'm comin' *after* ya' then hangs up the dang phone? What am I supposed to do, stand around here with a gun out the window? Like some cowboy?"

Dad never asked Mom's advice. On anything.

A quiet click down the hall indicated the door was now shut.

Tony frowned and strained to hear more. But silence filled the air.

Forget this. What could he do about it—except worry. He reached for the knob as he tried to wrap his head around the situation.

Trouble was nothing new to Dad. Trouble was his middle name. Lots of times Dad had expressed his concerns. But Dad was an arm-twister, a wheeler-dealer from way back. He riled up everyone. People disliked him. Hated him even. But they still did business with him. Yet there was something about Dad that kept them coming back for more. Go figure.

But nobody'd ever threatened Dad.

And now for someone to say "I'm comin' after you" and then hang up... A tightness gripped Tony's chest as he stepped outside and closed the door. His legs moved woodenly as he made his way to the train station.

Knowing Dad, until Tony was invited into Dad's business, he'd just have to keep his nose out of it and his ears open.

Saturday, 9:45 AM, August 2019

"Come on. Take me up to Citra. Please." Emily wheedled as Mom cracked an egg into the skillet.

All Emily wanted to do was talk Mom into going—so she could see whether the old place had fallen apart or was abandoned like she'd imagined in her dream, or whatever that was. And make sure Dad wasn't dead or something.

Mom said nothing, just pinched her lips together and dabbed at the eggs.

"You really *ought* to. Look at what you put us through last month—nearly getting us killed up there on the Suwannee."

11

Mom would not answer.

"Remember, I told you I didn't want to go to that awful retreat thing. But no, you had to sign us up anyway."

Mom raised her eyebrow and flipped over the eggs. She pointed her spatula at Emily. "Stop it. And lower your voice, young lady. We've settled all that. I've apologized to you. And you forgave me." She turned back to the stove. "Now please. Quit bringing it up."

But that wasn't the point. And Mom knew it.

Emily's cell phone vibrated in her hand. *Tony.* Her new best friend. She'd call him back in a minute. She pushed her cereal bowl away. "It's just this one time. Please take me out there. Citra's not that far."

"Emily!"

"I have to see our old place. You won't even need to get out of the car."

Mom glared into the frying pan.

"And you heard Grandma. Healing takes time. And family. And Dad's *my* family, even if you *are* divorced."

Mom turned off the stove and placed her hands on her hips. "Grandma doesn't know everything. You remember that."

Evidently Mom hadn't really changed.

"Well, she's right most of the time."

Mom arched an eyebrow.

"You never listen to her."

"Never listen to who?" Grandma, in her nightgown, stood in her kitchen doorway. She yawned. Emily and Mom had been living with her through the divorce, the second marriage, and past the imprisonment of Emily's stepfather, the lout. Grandma's two-story house sat in the town's historic district and was a whole lot better than their tiny wood-frame rental out in Citra.

Mom ignored Grandma's comment. She wasn't finished. "He's a drunk, Emily. A no-good, stinking drunk. We will not go out and check on him."

"I'm not asking you to check on Dad," Emily yelled.

Grandma crossed to the sink where she poured herself a cup of coffee. She kept her thoughts to herself.

"Tell her, Grandma."

"I'm staying out of this."

Mom scooped her eggs onto a plate and brought them across the room.

"He couldn't change while we were married," she said, plunking the dish onto the table, "so why would you think he's changed now? It's a waste of time."

"Stop yelling, Mom."

"You're setting yourself up for disappointment. Whether Grandma Rene agrees or not."

Grandma turned. "I haven't even expressed my opinion."

"Don't talk back to me." Mom stopped and turned. "Not you, Mother. I mean Emily."

"You should have stayed with Dad," Emily said. If she had, her stepfather Bill wouldn't have been around to attack and nearly rape her. Thank goodness Mom came home at lunch that day and stopped him. And they sure wouldn't have ended up at that creepy place on the Suwannee.

"Emily! Didn't you hear a word I said? We're not going through this again."

Emily thumped her spoon on the table. "I'm only asking for a peek. I want to see the house. Nobody has to get out. We don't have to talk to anybody. Can't I just look? Please?"

Grandma finally spoke. "A look? Could it hurt? It's just a house."

"Come on, Mom," Emily pleaded. She had her foot in the door now. "Dad won't see us. We'll just coast on by."

"He'll think I'm still interested, Emily. And I'm not. I don't want him coming around."

"He's *my* dad. Don't you think I have the right to see him?"

"Wait. I thought you wanted to see the house."

Emily stood and threw her wadded napkin in the trash. "I should have run away. Then I could have at least seen him." She marched out of the room and left Grandma staring at Mom and Mom staring at the table.

"All right. All right." Mom's voice followed Emily through the dining room. "But not today. And not right away. All I'm saying is I'll think about it."

Emily smiled and pushed open the screen door. She headed for the porch swing to return Tony's call.

Saturday, 9:59 AM, August 2019

Late! Now, instead of strolling leisurely by the old house as he'd hoped, and maybe catching a glimpse of the girl, he had to rush things up.

The bearded man, in his rubberized work boots, hustled past the big house in the historic district of Gaskille. He smoothed his bed-head with one hand and gripped his lunchbox and the other. He patted his pocket. Where was a dad-gummed comb when he needed it? If it hadn't been for that new alarm clock and the AM/PM mix-up, he'd be right on time. He couldn't afford to lose this new job. If he only had a car...

As he passed the big house's front walk, *Slam!* It was the front door. His head twisted ever so slightly, but *face forward!*

He caught himself. The last thing he needed was for the people in there, the girl, the mother, the grandmother, to catch him watching. His heart beat faster as he forced his face to the front and adjusted his sunglasses and hat. Only his eyes turned.

And there she strolled, a wavy-haired beauty, out to her front porch swing. Maybe the clock mix-up was worth being late after all.

Late as he was, one more minute wouldn't make a difference. At the corner electric pole he slipped inside the thick azaleas and parted the branches.

One minute. That's all. He'd allow himself one minute.

The sun blazed over the back of her corn-silk hair as she dialed up her cell phone. Her head tipped slightly as she spoke into it. He couldn't make out a word. Not that he was an eavesdropper.

The minute ticked by and he let go of the branch. *What a sweetheart.*

But duty called. He must get to work.

Saturday, 10:00 AM, August 2019

Tony pushed the broom along the wall outside the train station. His heart sat like a chunk of iron in his chest. Since Dad's conversation with Mom yesterday, Tony couldn't shake the memory of his fear-stricken voice. He'd hardly seen Dad since then, just long enough to get yelled at this morning, but the sound of it played over and over Tony's head.

Dad—*Vinnie*—always top dog, *afraid* of someone? Would someone really try to kill him? As much as Tony didn't get along with Dad, he didn't wish the man dead, for goodness

15

sake. Vinnie was his dad—even if he did follow Tony out of the house yelling this morning about him growing up and getting a real job instead of odd jobs like this at the train station.

Let Dad try to get a job these days.

Fine lot of gratitude Dad was showing with all that yelling. And here was Tony worrying about his welfare and not even know what in the tar was wrong. *Doggone it!*

Tony reached the end of the platform, shoved the sand hard over the edge, and turned to come back the other way. A movement on one of the train station's many benches caught Tony's eye. A strange man, still parked there an hour since his train dropped him off, showed no sign of budging. There he sat, focused on that small, worn paper spread across his knee.

The phone in Tony's pocket vibrated. He ignored it at first—but kept his gaze on the weird stranger with the violin case and beat-up jeans. He couldn't put his finger on it, but something was off about this guy.

He propped the broom against the train station's post and fumbled to catch his call. He hoped it was his girlfriend— girlfriend from *Tony's* point of view at least. He hoped the feeling was mutual.

The screen said *Vinnie*.

Rats. Tony let out a snort. *Not Dad again.* After all that yelling this morning, he was the last person on earth Tony wanted to hear from. It never failed with Dad; everything Tony did was wrong these days. If Tony answered, Dad would add some new chore or criticize with a sarcastic comment. He never took time to listen or ask why. About anything.

Tony sighed and lowered the phone. On the other hand, if he rejected Dad's calls he'd lose the phone, his lifeline. And boy, would Dad love that.

The phone buzzed again.

He lifted it up, but the vibrating stopped. Oh, well. He'd tried, hadn't he? Tony tucked the device under his arm, hooked up the ear-bud, and dialed Emily.

Her line rang just as another, much louder sound split the air—the long, multi-toned blast of a train horn. As engines approached they slowed around the bend of the Gaskille station. Tony glanced toward the trees that hid the curve, anticipating the sight of the train's front end bursting into view.

On the other end of the phone line, Emily answered his call right away as if she'd been waiting. He gave a fist-pump. Maybe she *did* like him back. He was certain about his feelings for her. The first time he'd spotted her was toward the end of the school year when she'd walked into his Math class as a new student. Instant adoration.

Just wait till she saw the surprise he had in store for her down at the town square.

Tony pulled the mic close to his lips. "Emily, you should come down here. The guy I told you about? He's still hanging around. He still hasn't called a taxi that I know of. Doesn't check his watch. Or his phone—if he even has one."

"Maybe he's going over to the Snack Station to eat. What's he carrying?"

Tony eyed the raggedy backpack and black case. "Not a lot." Some kind of instrument case.

"Homeless?"

Tony, a detective at heart, had plans to join the FBI one day. At the very least he'd be a sheriff's investigator. He'd turn 15 in a few days. College and a real job were only a few years beyond that. He needed all the experience this small town could offer. "Thin frame, ponytail, brown jacket with too-short sleeves. Homeless? *Maybe.* But something about him doesn't quite jive with the homeless look." Not to mention his mannerisms...

Emily said nothing.

"Doesn't *act* the part. Whatever that means. I'm not sure I can put my finger on it."

"You're probably making something out of nothing," Emily said. "He's waiting to get picked up, probably."

"Doesn't look like it. Since he got off that train I've cleaned all the windows, picked every shard of broken glass out of the rocks, and swept the platform. Everything. He hasn't moved an inch."

Static crackled over the phone as the latest train passed right on through the station without stopping. Freight only.

"Hit-men carry violin cases—with guns," he said. "You know, the Mafia. I bet you anything he's not a musician. Something's off. He's too clean cut, too *something*... and that paper he keeps studying. It's probably a hit list."

"Maybe you could stop a crime. Be a hero."

Little did she know. "Emily?" he whispered, moving a little further away from the man. "Hey, seriously. Maybe we should keep an eye on him."

Maybe this was the guy coming after Dad.

The rumble continued around him. It was an awesome feel and sound. Tony's favorite thing about the train station.

Emily's voice garbled over the line.

"Hold on a minute," he yelled. "I can't hear you."

He picked up the watering can and moved it beneath Bert's window. Tony wasn't supposed to water the hanging plants until all the guests left the station. Too much drainage and danger of slipping.

18

But the stranger on the bench wasn't going anywhere fast. He was holding up the works here. And Tony had things to do.

Tony swept around the door again and brushed a couple of previously missed cigarette butts into the dustpan.

"There's definitely an art to this, picking up trash with one hand on the broom. You know, not just everyone can do it." If he didn't keep talking Emily might hang up.

Emily didn't respond.

"But this guy won't leave. And if I don't water these petunias before I go, they're gonna be dead. And Bert will blame me. They're already half-wilted."

"Do I hear whining?"

"I need to get to the square." Yeah, and make a payment to the goat-cheese guy for Emily's surprise.

"Right, Farmer's Market day. I should go too."

All the more reason for him to go now.

Behind him the station doors opened and a couple of long-legged college-age girls burst out on the platform dragging overnight bags, most likely coming from the Greyhound Bus station around the building. They headed in the direction of The Snack Station. Their cigarette smoke swirled across his face, and he coughed as one of them looked right at him and flicked a half-smoked butt where he'd just swept.

Rude chicks. Tony frowned and swept it up. At 15, well, almost 15, Tony knew not to act like that. Hey, maybe Bert would notice and pay him something extra today. Bert was famous for his tight-fisted ways. Summer jobs were scarce, and Tony's odd jobs, all voluntary, depended on the generosity of his benefactors.

Well, at least it worked. Tony was earning something at least.

He searched for more trash and tried to keep the conversation going. "What did you and your mom find when you went shopping last night?"

"Good news. Grandma's getting me a poodle."

No way, that would ruin everything.

Tony leaned the broom away from his body. "Poodles are sneaky, don't you know? They climb on furniture and eat off the table. They run out the front door, and disappear when you go out to get the newspaper."

He glanced at the stranger who met his eye, smiled and looked away. A niggling thought stirred in the back of Tony's brain. He'd just about put his finger on the...

"Tony, why are you saying all these bad things? You know I want a dog. I miss Beggar. I miss him so bad I could cry."

Beggar, a stray Australian shepherd had saved her life at the Suwannee.

"But a poodle? Come on."

Tony stepped close to the window and checked out the stranger in its reflection. He felt like a spy.

"I love poodles. They're so pretty with their prissy little puffs. Besides, don't you like Lusmila's little poodle?"

"Yeah, but..."

"Forget it, Tony. I thought you'd be happy for me."

She might get mad and never answer his calls again. "All right, I'll shut up."

"Well, how old is that weird guy?" She had circled the conversation back to talking about the stranger.

"Give me a sec. I'm trying to act casual so he won't think I'm staring." Tony strode away down the line of freshly painted columns, peering into the trash cans, glancing back out of the corner of his eye every now and then. "Maybe 30 or 40."

"Take a picture."

"Heck no." Tony swatted at an imaginary fly. "You think I'm crazy? He'll open up that gun case and shoot me in the head."

Tony strode back to his watering can. Stranger or not Tony had to get this job finished and pick up his pay. He lifted its long spout over the plant nearest the bench. As expected, the water drained straight through the dried-out coir-lined container. He danced backward, out of the way.

The trickling drew the man's attention and he grinned toward the puddle that grew near Tony's feet before returning his gaze to the paper in his hand.

Tony turned away.

"Oh boy, he just looked at me," Tony whispered. "Water just poured through the basket. He probably thought something else." They laughed again. But that little something in the back of his brain was starting to click.

The man's lips seemed to be moving. "I'll try to get a peek at his hit list." Tony circled around to the window behind the bench and eased close enough to almost read it, but a breeze caught the note, and the man slapped it against his leg.

Tony jumped.

The stranger sat up straight and stretched his arm across the back of the bench.

"Forget it." Tony took the broom and stepped through the station's antique doors and into the building. He nodded over at Bert seated behind his well-worn counter.

But the thought in the back of Tony's brain had finally made its way to the front. "That's it!" he whispered to Emily. "It's the hands. His..." Tony clamped the phone below his jaw and opened the broom closet door. "It's the hands—they're manicured. And the heavy gold bracelet. I know gold, Emily. It's real gold."

"Wha...?"

Tony stuck the broom inside the closet door and shut it. He stepped to the desk so Bert could pay him. Most people were pretty generous with teenagers, and Tony'd found a niche with Bert. The man, though tight-fisted, hated any kind of physical labor, be it sweeping or picking up the broken glass out of the rocks, and was more than happy to chip in once a week for Tony's help at the Station.

Bert shoved a few dollars across the desk. "Thanks, Tony, good luck on your project."

"Thank you, Bert."

"Project?" Emily said. "What project?"

But that was one thing Tony couldn't tell her. He thrust the bills into his envelope and poked it back in his pocket. He needed to get this money down to the square, and most of all, keep his secret. "Oh, just something I'm saving up for."

When Tony stepped back out on the platform, the bench was empty.

But there on the floor lay the man's battered note. Tony stepped toward the bench and picked it up. It was some kind of list. *Freckles, Pony Tail, Dougie, Vinnie, The Rock.* All except for The Rock they were names of people. People Tony knew.

But Vinnie? His *dad?*

This had to be about Dad's phone call.

"I'll tell you what I think, Emily. Our stranger's a well-paid assassin or something. A hit man. A crazy man. But now he's gone. I'll meet you down at the square."

Tony ran off the far end of the platform with his arms flying and landed on the grass. A nesting duck flapped and hissed from under a nearby bush. "Sorry duck."

The street was empty.

Now what? A hit man on the loose? He'd have to find out where the guy went. Put a stop to whatever he was up to.

Chapter 2

The engineer guided his CSX freight train north, accelerating through long stretches of countryside along the tracks paralleling US 301. His fingers rested over the horn's lever. He squinted into the morning sun that streamed over the lakes and pastures and watched for the next series of whistle boards up near Hawthorne.

On US 301, the highway that led him through Hawthorne, Florida, Vinnie hurtled south in his shiny black Mercedes Benz Coupe. Brand new, and just the color he'd wanted. He smiled. What a cinch it had been to twist the dealer's arm and get the new car.

Saved $30,000 just because of some dirt he had on the old weasel. It paid to get around, didn't it? Paid good money.

He lifted his chin and grinned sideways at his handsome reflection on the darkly tinted windows. He leaned closer and checked for bits of lunch stuck between his teeth. With a twist of the rearview mirror, he examined himself from that angle, too. Uh-oh. Maybe it was time for a whitening.

He switched from a studious expression to a friendly one and admired himself once again. "You're lookin' pretty good, kiddo."

He ran his fingers through his hair and settled against the leather seat.

The steady sun beat down. It was enough to blind him. And

he'd forgotten his shades. He adjusted the air conditioner. Too hot today.

It was a perfect day for a dip in his spotless blue pool. Maybe he should call Tony, that no-good son of his, and get his lazy behind started on the pool. Not one bug, not one leaf did Vinnie want to see when he lowered himself into those crystal waters. Ahh, he could feel the coolness rising over his body right now.

He glanced in his rearview mirror. Where was all the traffic today? With one hand on the wheel, he reached for his cell phone in the console. Training his eyes on the screen he jabbed his thumb across the keys until Tony's number displayed. Great gadget, this phone.

He dialed. It rang twice. He raised the phone to scratch an itch on his nose. But blast it all, the thing quit ringing. He'd lost the call. Hung it right up.

What Vinnie should do was put in a list of names and numbers like Tony had. He gazed down at the tiny buttons and tried the number once again. His left hand guided the sleek Mercedes. It loped over the hills and highway as it approached the empty crossroad.

Then *Waaaooowwww! Waaaooowwww!* A train horn blared. Right there in his ear. Electricity shot through Vinnie's limbs. A train on the highway? He dropped the phone. Grabbed the wheel. Wrenched it off the road.

He hit the intersection. The Mercedes twirled. Barely missed the downed crossing gate. Nooo, what a mistake! There was no train on the road. *These* were the tracks. How could he have been so stupid? The train bore down. A one-eyed monster with a vibrating light. Huge. The horn blasted again. *Waaaooowwww! Waaaooowwwwwww!*

Seconds away. Pull. Pull to the right. Away from the tracks. Away from the monster.

The car spun. A weightless toy. He couldn't slow. Couldn't stop.

He squinted. Held his breath. Muscles clenched. He circled again. Back to the tracks. *Nooo!* The light trembled closer.

His foot. Pull it off the gas!

He lifted his leg. Shut his eyes. Twisted away from the window. *Don't hit. Don't hit.* The car twirled again. He dared to peek. A wall of train exploded by.

Iron wheels flew by his window. Sucked the air from his lungs. He couldn't scream. Couldn't breathe. He grabbed his head. Both hands.

His tires straightened. Dove into the ditch. His nose slammed the wheel. His head bounced back. Stars sparkled behind his eyes. The front end climbed. Weeds slapped windows. He grabbed the wheel. Pulled back. Nothing changed. The car surged, crunching the gravel between the cross ties. He stomped the brake. The car shuddered, as the iron monster groaned and thundered next to his head. His tears stung. Each gasp burned. Or was it his heart? His nostrils flared as he stared into the granite.

The stuff of his nightmares.

He squeezed his eyes shut. Jammed his fingertips into them, tried to stop the movie in his head—the kid's blood on the rocks.

Electricity ricocheted in his skull. He wheezed, tried to breathe. Pain stabbed his chest. The red on the rocks turned black. It always did.

A scream flew out of his throat. "Stop it! Stop it! I don't want to see it." He pulled his feet up, forgot the brakes. Tires strained in the gravel. He opened his eyes, whimpered, and stomped the brakes. The train rumbled on. He shifted into park and once again drew up sideways in the seat. He dug his fists into his eyes until white sparkles came. Gritted his teeth and screamed.

The blood. The blood.

It was that stupid kid's fault. The little jerk. He threw his own moron leg under the train. Vinnie didn't do it. If the boy had just given some thought to what he was doing instead of gettin' so close to the train.

Loser migrant.

The rumble continued. Vinnie pressed his thumbs into his ears. But it roared on.

An eternity passed, and the noise faded into the distance until he sat in the middle of a great silence. But the roar in his head continued.

The crunch of a car pulled up beside him in the crossroads. Doors opened and slammed. He peered over his shoulder. Some do-gooder couple approached. Tapped on his tinted windows. They couldn't see him in here. *Get lost.*

They cupped their hands against the windshield.

"Go away," he growled and sent them away with both hands, the rudest gestures he could think of. He cursed and snarled. Anything to run them off.

They left. Finally. Good riddance.

No one could see him like this. The tinted windows were the best thing about the car now. He buried his head in his arms, wiping snot on his knee.

The smell of urine hit his nose. He lifted his hands and looked down. His pants were sopping wet.

Chapter 3

Saturday, Noon

Tony jogged south, scanning the streets for two blocks, hoping to spot the stranger who'd gotten away, the one who might be after his dad. Whatever the guy was up to it was something sneaky. Right now though, he wished he'd remembered his housekey. He needed to swing by home for a minute.

But Mafia Guy, most likely headed downtown, wasn't disappearing so easy. Not on Tony's watch.

Tony pulled out his phone and punched Emily's number again. He slowed as he approached his family's Mediterranean-style home. Years ago it was a Coke bottling plant. Dad had gotten hold of some insider info on the city's downtown revitalization plan, and for little more than a song had snapped up the three-story beauty with its arched openings, tile roof, and wrought iron features. Tony snorted. *That* earned him some enemies.

Despite its location near the depot, which Dad claimed to hate, it made a handsome home, the envy of many.

Tony's phone vibrated. *Vinnie.* Not again. He took a breath. Whatever it took to keep the peace and keep Dad off his back. He punched the answer button and listened. Nodded. Dad wasn't big on greetings. "Yes, sir. I'll be there on time." Little did Dad know, Tony was already standing by the fence. "Yes, I'll skim the pool." Dad's detailed list of directions droned on. Like Tony didn't already know how to clean the pool. "Yes, sir, I'll get it done before you get home. Bye, Dad."

The cleaning would only take a few minutes. Tony kept up with it daily. But Dad had this thing about a sparkling clean pool. And though it would solve all his worries, Dad didn't want to cover his pool with a screen. He said it would look junky beside the old Spanish architecture of the home.

Tony extended his arms through the ten-foot wrought iron fence and jostled the thick foliage to get the maid's attention. "Lusmila!" Dad's hedges extended more than a foot through this side of the iron bars. So far no one from the city had complained. And they probably wouldn't. Dad had a way of getting what he wanted. Inside the fence, Lusmila sang away in Spanish as she backed around Dad's pool, sprinkling powder on the white marble surface, oblivious to his voice. As always, her little snowball poodle followed along in her footsteps. He'd give it a minute. The sunlight glared off Dad's statues—Jesus, Mary, saints, and angels. Tony squinted and turned a 360 to see if he could spot the bum nearby. So far nothing. If he did take the time to go inside, the man could slip by.

Lusmila finished her song. Tony shook the bushes again. "Hey! Lusmila!" But Lusmila flipped a switch and turned on the buffer. *Rats. Too late.*

He gave up and dialed Emily. At least he could talk until Lusmila finished.

"Hey you," Emily answered.

As they talked Tony dragged a tiny lime rock around on the sidewalk with his shoe, scribbling chalky lines. "Guess I'll be a little late. I've got to clean the pool."

"I'm..."

"Whoa, whoa, whoa," Tony interrupted, nearly dropping the phone. "There he goes. I see him, Emily! It's the guy. He's walking up the next block, headed for the square."

29

"Tony, I don't want to talk about your stinky old bum anymore. Why don't we just forget about him?"

The noise of the buffer stopped. "Hold on again." Tony whistled, a private signal between him and Lusmila.

It worked. Lusmila grinned and waved. *Finally.*

"Tony!" The childless widow had always doted on him. Years ago, Tony's mother and father had moved her into the single room on the top floor and allowed her to bring her poodle.

Teresita barked and twirled. Tony squatted and stuck his hand through to pet her, and she came to the fence, wagging.

Lusmila approached and Tony rose. "Hi, Lusmila, if you see Mom, could you please tell her I'm headed to the square? *Por favor?*" Lusmila liked to hear the Spanish words from his mouth. "I might be gone an hour." Not reporting in would get him in big trouble. Emily, the same age, had similar restrictions. It didn't seem so awful since he'd heard cops and FBI agents followed the same kind of rules.

She smiled and blew him a kiss. "Okay, *mijo*. See you later!"

Emily's voice came through his ear-bud. "Tony, I'm hanging up. You're not even listening to me."

Uh oh. "But I…"

"See you at the square. Gotta go." The phone went dead.

He'd have to fix this. Heading south, he sprinted past law offices, a feed store, and parking areas. Before he reached the farmer's market he smelled it—the kettle corn, cotton candy, and hot dogs. His mouth watered. But every penny counted right now. He rounded the corner, and the Gaskille farmer's market came into view. Running in place, he punched the traffic button and waited to cross the busy boulevard. This running wasn't half bad. Maybe next fall he'd drop a more boring class and sign up for cross-country. He should have thought of that last year. An agent had to be in good physical shape, right?

The light changed and he crossed, jogging past colorful tents dripping with ferns and orchids, stacked with clothes, and homemade articles. He slowed, tempted to take it all in. Instead he strode past the racks of handmade jewelry, candles, soaps, and pyramids of pickles, jellies, and golden honey that glittered like jewels in the sunshine. It wasn't what he was looking for. An elderly couple stopped abruptly in front of him, and he dodged, nearly tripping. They never even noticed. He passed by rows of metal chairs in front of the gazebo where spellbound adults listened to tiny tots play miniature violins. *Suzuki students from Gainesville,* the banner said. But as cute as they were, he kept moving and plowed through the crowd. He had business to take care of *before* Emily got there.

Emily darted back upstairs and grabbed her denim cross-body bag. At the bottom of the stairs she yelled out, "Mom, Grandma, I'm heading up to the farmer's market."

Mom appeared in the kitchen doorway.

Emily blew her a kiss. "I'll be back in an hour."

"Be safe, Emily."

The door slammed behind her and Emily bounded down the front steps and out the front walk between Grandma's blooming daylilies. The homes in Grandma's well-manicured neighborhood were about a hundred years old, the ancient oaks even older.

Emily's phone vibrated and she slowed, checking to see if it was Tony. Nope. It was Mom. *I love you*, it said. Emily texted back the same and turned onto the sidewalk. She glanced up and paused. Who was that coming up the sidewalk in a soiled mechanic's outfit?

Emily wasn't trying to be snobby. But old people from the neighborhood and elementary students walked these streets. Never laborers. So who was this old bearded guy with a lunchbox?

Their paths intersected at the end of Grandma's sidewalk. He stood to the side and waited as she passed by. He nodded, and acknowledged her politely with a dip of his head and tip of his hat, without a word. Sunglasses obscured his expression. She hurried on in his same direction, but sped up to keep from walking with him.

Strange. Nobody she knew did that hat-tipping thing. Not around here. Maybe on TV or in the old days. Most people just smiled, said 'morning,' or nothing at all. They didn't carry on much.

She hurried on. At the next corner she turned back slightly to catch another glimpse of him.

He seemed to be looking at her again, too. *Weird*. She picked up her pace.

Oh, brother, this was not what she needed, some old guy checking her out. *Shoot*. And she'd just come out of her own sidewalk, too.

On the far side of the square Tony found the vendor he was looking for—the one with goat cheeses, candies, soaps—and puppies for sale.

"Hi, Mr. Daniels," Tony said. He slid the envelope out of

his waist band and held it out to the middle aged farmer. "There you go. Twenty more and we'll be all square."

Mr. Daniels grinned back. "I'll get you a receipt." He folded back the corner of the tablecloth. "Want to take a look? I brought him with me today.

Tony bent down and peeked at the Australian shepherd pup. "Hey, there. Look at you. You've been growing." The dog lifted his head. His tail wagged, banging against the thin table leg.

"I've gotta call Emily," he told the man. "Just to show her. Remember, don't let on, okay?"

Tony sat down on the end of a bench overlooking the street. The crowd seemed a little thinner over here, and the only seat left was beside a very wide lady with a walker. He flopped down and made his call. After the brief talk he hung up. Oh, yeah, his sunglasses. He slid them down and stretched out his legs to people-watch while he waited for Emily to arrive.

As he lounged there, Mafia-guy appeared from the north, about 70 yards away.

Tony sat up straight and pushed the glasses back up. He leaned forward.

The man's backpack was slung over his shoulder, and he gripped the handle of his black violin case as he walked along. Hard to tell the guy's age under that unshaven scruff. Maybe 30? Forty? Emily would be a better judge.

Mafia-guy punched the traffic button, waited, then passed along the sidewalk on the other side of the street. He ambled along, gazing up and around, mostly at the buildings. Why would he study the street signs, comparing them to something on his paper? A second list of addresses? Tracking down his hits, probably.

Emily reached the farmer's market in double time. She wanted to see Tony, course, but slowed at the new textile tent on the corner. Scarves and fabrics the color of sunsets and tropical waters fluttered from its table and sides. The attendant, a very tall and robust woman, straightened her goods. A small sign out front advertised her tent as a charity for the suffering Nigerian Christian community.

Booths at the square changed from week to week at the Gaskille farmer's market, and this one Emily had never seen.

The woman flashed her a broad gold-toothed smile. A breeze wafted through her bright flowing clothes. "Would you like to see our products?" Her highly enunciated African accent rolled out like butter. The word *our* came out like *ou-ah*.

Emily didn't particularly need anything, though she wanted to see more of the woman's products. "Will you take a donation?"

"Yes, my child. Thank you very much. You are a believer?"

Emily nodded and dug out a dollar. That left nine in her purse.

The woman accepted Emily's dollar, and with a dip of her head placed it in her gray cash box. "You must see our belts."

She unhooked a green and yellow tapestry belt from a hook near the top of the tent, wrapped it around her own waist with a simple knot. She modeled it. "Nice, yes?"

Emily nodded enthusiastically. It was gorgeous. But the price tag, $15, was out of reach. "It would go great with a white blouse and jeans," she said.

"But what is more important, my dear, is de symbolism." The woman took off the belt and tied it in a loose knot forming a circle. "Hold dese up please. Let me show you."

Emily did.

"Hold de circle open."

Emily did, and the woman stuck her hands through. "Now pull de knot closed."

Why do that?

"You see. You can bind de devil's hands together." The woman took her hands out and untied the knot. "You must speak to de devil, I bind you up, you spirit of alcohol. You spirit of unforgiveness. I bind you up in de name of Jesus. Okay, young lady? You have de authority." Only it sounded like *au-tor-itee.*

"With a belt?"

"No, my child. No. You must do it with your mouth. In de name of Jesus. His name is the power. The belt is your reminder." Only it sounded like *you-ah.*

Emily nodded.

"Please give me your hand."

Emily complied and the woman wrapped the belt several times around her wrist. She formed a beautiful bow. It looked like a corsage for a prom.

"It is yours." Take it and pray, my child. Take it. And remember to pray. You can bind up dese evil things. Take control in de name of Jesus."

"Thank you. Thank you very much. But I don't have the money for this."

The woman closed her eyes and waved Emily away with the back of the hand. "It is enough, child. Enough." Then she went back to her business of folding and pinning her displays as if Emily weren't there.

What a strange conversation. As if the woman knew about her somehow. "Thank you again." She headed across the square to hunt for Tony.

Saturday, A Little Past Noon

At Gaskille's town square, the young man stood behind the work-tables of his Aunt Beth's kiddie-art booth. Against his will he'd been helping her out. *Supervised community service,* the judge called it. He bent low over the child's project and squirted glue over the kid's shoebox lid.

The child watched with big eyes.

"Now, pick whatever shape noodles you like, and make a picture," he told the child, pointing out the assortment of noodles in their individual bowls. "But don't take too long or your glue will dry."

The boy, about five, shifted on his high metal stool, eager to get started. His mother stood behind him at a safe distance gossiping with her friend but keeping a close eye on the boy.

"See mine?" The young man demonstrated one of his aunt's samples. "After yours is dry we'll coat it with gold paint like this one. A pirate's treasure chest for all your important stuff. All the big kids make these."

But as the child began his selections, the young man's attention was caught away.

Oh, yeah. There she was. That honey-blonde girl with the long hair. He slipped his hand behind him, picked up his phone. and swiped up the camera feature.

She faced away from him and was talking with that African woman over at the corner booth. They were messing with some kind of sash, tying it around the woman's hands. *Strange.* He clicked off a series of photos featuring her back side.

He knelt as if to take a picture of the child's artwork, then clicked off a few more pictures at a lower angle.

Last week was the first he'd noticed the girl. She'd even

passed by and eyed his aunt's booth. She'd smiled but hadn't stopped to do art.

He took a few more shots, but the little boy spilled a bowl of noodles. The child's mother, apologizing, darted over to clean them up.

"No problem," the young man assured her. In the meantime his honey-blonde was leaving. His head turned as she walked right past them toward the square's center.

Rats. Opportunity lost.

She strolled through the crowd to where a boy sat on a bench.

Rats again. The young man shut off his camera app. *So she's got a stupid boyfriend.*

The girl tapped her boyfriend on the shoulder.

Well, it isn't the end of the world. Maybe she'll come back—decorate a shoebox or draw a picture. He'd get a few more photos—maybe some close-ups of those cute ruffled shorts of hers while she sat at his art table.

Come to think of it, working his aunt's booth did have some perks.

Saturday, A Little Past Noon

Lunchtime. The bearded man opened his lunchbox on a bench in the square. He popped the top on his soda and set it down beside him.

Huh! A whole hour to eat his itty bitty peanut butter and jelly sandwich. Fifty-eight minutes too many. What a waste. With so much time to kill, boredom sent him strolling back to his apartment to eat this very same sandwich and take a quick nap.

But then—lucky him—on the way home he'd passed her again. He changed his plan and circled the block in order to come up here and catch another glimpse or watch her from a distance. She always seemed to hang out at the square.

He unwrapped his sandwich and bit off a chunk.

As he chewed, his sunglasses slid down, and he pushed them up, taking a deep breath to get control of his pulse. He'd let himself go to pot for so long the brisk walk had done a number on him.

Wait! He held the food in his mouth and stared. Stared hard. There she was. Again. Twice in one day. Right there in front of him behind the boy on that bench. The angle and the sun obscured her expression—but she wasn't looking at him, she was looking down at the boy who hadn't seen her yet. The boy waved his hand. Waved it at *him.* Did the boy recognize him? Know him from the automotive shop?

She tapped the boy on his shoulder then and it drew his attention away.

Hmm. So there was a boy.

The man tucked his lunchbox under his arm, grabbed his soda, and slipped through the crowd behind his bench. Too close for comfort.

Tony gazed across the open area at the man eating lunch on the bench. Who was the old guy staring at? Tony waved his hand but the man ignored it. No response at all. Just a focused stare. The man must be looking beyond him into the crowd.

A shadow passed over Tony's bench and a hand tapped his shoulder. He glanced around. *Emily.*

"Hey, you."

He scrambled up, inhaling a breath of her rose-scented perfume or whatever it was. "Emily." He grinned. "Hey." He circled the bench and pushed his sunglasses back up on his head. "Uh, gee, you smell good."

She smiled but said nothing.

Had he said the wrong thing? Better change topics. "I... I've got to show you something really neat. Something I came across."

"Really? Great!" She hesitated, "Oh, by the way," she held up her palms the way girls do when something's really exciting and gave a little squeak. "*I've* got some news. Grandma said the new poodle is a *miniature.*"

Tony forced a smile. No, that wasn't wonderful at all. That would mess things up. He needed to have a conversation with her grandma about Emily's birthday present on the 20th. And quick.

"Oh, I forgot." She rolled her eyes. "You hate poodles. Hater."

"Oh, yeah, that *is* nice!" he said.

"Faker."

He grinned. "Just come over here with me," he said, guiding her by the arm toward the goat-cheese man.

Mr. Daniels, watching from his booth, stood up and smiled. "Hi, there."

"Hi, Mr. Daniels," Tony winked, "Um, could my friend Emily take a look at your dog?"

"Sure, he's still down there under the table."

Tony lifted the table cloth, and Emily bent down. She said nothing at first, just stared with her mouth open. Then she crawled underneath the table with the dog. Her voice was muffled as she cooed and spoke to it.

Tony shrugged at Mr. Daniels and grinned.

"Oh, wow, Tony," Emily said, peering up at him. "He looks just like Beggar."

That dog, Beggar, had been Emily's main topic of conversation since she got back from her trip, and she'd described him well. Several times.

The dog's ears perked up and he wagged.

Off in the distance, the sound of an emergency vehicle grew more and more apparent. The dog whined and pinned his ears back. The sirens grew louder. Two full-sized fire engines came into view, honked to clear a path, and barreled toward the square from the east. They flew around the west side of the square, running a red light. Engines were a common sight with the fire station only blocks away. Pedestrians hustled out of the way as the trucks plowed down the hill to the south. They passed by Mafia-guy who was on the move again. He leaned over the hedges near the tattoo parlor. When he stood back up, the case and backpack were gone. Why would he hide them? Was it a bomb? A secret drop-off?

Emily climbed out from under the table. "Is he for sale?" she asked with a hint of emotion in her voice. Mr. Daniels looked sideways at Tony. He seemed unsure of what to say. "Well, this one here's sold. But we're having a new litter soon, if you can wait."

"Ohhh! Tony, *why* did you show me this *dog*? Now I won't be able to sleep thinking about him." She looked at Mr. Daniels. "Could I get first dibs on that new litter? Please?"

The man nodded. "Sure." He eyed Tony again.

Emily aimed her finger at Tony and squinted her eyes. "Forget the poodle."

Tony grinned, but his attention had shifted across the

street to Mafia-guy who strolled toward the sidewalk with his hands behind his back and his eyes on the sidewalk. What was with that guy?

The dog's owner offered them free samples, goat milk cheesecake, his specialty. They thanked him and took them back to the bench where Tony told Emily about the hit man, the bum, or whatever he was. They finished off the samples. "Don't look yet. But watch what he does out of the corner of your eye so he can't tell you're watching."

"I don't think he cares if we're watching, Tony."

The man circled the block twice and then Emily said, "So he's just walking around the street? Talking to himself?"

"He did that at the train station, too. Maybe there's a hidden microphone, maybe it's a Bluetooth. Or maybe he's crazy, one of those mass-shooters."

Emily's eyes grew wide. "Maybe it's a bomb!"

After several laps around the block, the man retrieved his case and backpack. Then he headed east along the Boulevard.

"Well, maybe it wasn't a bomb. What do *you* think is going on?" she said.

Tony pulled on his sunglasses and looked at her, "No idea. But it can't be good."

Emily shifted her purse. She had hung out with Tony as long as she could. She finally spoke up. "I'll let Grandma know about the dog, but it's time I got going. I told Mom I'd be back in an hour." Besides, she was tired of thinking about that homeless guy.

"Same thing here," he said, glancing at his phone. "Hey, what's that thing tied around your wrist?"

"Come with me a minute," she said. It would be easier to show him.

But when Emily led him over to the corner where the Nigerian woman had been there was another booth in its place, a booth with rustic wooden furniture.

"No way!" Emily said, touching the belt around her wrist. "The woman was just here. She gave me this!"

"Come on," Tony said. "Let's look around, maybe you forgot where she was." For the first time ever he took her by the hand. Maybe she could stay another minute or so.

They walked the entire perimeter of the market. But the woman's booth was nowhere to be found.

"I don't know what to tell you, Tony. She was here. And she couldn't have moved all that stuff out, and this furniture man moved all his stuff in so quick. She was right here on the corner. It was the first booth I came to."

Totally weird. The whole day was weird. She considered whether to tell him about the stranger with the beard, too. But there wasn't enough to tell him about that. She knew when to shut her mouth. And besides Tony might wonder about her sanity. He might never hold her hand again.

She lifted her wrist. If it wasn't for the belt tied around it she'd swear she was going crazy herself.

Tony squeezed her hand and let go. "I really need to take off. Dad's expecting me and I don't want to hear about it."

The texture of his hand remained with her all the way home. And so did the words of the Nigerian woman. "I bind you up in de name of Jesus."

She could pray that for her dad. With the belt as her reminder.

On his way through the square Tony passed the bench where the man had sat eating his lunch. The man was long gone, of course, but a thought finally inched its way to the front of Tony's brain. Something about the way the man had sat there, frozen, with that sandwich in his hand, staring. Of course he wasn't staring at Tony.

He'd been staring at Emily.

Chapter 4

Saturday, 3:00 PM

Vinnie coasted up the client's driveway in his black Mercedes. The heavily layered landscape and brick wall at the bottom of the first curve completely hid the mansion from the main road.

To have the honor, the pleasure, of viewing Esposito's estate—one had to be admitted through the gate. Like he had just now.

Soon enough he'd miss these meandering drives through Esposito's moss-draped oaks. Today he'd take it as slow and easy as possible, and savor the feel of the canopy. He couldn't help imagining one of those old Southern plantations at the end.

But this place wasn't like that. It was modern.

Vinnie imagined the place being his. He smiled and hung his elbow out the window, mesmerized by the reflection of the sky and giant branches passing over his mirror-like hood. Mixed with the rhythm of the tires as they rolled over the fancy brickwork, it made a delicious combination. Vinnie found it sad that Andres Esposito's last payment for the pool was due today, mostly because it ended Vinnie's excuse to return.

Vinnie hoped his men, a team of Mexicans, had set the man's statues up correctly. Today he would check behind them to make sure they'd cleaned up after themselves and hadn't broken anything. The man's pool had to be perfect. Vinnie didn't want to hear about problems later on or to have to send the men back to straighten things up. Better to have the team linger a few minutes. In fact, they were probably standing around his big white truck this very minute, waiting for the word to go home. And for some cash. Which he had. Pockets full of it.

Near the crest of the hill, Vinnie pulled up short at the base of the circular driveway, parked, and stepped out. He closed the door as quietly as possible. No need to draw attention. By parking this far back, it allowed him a longer stroll up to the door. It gave him time to study the place, the building and plants, all leisure-like. Maybe he'd get some ideas for himself. Not that he hadn't taken every opportunity to study things. Of course he had. The place was an eye-full, and he'd never had enough leisure to absorb it all. Without a doubt, though, it made his own three-story place seem pretty plain.

At the first landing, Vinnie paused next to an exotic potted fern and glanced around. A large stone wall blocked him from being seen from the windows. Not that he was doing anything wrong, but Esposito didn't need to see him admiring his entranceway. More than likely, there were cameras everywhere, and the Cuban had watched his approach. He'd probably be waiting at the door.

Raised voices floated down from an open window upstairs. Vinnie cocked his ear. A woman and man who must be Esposito, argued in Spanish. He'd love to understand the words, know a little of Esposito's goings-on. But the words meant nothing to him. Absolute diddly.

Horse-race problems? Could be. Esposito raced with the big-timers.

Money problems? Nah.

Marital problems? Oh, yeah. Vinnie had once caught a

glimpse of Esposito's young wife. How could he forget her? Lithe, beautiful, and a real fire-brand if that was her voice up there.

Vinnie laughed at his vision of Esposito's round belly, a middle aged fool alongside her. That had to be it, a marital spat. He nodded. Young versus old.

He paused on the second landing of the front steps, trying to glean what he could from the fracas. The tinkle of shattering glass raised his eyebrows. Ah, throwing things. Had to be something expensive. That was the only kind of stuff Esposito had around the place. Like a doggone museum in there. Couldn't have been Esposito. Guys didn't throw things.

At the third landing, Vinnie rang the bell.

A palpable silence now met his ears.

Vinnie crossed his arms and drummed his fingers. A couple of minutes passed.

Had they killed each other up there?

Should he ring again?

Only minutes ago, Esposito had buzzed Vinnie in through the gate. Could the guy forget so quickly?

The door swung open and there stood a slightly out-of-breath Esposito.

Vinnie swept his gaze across the man. No blood anywhere. This Cuban might even pass for Vinnie's brother. He'd have to remember that. If he ever needed a brother for anything.

"Vinnie! *Hombre!* How are you? How's the family?" With a wide smile as if nothing in the world had happened upstairs, Esposito opened his arms for a big embrace.

Uh-oh. These Latinos and their hugs. And him in these urine soaked pants. Would Esposito smell the dried pants? Maybe not. Too late now.

"Come, come." Esposito led Vinnie through a large foyer where a high waterfall trickled behind a black sculpture.

"Nice statue you got there, Esposito," Vinnie said. He'd seen it before, but he needed to get Esposito's mind on other things besides his smell. Vinnie twisted to get a better look as they passed by.

Esposito nodded. He paused near a large wine case filled with bottles. "Here," he said, and swung open the doors with a grand gesture. "Please, please, take one. This is such a special day for us. You and me."

"Tha—"

"No. Thank you. My wife and I appreciate the special touches you put into our pool," he said, gazing intently at Vinnie's face. "All the extra care. It is so beautiful. Please accept this small gift of our appreciation."

Vinnie opened his mouth again to speak, but the maid bustled into the room in her short black dress and little white apron. "*Senor*," she said and presented Esposito with a small note. Then she left.

Esposito studied it with a frown. "Excuse me, please, I'll be right back. Be my guest. Take a look at the wines, and find one that suits you. Sit down if you like."

After Esposito left the room, Vinnie hardly glanced at the wine. Being more interested in beer, he simply reached in, took a bottle, and shut the doors. Esposito would probably be gone a few minutes, so Vinnie took the opportunity to wander back into the foyer to check out the black statue.

The squabbling started upstairs again but with lowered voices. Vinnie sighed. Maybe they wouldn't drag it out too long.

Vinnie turned his back to the front door, his eyes glued to

the ball mounted smack-dab at eye level—the gargoyle's base. Long-taloned claws wrapped all the way around it, supporting the ebony creature's fearsome six-foot frame. His heart quickened. This creature would be perfect beside his pool.

How much had Esposito paid for it?

He focused again on the water streaming down the black marble wall behind the statue. The top had to be 15 feet in the air. Where would he put something like this? Near the bar?

The trickle and flow of the water over the small irregular steps created a musical effect. Vinnie liked marble and water, and this was a good mix. Whoever designed this did a good job.

Nice ferns, too, drooping out of the wall that way. Unusual. He had to get one of these.

He leaned over and stared through the pool's water. A mosaic of mirror lined the bottom and sides of the pool itself. Who would have thought to put mirrors in a pool? Nice touch. Its reflection doubled the number of black fantail fish fluttering over it. Black granite tiles sparkled on the floor around his feet, a natural extension of the mirrors and black grout in the pool. Fine. Very fine, indeed.

His focus returned to the large four-foot wings curling down around the gargoyle's squatting thighs. Muscular. Tough. Like him.

Flexing his biceps, he swept his gaze over the snarling face and illuminated eyes. A shudder passed through him. Vinnie laughed. He used to make faces and scare little kids just like this. With a flashlight under his chin.

What were its eyes made of, anyway? Marbles? Rubies? No way, Jose. They were just too big to be real rubies.

Esposito materialized at his elbow, and Vinnie jumped. When had the arguing stopped?

"I see you found some wine," Esposito said, eyeing the bottle. "Very good choice."

"Yes, thanks," Vinnie said, touching the bottle under his arm.

"Please, let's step outside and talk."

Vinnie followed Esposito out the back to his expansive pool area. Surrounded by high hedges, at first glance, it made Vinnie think of his own pool, especially now that his team had finally set up Esposito's tall white statuary, which up until this morning had been stored in crates inside Esposito's barn.

"Beautiful collection," Vinnie said, but then he actually took the time to focus on the figures. He shook his head. "They're…" Words failed to describe the perverted figures that contorted and twisted beside the crystal blue water.

His team of workers, all regular family-men, must have been shocked.

Esposito winked. "Carrara mines, Italian marble." He'd obviously mistaken Vinnie's hesitation as admiration. "Copies of the originals, though." He shrugged. "Who can tell?"

Vinnie remained speechless.

"Magnificent, aren't they?" Esposito turned to Vinnie, obvious pride on his face. "I went myself—to the mines. Ordered them personally. Come." He led Vinnie by the arm and introduced him to each of the figures by name.

"It… it must have taken a long time to make all these," Vinnie said.

What a pervert, this Esposito.

"Years. You have no idea. I couldn't wait to get this pool finished. To see them up like this. My beauties."

Vinnie followed, half-listening, and glanced at his men, out smoking behind the truck. They gazed back, apparently having run out of conversation. Probably dumb with shock. He needed to get them out of here.

"The statues are still so valuable," Esposito said, not letting it rest. "You have no concept of how much money is sitting around this pool."

Okay, okay, Vinnie couldn't care less about the Carrara mines. "Thanks, Esposito. This is all magnificent. But my men need to get home to their families now. Let's wrap up here so I can send them on their way." He had no intention of spending more time here. Was the man happy with the job or not? That's what Vinnie needed to know.

Now fork over the cash.

"That brings me to a small detail." Esposito looked down at his steepled fingers. "Let's step into the shade."

Oh, no. Not this.

Vinnie had heard this identical hem-hawing from others. It all started this same way. Bottom line, Esposito didn't have the cash. Vinnie wasn't about to tolerate a delay. He turned to Esposito.

"No, let's talk right here." Out of the corner of his eye he caught a movement in the open window upstairs. He glanced up. The woman stared down at them. "You don't have the cash, do you?" The final $20,000.

"But Vinnie," started the man, "I know that you are a reasonable man. The horse races are still on-going. Our small delay may only be a week."

Vinnie crossed his arms and stared hard at Esposito. "I've got men to pay. I can't tell them to come back next week. You know how this works, chum." In reality, they would get paid, but Esposito didn't need to know that. Vinnie had them covered.

"Look." The Cuban turned palms up, an effort to appease. He nodded toward the statues. "Take any one you want. Straight from Italy. The value is so much more than a mere twenty grand. Choose any one you like."

He should have expected this from the Cuban. Put a lot of work into something special and come out with the short end of the stick. Every time. Vinnie glared at him. "Any one, huh?" He pressed his lips together. He hated the repulsive figures around the pool.

"Sure."

Vinnie pointed with his thumb toward the house. "I'll take the black statue inside." It had to be worth more.

Esposito swallowed. "Inside?"

Vinnie raised his voice. "Yeah, the black one with the red eyes."

"But..."

"I said I'll take the black one."

"Andrés!"

Ah, the fiery wife, now. She must have pretty good ears.

Esposito glanced toward the window then back at Vinnie. "Please." His face twisted into a worried frown. "Let's just... just think about this a minute. That black statue has no value. I don't want to cheat you."

Really? Then why was his spit-fire wife getting involved? "I said I'll take it." Vinnie jerked his head toward the statues around the pool. "I don't want those." Yep, the corner by the bar would be the perfect place for his new black statue.

"Think, think, Vinnie, please. My wife—she spent a long time designing the black fountain." He lowered his voice to a whisper. "Really, it's a cheap statue. Just sentimental, that's all. Please, don't break her heart."

"Andrés!"

"You and I know just a little about the courts, don't we?"

Esposito clamped his lips and stared at the sky.

Vinnie could have sworn the guy was about to cry. He had him over a barrel. Hey, Vinnie was getting really good at this leverage business.

"What's it going to be? The statue? The legal system?"

Esposito turned and stomped into the house. "Tell your men not to break anything when they come through. And make it quick."

"Thank you. We'll see ourselves out."

The men moved the truck to the front of the house, and unlike earlier, a deathly silence filled the foyer as the men turned off the pump and detached the statue from the pump and hoses. Heavier and more bulky than he'd realized, it required all of Vinnie's men to get the slippery figure into the truck without dropping or smashing it. He'd have to build his own rock wall. "Don't lose the eyes, now," he said as they jockeyed it in sideways and secured it to the rails inside the truck. With a snap, he closed the padlock and patted the back of the truck as the men drove off. Pretty good deal.

Some things were better than money.

Barter.

Winning.

Fine things. And tax free.

With a satisfied grin on his face, Vinnie brushed his hands off and traipsed away from the departing truck, taking a shortcut across the fine shrubbery, and making his way to his car at the base of the loop.

Once again a torrent of Spanish curses burst loose from upstairs, this time with the shattering of multiple glass items.

Vinnie winced and chuckled as he started the engine. She

must've forgotten about Vinnie's vehicle still parked in the loop.

He circled the driveway, quicker this time than when he arrived.

The stink of urine still filled his nose. The windows went down. He needed to get the car detailed before the smell set in.

And he couldn't care less anymore if Esposito had noticed.

Chapter 5

Saturday, 5:00 PM

Out by the pool Tony put a marker in his book and leaned back with his eyes closed. The radio's Best Ten countdown played through his earplug as he enjoyed a few peaceful minutes in the sun.

A click sounded and then a hum. The electronic gates opened on the left side of the house.

Tony roused and craned his neck to see who was coming in.

Dad's black Mercedes slipped forward along the tall hedges and parked as usual. The large white utility truck parked on its left. His team of five men jumped out and pulled open its double back doors. What could they be doing?

Dad hopped out of his car, directing the men and unbuttoning his shirt at the same time. As usual, he could never wait to get into the pool. From the back of the van, the men guided a loaded dolly down the ramp. Strapped to it was a large object wrapped in a utility quilt. "Pull it up right here," Dad said.

Mom opened the back door a crack and stuck her head out, watching.

"Hey, Tony. Tony!" Dad said, waving a hand and striding in his direction. "Get up and get these fellows a beer, pronto. Including me—six altogether."

Lulled into a stupor by the sun, Tony stood and headed to the bar.

The men lost no time scuttling the dolly around to the

front of the bar and unwrapping the huge object. Some kind of black statue.

Tony reached in the refrigerator and lined up the bottles on the counter. He popped the tops and brought them out all at once with his fingers around the necks. Good trick if he ever decided to do table-waiting.

He brought them around and set them on the patio table near the men who stood back, gawking at the statue.

Vinnie admired the thing from the opposite side of the pool.

Tony circled around to get a better view. Pretty ugly if you asked him.

Mom and Lusmila emerged through the French doors.

"What is that?" Mom said.

Lusmila shrugged. "At least eets no naked lady."

"Oh? Yes, it *is* naked. Take a closer look."

"Oh. I see," Lusmila said, her hand lifting to her mouth.

Teresita barked through the glass, all five pounds of her bouncing back and forth.

Vinnie directed, and the men turned the statue sideways so its clawed hands and snarling face stared toward the house. Mom pressed her hands against her cheeks. "Ohh! Look at that awful thing. Vinnie's dragged a *gargoyle* onto our property?"

Lusmila harrumphed then retreated into the kitchen. "Ooh, boy."

The workers folded the quilts and packed them into the van.

Still in his long pants, Vinnie dug out his wallet and called for Tony.

He peeled off five $100 bills. "Give the guys one each. This was their day off, and they did some extra work for me. Give 'em a big thank you for me."

55

He thrust the money at Tony and grabbed a pair of drying swim trunks off the back of a chair.

Tony paid off the men, who drove away together in an old beater parked by the street.

When Tony returned Dad was already submerged in the water with his arms up over the edge of the pool and beer in his hand. His gold Italian horn necklace glimmered through the water, contrasting with his dark chest.

Mom stormed over, clearly upset. "Vinnie, could we talk, honey?"

Tony inhaled. It looked like his own question for Dad would have to wait.

Vinnie took a swig. "What? You don't like somethin'?"

"Honey, I really feel uncomfortable about this thing. It looks demonic."

"Yeah, well before you start in on me, I knew you weren't going to like it. I knew it. And I don't wanna hear it."

Mom leaned toward him and swept her arm across the statuary vista of Jesus, Mary, horses, saints, and a naked Venus statue. "Don't you have enough? And besides, the new one doesn't match. These are all white."

"Look, how about I get you that grand piano you been buggin' me about. No big deal."

"That doesn't get rid of this ugly thing."

"You leave me and my toys alone." He took a long swig of beer. Then leaving the bottle up on the concrete, he ducked below the surface, wetting his thinning hair. Coming back up he pushed the water and his hair back with two hands. "Now, this statue, this *payment* I've received, well, it's got style. Lookie there, see those nice eyes and wings?" He chuckled. "Baby, nobody will mess with Vinnie with this thing here."

56

Mom crossed her arms and tapped her foot.

It sounded like Dad had probably created some new enemies.

Vinnie hollered over to Tony. "Whaddya say about this here nice statue, son? You like this? Like it watchin' over the place? Huh?"

Tony shrugged. He didn't need to get involved.

"Yeah, go on, ignore me. Stupid, just like the rest of 'em. Can't even speak when he's spoken to. No respect for the old man."

Mom turned around and marched back into the house. Tony stalked off behind her. The French doors slammed behind him. Teresita bounced around, jumping to be picked up.

He ignored the dog and gritted his teeth. "I *hate* Dad."

Outside, his father continued to yell, his voice penetrating the French doors, "And Lusmila is going to sweep around it, work around it—just like all my other statues. It's no different. So get used to it, Nancy, woman. I don't wanna *hear* what you don't *like*."

Dad lifted his beer and toasted the statue.

Mom put her hand on Tony's shoulder. "Ignore it, Tony. Don't let hate poison you. It's not worth it. Try to understand him. Even if we don't agree. He doesn't really mean a lot of what he says. He's just spouting off."

Tony grabbed a shirt where he'd thrown it over the back of a dining room chair. He stepped toward the front door. "I'm going for a walk."

"Tony, Emily'll be here in a few minutes for her piano lesson, and I've invited her to stay for your birthday dinner."

"Yeah, I forgot. Happy birthday to me."

"Tony, don't take this out on me."

"Okay. But I'm still going for a walk." He held onto the door a second longer and clenched his jaw. "And I still hate him. I. Hate. His. Evil. Guts."

He slammed the door and strode around the corner to the square.

Forget asking Dad for anything. His chance was lost. He'd probably said no, anyway. Every time Tony asked Dad for something, he said to go earn it. Like Tony wasn't already trying.

Tony wasn't asking for a handout.

Why wouldn't Dad let Tony work part time? Even for a day?

He cared more about his Mexican workers than his own son. Tony could have bought five bikes with the money he'd just handed out to those men.

If he could gather up enough for a bike, he wouldn't have to borrow one. Then he could run more errands, get more done, earn more money. It was summer, after all, and time was ticking. And he had important things to pay for. One in particular.

Somehow he'd still have to approach Dad.

Saturday, 5:30 PM

Emily pushed open the screen door and stepped out to check the mail.

She lifted the lid on the mailbox. In Gaskille, the postman delivered mail right up on the porch.

Aha! The mail had come. She pulled out a lone advertisement from Penney's and flipped through it to the new line of school clothes. *Not bad. Mom should see these.*

She folded it back and reached for the door. But a movement out by the road caught her eye.

The bearded man. *Not again.*

Emily froze as their gazes met—his sunglasses and her eyes.

He nodded but didn't wave. Just switched his lunchbox from one hand to the other and kept on walking. *What was he looking at?*

She swung the screen door closed and latched it tight. Her heart hammered. Could it be a coincidence that she kept seeing him? Was he stalking her?

Why was he always looking her way?

Chapter 6

V innie wrapped his fingertips around the icy beer bottle and inched his way down the side of the pool into the deeper water. This daily routine in the pool was so relaxing. How could anyone live without a pool? He took a long cool sip, set the beer bottle on the concrete and hung his arms over the concrete ledge. Gazing beyond the amber glass, his eyes drifted to nothing in particular at first, then over on the black statue.

"Nancy, you might be right," he mumbled.

She'd mentioned one thing he hadn't considered. The new statue didn't fit alongside his other white ones. Why hadn't he thought of that back at Esposito's place? He could have asked for one of those fancy leaping horses near Esposito's entrance gate.

Or one of those *others*.

He chuckled out loud and took a swig. "Nancy, woman, you'd have had a lot more to say about one of those, honey."

Yeah, a white marble horse would have been a better match.

He studied the statue. Without the waterfall it wasn't so grand.

One thing was for sure now. There would be no waterfall. Not out here, anyway. It wouldn't work. Of course, the figure did blend into the dark background of hedges. That worked.

Vinnie pushed off the side of the pool with his toes. He slipped through the water to the opposite side, grabbed onto the ledge and hung there, admiring his prize from a new angle. It sure was fine, though. He traced his eyes over the fine black figure. And look at those red eyes. What a great concept, a very good idea, effective. Scary. And such an easy deal. Yeah, he should keep the thing. This corner was a good place for it, guarding the bar like that. The tall foliage almost worked like the waterfall. He chuckled. Might be kind of a humorous surprise if someone wasn't paying much attention. Yeah, yeah, yeah, he'd keep it.

Vinnie floated away on his back. With all this protection, who could touch him now? He stared into the clouds. He had Jesus, Mary, a wide assortment of angels, and now this.

Chapter 7

Saturday, 5:30 PM

At the square Tony sprawled on the bench for the second time that day. He clamped his lips together and folded his arms across his chest. Pushing his sunglasses up on his nose, he glared across the panorama. His guts boiled. With only one son, Dad had to keep calling him stupid. Every day. Tony did what he was supposed to, whatever Dad asked. So why couldn't Dad get off his back? Just be a regular dad?

The phone in his pocket vibrated. He reached for it. Emily. "Hey."

"Happy birthday, I'm headed over for my lesson right now. You home?"

"No, I'm at the square."

"Well, your mom invited me to stay for dinner and your birthday cake. Be sure you get back."

"Yeah, wait till you see my dad's newest statue."

"Statue?"

Tony turned sideways and put a shoe up on the seat. He propped his elbow on the back of the bench. "Yeah, looks like a de..." His gaze landed across the street. On the Mafia-guy in his ponytail. He seemed to be in deep conversation with some other homeless guy.

The hit-man stood up with his violin case and nodded to the other guy. Tony sat transfixed.

"Looks like what?" Emily persisted.

"Um, some naked squatting devil. Real ugly."

"You've got to be kidding. I'm so sorry, Tony."

Mafia-guy strode away from the square, going east along the boulevard. He cut north between two buildings. Tony needed to find out more about him. "Have a good lesson, Emily. I gotta go. We can talk more later when I get to the house."

Sprinting now, Tony thrust the phone into his pants pocket, and followed Mafia-guy's steps. The man turned left onto Third Avenue, but when Tony reached the corner the street was empty. Tony slowed to a jog. He scanned left and right. There! To the right. Tony veered off. Maybe he'd better keep some distance between them. He slowed to a walk again beside the commercial laundry and stepped behind a shrub. He'd give the man three seconds then step out. One, two, three. He stepped out.

Well, that was stupid. Where'd the guy go?

Tony hit the sidewalk running east and zipped through the laundry's parking lot. He jogged through a tree-filled lot opposite some kids playing in the dirt. That couldn't be it. He studied the shade-obscured buildings. If the guy was standing behind one of them... nah, probably not.

A neglected clapboard building, probably abandoned, butted up to the trees. He jogged past it to the next street. And again... *nada.* He paused, glanced from side to side and loped five more blocks before stopping. He threw up his hands. Nothing.

The guy couldn't have known he was being followed. Shouldn't have needed to hide. Man! Somewhere in this area he'd left the sidewalk.

Tony headed back to the square. The man's actions were just too strange to ignore. That list, searching the streets, talking to bums, the case, hiding the case in the bushes—all around the same time Dad got that call. The guy was up to something.

And now disappearing...

A black thought crept in. Maybe Dad deserved what he got. *Hah. No.* Tony shoved the thought back down. He had to stop this. He couldn't just sit back and let it play out. That wouldn't be right.

Chapter 8

Saturday, 6:30 PM

Tony saluted Lusmila through the kitchen door from where he sat at the dining room table finishing off his last bite of his chocolate birthday cake. He swallowed. "Lusmila," he said, "this is the best thing I've ever tasted."

She gave him a big smile and blew him a kiss. "*Feliz cumpleaños*, Tony." Then she grinned at Emily. "Every cake is the best thing he's ever tasted." With a happy shrug she turned back to the kitchen to wipe the counters and tidy up.

Dad, seated at the end of the table, gestured toward the two small gifts in the fruit bowl in the middle of the table. "Gonna open your gifts?"

"Oh, yes, the gifts. I thought you'd never ask." Tony reached into the bowl. "And what's this?" he said, picking up the larger one, a blue foil package. "It says, *from Emily*."

"Remember that book about the Chinese man and his ducks? The one we read in English class at the end of the year?"

"Yeah, that was a good book," he said, giving the package a sniff. "Is it a roast duck?"

"Yeah, right. Well, I knew how much you liked it. So I made you this little surprise."

Tony tore off the paper. Inside was a cardboard box. "Should I give it a little shake?"

"No, no. It might break."

He lifted the flaps. Inside sat three yellow ceramic ducks

with orange beaks. Tony grinned and lined them up next to the salt and pepper shakers. "That's really nice, Emily."

"It's a little different. I hope you don't think it's sissy."

"What? It's thoughtful. You knew I liked that book, and you were thinking of me. These are awesome. When did you have time?"

"Just after the Suwannee nightmare." Her downcast gaze stopped Tony from commenting on that. The raw wounds were still there. Maybe painting the ducks had been therapeutic.

"I love them. Thank you."

"So do I," Mom pulled a small gift and card out of the bowl in the middle of the table. "Are you going to open mine?"

Inside Tony found a $50 gift certificate to The Game Joint. "Awesome!"

Mom stretched her hand across the table. "I apologize, Tony. I couldn't remember the names of all your games, so I thought it best you go down and pick out what you like."

"Are you kidding? I love this. I need to take a look at the new things they've got, anyway."

His father shoved a chunk of chocolate cake into his mouth. "Happy birthday, Tony."

"Thank you, everyone. I really appreciate the nice birthday gifts," he said, and then even louder, directed the next part at Lusmila. "I especially loved the cake and the steak dinner."

Lusmila peered through the doorway and tossed him another kiss. "So glad you enjoyed it, *mijo*." Then she stepped around the table collecting dishes. "*De nada*."

The demon Callous leaned his amber-toothed grin near Vinnie's ear. His stinking breath rolled out between warty lips.

"Remember?" he whispered. "What's under the bed in there?"

Vinnie took another sip of his wine. Looked like he was thinking things over.

Tyrant drummed his fingertips together next to Vinnie's other ear. He wiped a string of drool and leaned in to add his two cents. "Don't let that woman tell you what to do. Make sure she knows you're the boss. Keep her in her place."

"You talk too much, stupid," his partner said.

Tyrant let Callous have it with two fists over the head.

Callous' broken amber teeth clacked together.

"Don't tell me what you think. I don't care."

"Loser, loser." Callous turned his attention back to Vinnie.

Steaming, Tyrant did the same.

"One more gift," Dad said. "Nancy, woman, run in there and get that gift out from under our bed."

Mom drove a sharp look into Vinnie. She furrowed her brow. Lusmila grabbed a dish and scuttled back into the kitchen. "Are you sure this is the right time, honey?"

Dad wiped his wrist across his lips and burped. "Woman, you know it is. Tony here is *the man* now, and it's time for him to step a rung up the ladder. Just trot on in there and get it."

She narrowed her eyes at him.

"Get it, Nancy," he said, using that tone that forbade rebuttals. He glanced through the kitchen door to Lusmila as Nancy rose to comply. He sniffed his glass, his fingers. "Something stinks in here."

Tony traded a look with Emily as they waited for Mom to come back. Dad said nothing, just drained his glass of wine. Lusmila reappeared and filled Vinnie's glass. Her hand shook, and wine spilled on the tablecloth. "I'm so sorry, Mr. Vinnie." She dabbed it with a napkin and hurried back to the kitchen.

In a minute, Mom returned, holding what appeared to be an ancient black violin case. She gripped its handle with both hands and gave Tony a sideways glance. It seemed more apologetic than anything. It changed into a glare for Dad as she lifted the case across the table to Tony.

Tony watched the faces around him. "Wh-what's up with this? A violin?"

Mom kept her gaze on Dad as she picked up her napkin and flopped down ungracefully into her chair. She crossed her arms. "This wasn't the way we planned it. Go ahead, Vinnie. Just tell him."

Vinnie stacked his silverware on his plate. "I changed my mind, Nancy. This is the *day*, and this is the *way*." He pushed the plate away from himself. "Open the case, son. Happy birthday from Dad and Mom here." Vinnie leaned back in his chair, both arms extended on his arm rests. He drummed his fingers on the tablecloth, watching Tony.

No one said anything as Tony opened the case. A violin. He glanced up at his mother who now seemed to be fighting back tears. "Mom? Dad? Thank you. But—why did you get me a violin?"

"Honey—" his mother began.

"It's from your grandparents," Vinnie interrupted.

Oh, grandparents. "Yours, mom? I didn't know anyone in our family played this." All four grandparents had been gone for years. Naturally, it would have been her parents, she was the pianist in the family.

"No, honey…"

"Mine, either." Dad, still drumming, raised a brow.

After a brief glance in the case, Tony latched it back, more interested in their answers than the instrument. He wasn't a musician. Didn't know a thing about music. "I don't get it then. What grandparents?"

Dad looked back at Mom who stared at her lap. Was she crying? "It's time you know, son, as a man should."

"Know what?"

"You're adopted, son, adopted. This belonged to your grandfather. On your own side of the family."

Tony swallowed. What kind of sick joke was this? It couldn't possibly be real. He wasn't adopted.

He stood. "You're just kidding, right?"

Mom kept her eyes on her lap and shook her head.

Dad just sat there with some kind of expectation on his face like Tony should have something happy to say.

Dizzy and drugged with confusion, Tony stood. He had to get his head on straight.

"Tell me you're joking. This is sick. You can't mean it."

He glanced around the table. Emily gazed up with tears of disbelief in her eyes and her hand over her mouth. Dad was still staring at him.

Tony waved an arm. "I'm adopted?"

Silence.

"You waited until I'm 15 years old to tell me I'm adopted?"

He turned and walked out of the silent room.

Of all the cruel tricks. Traitors!

Chapter 9

T ony plodded robotically down the marble tiles of the hall to his bedroom. All he wanted was to be out of the dining room. Away from the traitors. Especially Dad. A loud buzzing filled his head. That, mixed with the garbled conversation from the dining room, his mother's pleadings and the raised voice of his father defending himself.

A pattering of feet indicated Emily had followed him. She caught up and touched his back as he entered his bedroom door. Somehow he still held the gift in his hand. The violin. Should he set it on the floor by his bed or throw it? Finally he just slumped to the floor. He spread his fingers over the case, the only true piece of his past—his past that felt like a lie. How had he never heard the first hint about it? And now it had just slugged him in the head like a baseball bat.

Should he love the gift or hate it? Who the heck *was* he now, anyway?

Emily knelt on the floor opposite him.

"Shut the door," he mumbled, and buried his face on his knees.

Before Emily could stand, Mom appeared at the door. Teresita whined at her feet. Even the poodle seemed to realize something was wrong.

"Honey, forgive me," Mom said, hesitating. "I didn't want it to be this way, either."

Tony turned his flooded eyes to her. "Am I really adopted?"

"Think of it this way, honey. You were picked out. You were

70

so wanted, so desired, so loved. We loved you so much we brought you home with us."

"But what…?"

Mom sank to the floor beside him and reached her arm around his shoulders. Emily stayed where she was on the other side. Tears streamed down her cheeks.

Mom spoke softly. "Your real mother and father died in a car crash. Then your grandmother and grandfather took you in."

Tony wiped his nose with the back of his arm, and Emily offered him the Kleenex box off his desk.

"But what happened to them, my grandparents?" he asked, taking the box.

Mom touched his cheek. "They were old and broken-hearted, and first your grandmother, then your grandfather, died right afterward, honey, just a few months apart."

A long silence passed as Tony digested this information. "I've just been passed around, like a raggedy old t-shirt."

"No, honey, *chosen*, you were *chosen*. Things happen for a reason. We wanted a child so bad, and there you were, all we ever wanted."

Tony hugged Mom back, "Mom, I can't even think about this, it's all so—"

"I know, and I'm sorry it happened like this. You saw I had no choice."

"I know you didn't. I told you. I hate his guts. But now," Tony said, sniffing, "I hate him even more. I'm glad we're not related." Tony poked the violin case with his sneaker. "What about this? Whose was it?"

Mom laid her hand on the case. "This was your grandfather's, your mother's father. He was a concert violinist."

71

"Okay, well, that's one good thing."

Mom gave him another squeeze. "Oh, it's all okay, Tony. You have a family. It's us. We love you so much. Your dad does, too, Tony, he's just rough around the edges." She reached over and took Emily's hand as she said that.

"Why didn't you tell me, Mom?" His voice cracked.

"Your dad wanted to wait."

"Wait? Wait for what?"

"For just the right time."

"Oh, like for a crushing happy-birthday blow? That's so sweet of him." Tony grabbed two fistfuls of hair and shoved the case under his bed with his foot.

"Honey, you know he has a hard time sometimes."

"Yeah? Well, how about this..." He looked at his mother and steeled his eyes. "The way I feel about him, this is the best birthday gift ever."

Sunday, 12:12 AM

Emily tossed and turned. Sleep refused to come. She lifted her head and checked the time. *Noooo! Midnight already?* She pulled the sheet over her head and closed her eyes. If she didn't get some sleep there'd be payback in church tomorrow. The disturbing memory of Tony's distraught face looped once again across her mind.

Poor guy. What a cruel way to find out he was adopted. And on his birthday, no less. His dad, Vinnie, ought to be punished for the way he treated people, and especially his own—well, *adopted*—flesh and blood.

She flipped over on her side and wrapped an arm around her pillow.

Then there was that other haunting picture that wouldn't leave her mind alone. Emily couldn't be sure if it was her imagination, a vision, a dream, or what. But it was the picture of her family's old house in Citra. Mom had finally walked off from the place and left Dad to his own drunk devices. Emily couldn't shake off the image—those dirty dishes in the sink, the empty bean cans, the mouse droppings on the table, the beer bottles all over the floor, the dried puke around the toilet. And saddest of all, Mom's curtains, always starched and white, now stained and limp, hanging out the kitchen window.

Was their old house really like that now? Mom had kept it so clean before. And if it was like that, then Dad must—she hated to think about it. But she had to know.

Emily closed her eyes again. Mom just *had* to take her out there. Emily had to see. See for herself that it wasn't true.

Was Dad really so bad off? What could have happened to make him leave the house deserted?

Had he drowned in Orange Lake? Gotten caught in a storm while fishing? There were plenty of summer storms. Or that pit bull on Dad's street—could Dad have wandered into its pen? It *had* been killing cats before they'd left.

Earlier, back at the Suwannee, Emily had pushed aside her temptation and decided to not run away and try to help Dad. If Mom hadn't been able to fix him, then how could Emily do it? Like Mom said, he'd had his chance. Fourteen years with Dad hadn't changed anything. Why would now be any different?

She closed her eyes and tried for a long time to imagine lambs jumping over fences.

Crash! A tinkle of broken glass from downstairs. Then silence.

Emily sat up. The clock on her dresser said 1:11 AM. She glanced at the dark hallway outside her door.

She stuck her foot out and touched the floor. "Mom?" Had she or Grandma fallen? Or dropped something? She pulled back the covers and tiptoed into the hall. She peeked into Mom's room. But there she lay, undisturbed, and snoring peacefully.

Uh-oh. It must be Grandma. "Grandma?" She flipped on the hall light and flew downstairs. On went the rest of the lights, dining room, kitchen, and the front two rooms.

The rooms were empty. Silent. Except for the hum of the refrigerator.

Maybe the noise came from upstairs. She raced back up. "Grandma?" She swung through Grandma's doorway, but she, too, lay sound asleep.

Oh, no. Maybe it was a break-in.

Emily eased back out of Grandma's room. Without a sound she opened the upstairs closet and got out the broom. She threw it over her shoulder like a baseball bat and crept back down, gripping the rail. At the bottom she checked each room again and turned off the lights one by one.

Except for the glow from the streetlights, darkness filled the downstairs.

On tiptoes she moved from room to room. She scanned every window for the glint of broken glass.

Nothing. What had made the crash? The noise was too real to be a dream. Or *was* it a dream?

Back upstairs, having found nothing, Emily crawled into bed again. She glanced at the clock. 1:30 AM. Beside the clock hung the African woman's colorful belt, suspended from the mirror above and now strangely transformed into the gray and white of night.

Her prayer reminder.

If the crash was just a dream, maybe she should pray. It might be a warning.

She sat up and grabbed her pillow. "Lord, thank you for the reminder. If someone's in danger please protect them. Send angels to protect my dad from all harm." Then she prayed the words she'd been praying every day since she met the African woman. "And I bind up, in Jesus name, all spirits of alcohol and any other evil spirit in him or over him. Anything not coming from you, Lord, I bind it up. In Jesus name, amen. Oh, and please bring him and Mom back together so we can be a family again."

Darkness lay deep over the quiet city, especially on the corner near the Buy It Less Grocery, the last store of the night to close. The man held a gallon of milk in one hand and his brown bag of potatoes, eggs, bread, and hot dogs in the other. The manager had just locked the doors behind him as he trudged toward the street corner to cross the eight lanes of the boulevard.

The man waited for the sign to change to the little walking figure. Even with scant traffic he paused for the signal. Above him buzzed and flickered the only good streetlamp within a quarter mile. It was more off than on, and threatened to fail completely. Across the pavement lay a wilderness of empty parking spots and a deserted plaza.

The lights changed and the little walking figure blinked for him to cross the road. On he plodded, across one, two, three lanes.

The tall angel stood on the opposite side. He straightened. The command had come. "Protect!"

Ever alert, he searched for the danger. *Mmm hmm.* And here came the demon around the corner. He recognized the familiar dark cloud moving along inside the lifted truck. The driver's *controller.*

The vehicle, with its windows down, barreled forward at a hideous speed for this small town. Its roaring engine and its top-decibel music vibrated the dark windows of the plaza. The truck surged forward—heedless of the red light or the man in its path.

Near the red light a bottle flew out the truck's window. It twirled up and over the cab.

In less than a flicker, the angel snatched his man across the street as wheels, as high as the man's chest, blurred past.

Protection accomplished.

The bottle landed on the asphalt and shattered into a million amber gemstones. Right where the man had stood.

A clueless *"Yee haaa!"* drifted out the window and faded into the distance.

The man with the bag now stood on the opposite corner. He turned and stared back at the middle of the street—and from the expression on his face likely wondered how in the world he'd gotten across the road so fast.

Sunday morning Emily climbed out of bed late. Tony would be waiting for her at church. She barely had time to wash up, dress, and dab on a little mascara. She gulped down the eggs and bacon Grandma fixed for her, and raced out to Mom's car.

She sat with Grandma in the back seat. "Mom, don't forget what you told me. I'm counting on you taking me out to Citra to see things."

Mom raised an eyebrow and looked at her in the rear-view mirror. Grandma patted Emily's leg and held a finger in front of her lips. She mouthed a silent word. "Patience."

At church Tony waited alone at the front door for Emily. The music had already started inside. He nudged Emily and pointed upstairs with a questioning look on his face. Emily understood and turned to Mom and Grandma. "Do you care if Tony and I sit up in the balcony?"

"Go right ahead," Mom said. "Just behave yourselves and come straight down afterward."

As they walked away, Emily tossed Mom a grin over her shoulder. "See you in a little bit."

Up in the balcony Emily sat at the end of the pew. The preacher's voice and her lack of sleep blended perfectly, and before long she was fighting to stay awake. She finally slumped against the corner and closed her eyes.

She dreamed that church was over and Mom had driven them all to Citra. And there, once again, were the mouse droppings, the bean cans, the beer bottles, and blowing curtains.

Emily woke with a start. The preacher was still preaching, and Tony seemed intent on what the preacher was saying. She re-closed her eyes.

Once again she drifted off, haunted by the same dismal dream. But this time a diapered baby stood in the middle of the filthy kitchen.

The organ began to play and Emily jerked awake again. Tony was busy turning pages in his hymnal. She straightened, grabbed one side of his book, and sang along. It woke her up enough to prevent her from falling asleep again during the final prayer.

She promised herself to get more sleep tonight.

After the dismissal, Tony took her by the hand and led her toward the stairs. She smiled and glanced ahead toward the exit. But what she saw beneath its arch froze her blood. She grabbed Tony's arm with both hands. "Wait!"

"What's going on?"

She looked up at Tony. "It was *him*. The man with the beard. Up here. With us. In the balcony." Her voice cracked. "I think he might be following me around."

No way, José! Tony let go of her hand and dove through the arch. No old geezer was going to follow *his* girl around.

The stairs were clogged with people. He could have pushed past everyone, but it was church, after all. But if someone really was following Emily around, Tony needed to at least see who she was talking about.

The logjam in the stairwell moved like molasses. It was all Tony could do to keep from saying, "C'mon, let's go." At the bottom of the stairs he broke free and bolted out the front door. He turned left and right. Looked everywhere. Emily's mom stood near the sidewalk. He waved. But no one in this crowd had a beard.

He headed back inside and met Emily at the bottom of the stairs. Could it just be her nerves? Or her drowsiness? He had caught her napping upstairs. She'd been through so much at the Suwannee. Nearly died. What could he say to take away her worry?

"Find him?" she said as they crossed the foyer.

Tony shook his head. "Your mom's out front."

Emily said nothing as she followed him into the sunlight.

"You know, if he *was* in church," Tony said, "that's a good sign. Maybe he's just a nice guy and you keep crossing paths. Maybe it's nothing. Has he done anything suspicious?"

"*If* he was? He *was* there. I saw him."

"I'm sorry, Emily, I didn't mean it to sound like that."

"It's—it's just the way he notices me. I can't put my finger on it. Ohh! Maybe I'm crazy."

"No, no. I don't think you're crazy. Tell you what, just be polite and keep an eye open. Let me know if anything gives. Can you do that?"

She nodded.

Maybe the guy was harmless. Maybe.

Chapter 10

Vinnie's "friend" Eve, long ago known to her family as Freckles, stepped into the assisted living center's activity room and glanced up at the clock. A few seconds more and the jaunty music at the end of Matlock would finish up. She grinned at Mr. Shay's rapt expression, unwilling to interrupt any part of his favorite show. After the last note, she leaned near his wheelchair. "Ready to go back to your room? We can get your pajamas on and get you all nestled in. Then we can turn your TV on if you like."

Her own son Billy was probably sound asleep right now in the corporate nursery down the hall. Poor Billy. But he never complained. He loved it here, being around all the old people, and they loved him too. The center was part of his life. And where could she possibly afford to work without this built-in nursery?

"I'd like that, Eve, honey." Mr. Shay unlocked his wheels and gave a little wave to his friends as he whirled the chair toward the door. "Good night, Mrs. Waldron, Mrs. Marcum." Eve took over the driving, and the light clicking of the wheels echoed down the otherwise quiet hall as she pushed him to its far end. Things had settled down for the night. All the visitors were pretty much gone.

What meager few there had been.

Blue light flickered across the faces of other residents. Some had already fallen asleep in front of their sets. Mr. Shay liked to push bedtime as far as he could, but the night nurse with the meds would soon be stopping by his room. She'd blame Eve if he wasn't there.

"What'll it be tonight, Mr. Shay? Polar bear pajamas, airplanes, or trains?" Mr. Shay loved the flannel pajamas his late wife had made him and said he wanted these three pairs to last "until Jesus came."

"Why don't you pick for me?"

"How about airplanes?"

"That'll do. That'll do. I appreciate you waiting until the show was over back there. Some nights the aides just come on in and bust up my show. Won't even wait until the music is done. I love that theme song. Don't you, honey?"

"I sure do."

"It's the little things that count. I believe you're the nicest gal we have here at the home. I'm not just a number on a room to you."

"Aww, thank you, Mr. Shay, but I think you just like redheads, right? Isn't that it?"

Mr. Shay cackled over that. "You bet I do. And I bet you have a dozen boyfriends lined up out there to take you out, don't you?"

It was Eve's turn to laugh. "I don't think so. But there is one special one. His name is Sammy."

Maybe she shouldn't have mentioned him, though. Sammy had made himself a little scarce lately.

"Here we are, now. Let me help you out of this chair and into those nice fresh pajamas."

Eve smoothed his blanket around Mr. Shay's thin shoulders. "Is there anything else you need?"

He pulled his arms back out and sat up. "Yes, the Bible

over there, can you hand it to me? Maybe we'd better jack this bed up a little, too. I need to have my devotionals before I go to sleep."

She raised the bed and handed him the Bible. A picture fell out on his blanket, and she picked it up. "Oh, my, who is this pretty girl?"

"That's my daughter. She's all I have left. You remind me of her. She's way up in Wisconsin right now. Coming down at Christmas, though."

"I know you miss her."

"The light of my life."

Eve blinked back tears. If she could just do more for him. Mr. Shay's wife had been gone since last year. Poor man had no visitors.

"You know what I like about you, Mr. Shay? You don't get to see your daughter very much, but every time I see you, you're busy cheering on the others. You never complain."

"Well, who wants to hear an old man complain? I know I don't." He laughed.

Mr. Shay rested his blue-veined hand across hers on the bedrail. "Honey, I know you have to head home in a little bit. You be careful out on those dark streets. Keep your seatbelt on and your doors locked. Promise me?"

"Don't worry, Mr. Shay. They have a security guard that can walk me out, a very nice guy whose name is Mark. And I always use my seatbelt."

"Thanks for being so good to me, honey. I bet your mom and dad are so proud of you."

It was all she could do not to choke on that. "They're gone now, but thank you."

"I want to see that little redheaded boy of yours next time

he's around. Tell him to come by and give Mr. Shay a big hug."

"You have a good night's sleep now, Mr. Shay." She turned back at the doorway. "And like my daddy used to tell me, sleep tight, and don't let the bed bugs bite."

At least that's what he'd said up until the time he'd walked out on Mamma and her and Pony Tail. God bless him. Wherever he was.

At 11:00, Eve punched out on the time clock and went by the nursery. Billy was sound asleep on his little cot. She knelt down and shook him. He was way too big to carry anymore.

"Wake up, Billy. We've got to head on home." He sat up. Eve pressed his warm little cheek against hers and hugged him tight. Mr. Shay's words came back to mind. "The light of my life." What would her life be without Billy right now?

"Let's go," she whispered, a lump in her throat. Picking up his backpack, she took his hand. Why was she so emotional tonight?

As they approached the glass doors, the night guard's glowing cigarette flew into the bushes before he opened the door from the outside. His nicotine cloud hovered over the exit. She held her breath. Hopefully the cigarette smoke wouldn't set off one of her migraines.

The guard walked them all the way out to the car and even lifted Billy into his car seat.

"Oh, man, Billy, you're gettin' to be as heavy as a grown-up cowboy."

Billy grinned, mostly still sleep.

"Thank you, Mark," Eve said. "It's so hard to wrangle him into his seat when he's half out of it. You're the best."

"You're welcome, ma'am." He tipped his hat. "Have a good night. Drive safe."

Before the car even left the parking space Billy was sound asleep again. Poor little guy, getting dragged from pillar to post. But what could she do better? So many people had it worse than her, too.

Out on the road, traffic was light at this time of night. She checked her door locks as she drove down Highway 200 and pressed on the gas. No way she was feeling sorry for herself. She'd made up her mind about that. Mr. Shay would be proud of her on that count. She tried to recall what kind of leftovers she had back at the house. Not a thing. Billy had eaten back at the nursing home. But she hadn't and wasn't about to stop at a grocery store with him asleep. Fast food it was. She turned the car around and headed over to the only place still open this time of night, Burger Bob's. In the future she should plan better than this, but it would have to do for now, even though for weeks now she'd fallen prey to lazy eating patterns.

At the drive-up window she placed her order for a dollar burger, a courtesy cup of water, and a side salad. It was slow coming. She sighed. Maybe one day she'd have an excuse to use those pretty red plates she'd set out on her table at home.

The burger came, and Eve pulled into a parking space. She devoured the meal and used the flattened bag on her lap as a placemat. She ate the salad piece by piece with no dressing and drank the water. There was no time for sitting down at the table and picking over food. What she needed was a hot shower and a cozy bed for her tired bones.

Chapter 11

Monday, 7:00 AM

Emily groaned and opened her eyes. Her sweet sleep was ruined. There stood Grandma jiggling her shoulder.

"Wake up, Emily. Rise and shine!" Grandma wore a mischievous grin. "You said you wanted to spend more time with me. How about a little early morning walk?"

"Grandma!" she whined, raising up to see the clock. She slumped back against the pillow. "C'mon, it's only seven a.m." So much for catching up on sleep. A promise was a promise though. "Gimme five minutes, okay?"

Grandma headed downstairs. "Eggs and bacon on your plate! I'll be out in the laundry room folding towels."

Emily gobbled down her breakfast and caught up with Grandma. They locked the door and headed down the hill in the opposite direction from town. Mom was inside getting ready for a job interview at a school, a position with better hours. Attendance clerk, or something.

"Early's better, it's not so hot outside," Grandma said.

Emily nodded.

At the intersection of Eleventh Street at the bottom of the hill Emily stopped to straighten her shoelace. When she stood back up, the bearded man rounded the corner in his work uniform and sunglasses and tipped his hat in greeting. Emily stared, speechless.

Grandma had no trouble greeting him. She spoke right up and told him good morning.

Like before, the wordless man stepped to the side with his lunchbox, bowed slightly, and then moved along.

Emily grabbed Grandma by the elbow and kept walking. "How are you doing, Grandma? I mean, walking." She tried to keep her voice steady. No way was she going to let on about her nervousness to Grandma.

"Now that y'all are back from that Suwannee place, I'm the greatest I've ever been."

Well, Emily wasn't great. Not with that bearded guy popping up everywhere and creeping her out. But then, he hadn't done anything. Not *anything*. He'd been polite. He wasn't really *following* her anywhere. He just *showed up* everywhere. And turned around to watch her like he'd done the other day. Her fingers trembled around Grandma's elbow.

"You can let me go, now. I'm not frail. I'm not going to fall over."

Emily dropped her hand. "Sorry, Grandma."

Maybe Emily was just being paranoid since that Suwannee thing in June. If she turned around right this minute, the guy would probably be marching away in his work outfit, and tending to his own business, like a man going to work.

She told herself not to turn around. But she couldn't resist. She turned.

And once again, in mid-stride, the bearded man had done the same thing. They met each other's gaze and turned away at the same time.

Oh, dear. Oh, dear. If her dad were here he would help her. *Lord, wherever Daddy is, please help him. Fix him. Bring him back home. Bind up that spirit of alcohol. In Jesus's name.*

In the meantime, should she tell Tony? Maybe. Maybe not.

Tony had his own problems. And he was too busy playing detective and chasing that Mafia man.

Now *that guy* was probably nothing.

Monday, 10:00 AM

Tony stepped over cracks in the sidewalk as he ambled south along Third Street. A mockingbird trilled from a nearby sabal palm. He glanced up at their sunlit tips and beyond them at the cottony clouds. Not a bird in the sky. Days ago, in this very neighborhood, he'd glimpsed a striking swallowtail kite with its forked tail and long black-tipped wings flying over. With a white body and Shamu-like markings, the kite had been only 20 feet away—almost close enough to touch. Its nest would be high, most likely in one of the tall pines down by the tracks.

The black and white of his own life had now turned cloudy gray. Nothing sharp. Nothing clear. His last name—Vinetti— what did that really say about him? Nothing at all, now.

Half a block ahead, a woman in a white bathrobe struggled one-handed with a deflated kiddie pool she was dragging to the curb. Her other hand held a cigarette. It was Claire, Dad's friend. Claire had the longest blond hair in town. Tied back with a ribbon, it earned her the name Pony Tail, one that Dad used, and one that just seemed to fit. Claire finally parked the cigarette in her mouth and heaved one end of the pool onto the trash pile with both hands. Her mountain of trash consisted mostly of blackened wood.

Burnt up, just like Tony's identity. Up in smoke with that one sentence. *You're adopted.*

Just how was he supposed to regard himself? If he'd grown

up with the facts it might have changed things. He could have coped better.

By the time Tony reached her pile of trash, Claire had crossed back through the gravel parking lot of her beauty parlor/home and was standing in her backyard. The sign around front said *Sheer Grace Beauty Salon. Closed.*

He waved. "Miss Pony Tail."

Whoops. Bad old habit.

How could he forget the way she'd snapped at him a few weeks back, a reaction so opposite her good nature, he'd never seen it coming. "I prefer not to be called by that nickname. Ever again. I don't care what your dad calls me. No one else uses that nickname." She pointed her finger at his nose. "I've never said anything to you before, but you're old enough now to understand. Do you hear me, young man?"

The little speech still stung. Try it again. "Sorry, I mean Miss Claire. Hi."

Claire took the cigarette out of her mouth and turned around, clutching her robe together and crossing her arms. A long black mark streaked diagonally across the front of the robe.

"Hi, Tony. Happy Monday."

She didn't sound too happy. At least she wasn't gritting her teeth at him today.

"I didn't mean for anyone to see me in this old getup."

Tony pointed toward the pile of burnt boards. "What burned? You need some help?"

Claire frowned like he should already know. "You didn't hear all the fire engines on Saturday?"

He thought a minute and remembered. "Oh, yeah. I guess I did, but didn't think anything of it." They'd come barreling by the square.

"The neighbor kids—trying to barbeque. Caught the bamboo on fire in back of my house. What a torch!" she said, waving the cigarette in an arc. "I thought they were going to burn the whole neighborhood down." She returned the cigarette to her mouth, closed her eyes, and gave it a draw. "Where are you headed, Tony?"

"Headed to get the nurses' lunch orders down at the nursing home."

"You make any money like that?"

"Just tips. There are no other jobs."

"Bet you get more lunch orders that way—going down there in person. Those nurses see a handsome young man like you and they just have to place an order."

Tony's cheeks warmed. "Larry's does get more orders like that. And it's a lot more trouble. But it's one look at Larry's menu, not me, that helps. Who wants instant potatoes and macaroni glop? You know about nursing home food."

She took another puff. "You're quite an entrepreneur, Tony."

"Thanks, Miss Claire. Guys need cash, you know. For stuff."

"Yeah? Well," she said, "we girls need cash for stuff too, honey."

Tony laughed. "Before I forget," he held up one finger, "Dad…" He hesitated to say it now. "Dad—sends his regards." Tony had standing orders to bring his regards to Pony Tail, Freckles, and Mr. Doug each time Tony saw them. For what, he couldn't say, just some childhood friendship deal.

Claire moved her hands to her hips, raising her eyebrows like an owl over her prey, "So Vinnie Vinetti sends his regards? I *bet* he does." She nodded sarcastically. "You thank him for me, Tony. You thank him."

Maybe he should just forget saying that, too, from now on.

"You're such a nice kid, Tony." She flicked her cigarette,

89

mumbling as she walked toward the back steps. "But you absolutely have no idea the message you are passing on when you say that, do you? Vinnie can't let history rest, can he? He just has to pick at the scab."

What was Claire talking about?

She sat down on the top step and tucked her robe around her legs. "Well, if you really want to earn a few bucks I guess you can help. I'm trying to get this stuff out to the road before the garbage man arrives."

Best to move on to a new subject. "What happened to your little kiddie pool? It looks brand new." What was Claire doing with a kiddie pool, anyway?

"Had a hole in it. I was dipping out some tadpoles and drat it all, I burned a hole in the thing. She flashed a steak knife from off the steps and slapped it back down. "I finished it off with this."

Tony tucked his chin back. She was certainly wound up this morning.

"Sure, I've got a few minutes," he said.

Claire pointed to the burned clutter that had once been a shed. "Just haul that junk out to the curb and toss it up there with the rest."

He stepped toward the rubble.

"Sorry I don't have gloves. But keep it neat. I don't want the garbage man mad at me."

Claire rose as he tugged at the burned wood.

"Miss Claire, do you see anything under here you want to save?"

"I've picked through it already. But I couldn't reach my in-laws' Bible under there. Strange, it's hardly scorched at all."

Claire returned to the back steps as Tony set to work and

dug out the Bible. It only took a few minutes to drag the larger debris to the street, rake through the ashes, and bag the rest. Not much to it. The shed had been pretty small. He wiped his sooty hands on the grass and brought the Bible over to her.

"I've heard of Bibles coming through fires before."

"Yeah?"

"Yeah, like protected real estate," he said. He reached in his pocket and checked the time on his phone. "I've really got to go."

"Wait here." She darted inside and returned with a new bar of Lava soap which she tossed into his hands. "This should help."

Tony scrubbed up, wiped the water on his pants.

She offered a ten-dollar bill.

He took it. "Thank you, Miss Claire."

"Everything okay with you, Tony?"

"Yeah, yeah. Been doing some thinking, that's all. Bye, now."

She waved as he turned to walk away. "Hey, Tony, you going to Summer Crafts on the Square this Wednesday?"

"Yeah, maybe." But only because of Emily.

"Emily going?"

He smiled and felt the color rise in his face.

She grinned like she'd meant to stir him up. "And one other thing, on another subject. You think you'll be seeing my sister?"

"Freckles? I mean Eve? Just about every time I go to the nursing home."

"Then please. Take her something."

Tony drummed his fingers against his leg as Claire raced in the house. He'd spent enough time here already.

Claire re-emerged with a white gift-box. She held it out as she descended the steps. "Please, take a look at this."

This was eating up his time.

She took off the lid and pulled away the white tissue paper. A toddler's blue dress shirt, a bow-tie, and suspenders lay underneath. "I made it for Boogie. Won't he be the sweetest little thing in this?"

"That's nice, Miss Claire. And I hate to rush this, but I really have to run now."

Claire pushed the tissue paper back in place and closed the box. "Well, would you make sure Eve takes it? I keep trying, but she just won't let Boogie come over here or be around me. My only sister, and I can't even get together with her. I love that child so much. Make sure she takes it, Tony."

He took the box and turned away. "I'll make sure."

Claire walked along with him past where the blue kiddie pool lay sandwiched between the black boards. "I kept the pool full and clean for little Boogie. But he never even used it, and now there it is in the trash."

"I think that's real nice," Tony offered, the mention of trash bringing back the memory of the hit man's list.

Maybe he should bring that up. Her name was on it. Nah, she'd keep him talking. He'd better wait. And then there was Dad's name on the list. He snorted. Dad had probably earned a place on the list, whatever it was. But not Pony Tail. She wouldn't hurt a flea. Still, he'd wait to mention it.

"I keep hoping," Claire said.

Tony clutched the box to his chest and moved down the sidewalk. "You know what they say; Love conquers all. She'll come around."

He waved back at Claire. "See you later."

Within steps the gift-box's overpowering cigarette odor forced him to lower it to his side. Claire probably had no idea.

It was no wonder Eve didn't want the kid around the woman's house. If he had a sister or brother, though, nothing would keep Tony away, not even cigarette smoke.

But he was adopted. No brothers or sisters. Tony was as alone as a pixel on a world map.

Chapter 12

As she waited on the clerk to return with her paperwork, Eve gazed out through the plate glass window of Golden's Furniture Store. She should have parked her battered vehicle on the far side, away from the windows, so it wasn't juxtaposed to the fine decor inside the store. This view only exaggerated its nicks and dents. She picked up her phone, glanced at the time, then dialed. She had to share her good news.

Billy, next to her on the sofa, perked up. "Who you calling, Mommy?"

She patted Billy's leg. "Just my new friend Sue. If she's on break."

Sue, who worked at Larry's Restaurant, had met Eve's childhood friend Doug one day on his lunch break. And now they were an item.

Sue answered right away, "Hey, perfect timing."

"You'll think I'm crazy, Sue. But I did it."

"C'mon, don't make me guess."

"Well, maybe I should have spent Mom's inheritance money on a newer model car... But you know that white leather furniture I told you about?"

"You didn't."

"Call me impulsive. They're delivering tomorrow."

"Wow, Eve, I thought you'd pick the brown leather."

Probably because of Billy.

"White's pretty, too. And I don't think you're impulsive. How else are you ever going to accumulate nice things if you don't take the opportunity? When will you ever have a lump sum of money like this again?"

"Thanks. I was just looking at my run-down car out there and feeling kind of guilty."

"Don't be. If you fritter your money away on dollar-store items it will keep you in a rut, and you'll never have nice things."

"I've been forced to live like that."

"No, no, no. Not a criticism. Your ex cleaned you out. I've been there, too. This is a good way to lift you out of that rut, is all."

"The weasel. I hope he's happy with his new teenage wife and baby and all of my beautiful belongings that he stole."

"Where's the love? How'd you ever get stuck with such a dud, anyway? I hope your boyfriend Sammy is better than him."

"My ex might as well have taken a gun and shot Billy. There's not much difference in that and what he did."

"You think my Doug would ever treat me like that?"

"Are you kidding? Doug? He's as faithful as they come. As for the weasel, I'm steering clear of logic next time. I'm going with my heart."

"Just don't get in a hurry."

"Right now, I'm dealing with other issues. But you can bet I won't get stuck like that again." Sue had no way to understand the whole picture yet. Not in the short time they'd been friends. And today was not the right day to get into it. "Hey, I'd better talk to you later. Just wanted to share. I'm about to sign the paperwork here."

After the call Eve tossed the phone into her purse. She

gave Billy's shoulders a rub and glanced around the store. She hadn't planned to spend the entire day in the place. Where had that saleslady gone? Her eyes drifted beyond the window again where her vehicle baked in the late morning sun. The hood of her car had been covered with dew when she first drove up, but now it had evaporated.

Just like the dew of her youth. She stared harder through the window glass, hoping that the watery speck forming in her vision was just something on the glass, like the sun radiating off a water drop. And not a migraine aura. Not today. She hadn't had one of her monster headaches for two weeks.

But as she turned away from the window, the colorful speck moved too. She closed her eyes. *Noooo.* That's how they always started.

A sales assistant sat down beside her with the invoice. "Are you all set to receive the furniture at home? We'd like the men to be able to set the pieces in place with a minimum of shuffling."

Eve turned, experimenting with the spot. The bright aura continued to follow her visual path. Not good at all. *Please, God, no more migraines. Please.*

Her attention returned to the woman and her purchase. "Oh, the room's been empty for a week. A neighbor helped me out." Actually, her fellow renter, in return for taking whatever he wanted, had hauled her furniture off to the Salvation Army. "We are so ready. The walls are painted, the curtains are clean. The carpet's been shampooed. It'll be a snap for your guys. Little Billy helped too. He'll miss flying airplanes and riding his "horsie" around the empty space."

The saleslady smiled down at Billy. "You've been awfully good sitting here this long."

Billy smiled and concentrated on his Etch-A-Sketch, the

same kind Eve had played with as a child, back in the trailer park—back when everyone called her Freckles.

She smiled and kissed the top of his head. "You couldn't ask for a more patient little boy." She glanced down at his toy. The warbly brightness had grown. It now covered half of the toy's screen.

The sales lady pointed to the bottom of the invoice. "I've added in the delivery charges here at the bottom."

"That's fine. Like I said, there's no way I could get the furniture home by myself." Eve reached in her purse for the checkbook, and a stab of pain hit her over the right ear. She winced. Maybe if she ignored it, or sat still a few minutes, it would go away, or not grow worse. The saleslady sat beside her on the sofa as she wrote.

"I'm sorry about your mother. You mentioned this was your inheritance money from her."

"I did, and thank you."

How long had Mom sacrificed her comforts in order to save these few thousand dollars for Eve and her sister? Every conceivable argument had failed to pry Mom out of that little roach-infested trailer and its stored memories.

"The white leather chair and sofa set, it's a beautiful choice. I was worried about it at first, with a little boy in the house. You know what I mean. But…"

The pain above Eve's ear morphed now from narrow stabs to wide throbs and took her breath away. How was she going to get home like this?

"…he's such a good little boy, you should have no worries at all."

Eve gasped and handed Billy her purse. She tried to move only her eyes. Experience told her if she tipped or turned her head too fast the pain would be worse. "Billy, reach into my bag, please, and get my headache medicine," she whispered.

Billy jumped to, and started digging for the prescription bottle.

The sales lady motioned to a wandering assistant on the floor. "Myrna, come over here." She turned back to Eve, "Let Myrna here get you something to drink with that. We've got Coke, coffee, water. Just name it."

By now, Eve's eyes were watering. "Whatever is quick and easy, thank you."

Myrna studied Eve's face and darted away.

"And, oh, that beautiful red Buddha you bought," the sales-lady continued.

If she would just quit talking so much.

"Such a good decision. Just rub its cute little tummy. I've heard it'll bring you good luck or something."

Eve wrinkled her brow at the next throb. "I almost passed it up," she whispered, trying to hold back the throb.

"And don't you love that red marble belly? He reminds me of a little bowling ball."

Eve was glad she'd bought it while she had the cash. It matched her red dishes, her inspiration pieces.

But right now, all she wanted was to get home, pull those heavy red curtains closed, and lie down. Maybe she wouldn't throw up this time. Thank the Lord she didn't have to go to work. There was no way she could afford another sick day. Not if she wanted to keep her job.

Now if her ex would just come through with his child support check, she could rest easy.

Myrna returned with a pointy paper cup of water. Trembling, Eve popped in the pill and took a drink. It shouldn't be long before it took effect. If she could get home maybe she could make it through the day and be ready for the furniture delivery tomorrow.

"Here, Mommy, your sunglasses."

That bright sunshine would kill her if she didn't have these on in the car.

She shoved them on and squinted through the store's front windows. "Thank you, Billy." Dropping the paperwork in her bag she stood.

Billy followed her example by holding his Etch-A-Sketch under his arm. His other hand reached for hers. "I'll help you get to the car."

The saleslady followed them outside and helped Billy get buckled into his car seat. She tousled his hair. "You're a sweet boy, just like my little grandson. You stay that way, okay? Bye, bye." She shut the door and waved as Eve started the engine. "Thank you now. Be safe driving home, honey."

With a huge sigh, Eve backed out and headed home. Finally.

At the SE 35th Street Bridge, her cell phone rang. The screen told her it was Sammy.

She hit the green button. "Honey, how are you?" The fact that her boyfriend hadn't called for three or four days was not unusual in his line of work.

"I'm sorry. Lots of case work. Depositions. Court. You know how it is. Especially lately. Practically living at the courthouse."

"So, what's up?" Something about his voice sounded off.

"Hey. You—you don't sound too good." He always picked up on it when she had these migraines.

"Well, I did go down to the furni—"

"You've got another headache, don't you?"

"Well, I—"

99

"Eve, let's just stop this."

She held her breath. "What do you mean?"

"I mean, I just can't do this anymore, this headache thing and all. I just can't take it on; it's just not the life for me."

"You mean—"

"You're a good girl, Eve."

What could she say?

"I just can't do this anymore. And there's no sense pretending."

Eve's mind drew a silent blank. He was just like all the others. Was the world full of heels? But the sad thing was, she didn't blame him at all.

"Good-bye, Eve."

She slowly closed the phone and dropped it on the passenger seat. Oh, gosh. *Bam.* Just like that? She should have seen this coming. Numbness spread across her nose, ripening her eyes for a different kind of tears.

How could her day get any worse? The slow throb hammered above her ears.

Her cell phone rang. Maybe Sammy was sorry and had changed his mind. She read the screen.

No. It was the nursing home. Her boss.

This couldn't be good, either. She clicked the green button. A whisper was all she could manage with the lump in her throat. "Hello?"

"Eve, could you come to work early, as soon as possible? One of our girls has the flu and can't come in. She's really bad off."

Oh, this was the last thing she needed. "Nobody else can do it?"

"Not today. We really need your help, especially after you've taken so many sick days. Help us out?"

She pressed a tissue against her nose. "I'm heading home now. Let me change and pack Billy's bag."

She could hardly see the traffic lights through her tears, but she kept driving. Somehow she would get through all this. A better day was coming. She wiped her eyes and glanced at the blurry image of Billy in the backseat. And her son wasn't going to suffer for it.

Chapter 13

T ony left Claire's and plodded south again along Third Street toward Summit Nursing Home. This route, a few blocks out of the way, passed by Emily's house. As he rounded the mammoth camellia bushes of her next-door-neighbor's yard, Emily's porch came into view. On its far side, almost out of sight, sat Emily with her book, the sun at her back, her long wavy hair lit up like silk. He never ceased to be amazed at the number of books she read, hundreds and hundreds by now, if not more. The only ones she'd ever complained about were the propaganda books they'd assigned while she was at the Suwannee. Emily was so smart he wondered why someone like her would even talk to an ordinary guy like him.

He stepped up to the back of her mother's car. It was parked under her Grandma's gnarly old cedar tree. "Emily!" he hollered, and waved one arm.

She looked up and waved, "Tony!" In two seconds, she'd slid her book into the chair and loped down the front steps. Man alive. She had to be the prettiest and best girl he'd ever met. If she ever moved back to Citra, he'd find a way to follow.

Emily skip-walked up to him, tucking a strand of hair behind her ears. Then she stuffed her hands into the back pockets of her denim shorts with a tip of her head and a smile.

So different from those groupie girls at school.

"Hey, where are you headed?" she said.

"Lunch orders again."

"You any better today?"

Still holding the box, he folded his arms over his chest and dug a toe into the dirt. "After the big surprise? You really have to ask? Better, though, now that I've seen you."

"Aw, thanks. But are you coping?"

The way Tony felt, he shouldn't call Vinnie Dad anymore. "Is hating Vinnie's guts coping?"

She stared at the ground by his feet then looked up at his face. "Grandma says hating is like poison inside you. Don't let it eat you up, Tony."

"You've got to be kidding. How can I not hate him?" He struck a pose mimicking Vinnie. "*No big deal, Tony, but you were adopted. Ha, just thought you'd like that little information for your 15th birthday. And, oh, by the way, happy birthday, kiddo, here's a dusty old present from your dead grandfather.*"

"Your dad just lacks social skills. He's always that way; it's not just today. He really does love you."

"Ha!" Tony's voice came out a little too loud for the circumstances. He quickly lowered it. "He's not my father, remember? He doesn't love me, and I know that. He calls me stupid. All the time." He stopped talking for a beat to keep his voice from cracking. "And just the other day…"Tony shook his head. He'd better stop. She didn't need to know it all. "You just can't imagine. And I'm not trying to get your sympathy. It's just the way things are."

"I'm sorry, Tony. I wish I knew just what to say, but here's a hug." She wrapped her arms around him and squeezed. "I know you can use it."

He stared into the trees over the top of her head and blinked back the burn. What he wanted to say was, "Thanks, Emily," but he couldn't trust his voice. So he kept his mouth shut.

Emily squeezed again and backed away. She punched him lightly on the shoulder. "Hey, you'd better go get those lunch orders. I don't want to hold you up."

Tony cleared his throat and reached for her hand. "I don't mean to hate him, but right now it's all I can do. I'm not sure who I am right now." He frowned. "I just can't wrap my head around it. Who I am, who I thought I was, is all a lie. It's like, where do I fit?"

Emily pointed to his heart. "The person in here is the same as he was before," she said. "And I like that person. Very much."

Tony inhaled a jerky breath. "Thanks for that. It's just going to take some time to straighten my head out."

"One other thing about it, Tony. If you hadn't been adopted, I never would have met you."

He gave her hand a squeeze and cleared his throat again, stalling for what to say. "Thanks. You're right. That never would have happened. I'll see you later, okay?"

"There's gotta be a reason, Tony." She waved her fingertips as he turned. "God has a plan for you, and this all figures in."

Tony threw her a half-smile and a wave over his shoulder as he walked away. He'd have to think about that.

What kind of plan would God have for a mere pixel on the map?

If he had distant relatives, aunts, uncles—somebody, then he would be somebody. A part of something.

Chapter 14

Monday, 11 AM

Tony took a shortcut through the Summit Nursing Home parking lot. This time of day, there were few visitors, and most of the cars in the lot belonged to the nurses and aides. A cool breeze rustled the patio elms, providing brief respite from the thick vapor of humidity that hung over the asphalt. A metal-on-metal creak groaned from one of the cars, and he turned. The door of a dark blue Toyota hung open, and out stepped a long thin leg in nurse's aide scrubs. The old beater certainly didn't match the pretty redhead inside. Only one lady in town wore such long wavy red hair, and that was Freckles. The prettiest employee at the nursing home.

"Hi, Freckles," he said. "Just getting to work?"

When she turned, her face was blotchy and her eyes red and puffy. She dabbed a Kleenex under her nose.

"Wow, are you okay?"

"No, no. Hi, Tony," she said, her voice muffled. "I'm waiting to clock in."

"What's wrong? Why are you crying? Is Billy okay?"

"Billy's fine," she said, waving her Kleenex at Tony. "It's me. Just problems."

"Sorry, I don't mean to be nosy."

Eve blew her nose and placed her other foot on the ground. "No, and you probably wouldn't understand anyway. I'll be fine."

Tony stood beside the door, not sure if he should mention Claire's box in his hands right now.

"It's boyfriends, Tony. Headaches. Job. Nothing anyone can do anything about." She looked up at the treetops. "I'm so sick of being sick. Nobody wants a sick girlfriend."

"Be glad you found out now. They aren't worth having if they can't understand your headaches." Maybe he should just stick the box in her backseat and say nothing.

"It's not only that. I'm getting pressure at the job too. I've taken too many sick days off, and they're losing patience. They called me in today, and I'm already sick. I can't turn them down. I can't afford to lose my job."

"No wonder you're stressed, Freck—Eve, I mean. That's a lot to worry about."

"Thanks, Tony. Sorry to dump on you. But I really have to go clock in. Keep this to yourself."

"Definitely." He glanced up, almost deciding against saying it, but it came out anyway, force of habit, "My dad—"

"You are a nice boy, Tony," she said, glaring at him with those tear-stained eyes. "But when you say those words you have no idea what you're saying. Don't ever say that to me again, okay? Do me that favor."

Tony looked at her, dumbfounded. Smacked down twice about the same thing. Was it Dad? Everybody else hated him too? Just what was the big deal?

"I'm not mad at you. Just please, don't tell me that again."

"Sure, Fre—"

"Nope. Not that either. Call me Eve."

"O... Okay, Eve. I'll try to remember. Sorry."

"I'll be inside in a minute. You go on, now, and get your lunch orders." She grabbed his wrist and patted the back of his hand. She smiled. "It's not you, Tony. You really are a sweetie. Not like some people I know."

Tony glanced down at the box in his hand that Claire had given him and thrust it through the door toward Eve. "Your sister Claire, she sent you something."

Eve backed away with her palms up. Like someone had given her a snake. "Oh, no. Take that away. Not in here."

"But it's a gift. For Billy."

She handed him the key. "I appreciate it and all that. But put it in the trunk. Go ahead, just stick it back there."

Tony hesitated. "Okay, if you say so." He stepped around and unlocked the trunk. In the bottom of the trunk were other brand new toddler clothes sitting inside open gift boxes.

Of course, the cigarette smell would drive a person away, but if these were from Claire, why didn't Eve wash the clothes and keep them? At least be nice to her sister.

Chapter 15

Vinnie hit the remote as he swung his car into his driveway. He drummed his fingers on the steering wheel as the automatic gate opened. "C'mon, c'mon! Slow as molasses," he griped, then whipped inside and threw the Mercedes into park. His shirt was off before his feet hit the ground.

He slung it over the back of a poolside chair and kicked off his shoes and socks. Before undoing his belt buckle, he thought better and glanced toward the French doors. It would be just his luck someone—like Lusmila—would see him in his red-plaid drawers. Or that little girl Emily, Tony's friend, she might drop by. And then where would he be? Trapped in the pool in his undershorts until she left. He'd better go on inside and put on some trunks.

He stepped toward the house. All the windows were dark. Where was everybody?

Vinnie unlocked the French doors and laid his keys on the dining room table. "Lusmila? Nancy? Tony? Anybody here?" He stepped inside the bathroom. His big toe hit a dog treat and sent it spinning across the floor. "Stupid mutt." The damp swimming trunks hung over the shower rod from this morning. Better than his boxers, anyway. He changed, grabbed a towel, then stooped to pick up the dog treat. "Teresita? Anybody here?" Must be out shopping.

Back in the kitchen, he set the treat on the kitchen counter and searched through the refrigerator until he came up with some smoked turkey meat. Using up the last of the mayonnaise, he constructed a masterpiece of a sandwich with meat, mustard, tomatoes, lettuce and onions on rye. How was that for a Dagwood sandwich? He could shove half of it into his maw right now, but no, he'd be decent and eat in style out by the pool.

The last piece of Tony's chocolate birthday cake beckoned to him from the cake plate on the counter. He lifted the glass lid and scooped it onto the plate between the two sandwich halves. Licking his fingers, he left the mayonnaise jar and cold cuts for Lusmila to put up. Finding an ice-cold beer in the fridge, he set it on the tray with the sandwich and cell phone. Then he carried his nice little picnic out the back door. Vinnie hadn't lost his bachelor skills at all.

The cell phone rang, vibrating the tray. Who would that be? Hopefully a new client. Vinnie could use some fresh money after the pool fiasco. But this was a new number. Placing the tray on the back steps, he grabbed the phone.

"Hello? Vinnie here."

No answer. Faint noises speckled the background. *Somebody* was on the line.

"Hello? You'll have to speak up. I can't hear you."

Again, no answer. The background noise continued.

"This is Vinnie. Can I help you?"

The caller disconnected.

Vinnie hung up too. "Stupid." Then he slid the phone back on the tray and moved toward the pool. Perched on the side of the pool, he set the tray on his lap. Crumbs fell in the water as he licked the icing off the chocolate cake. Let the filter catch the crumbs. Or Tony. Within a couple of minutes he polished off the rest of the food and left the tray near the steps. Grabbing the beer, he guzzled half of it down, burped loudly, and lowered himself into the water. Just the kind of lunch break he needed. The cool water rose over his chest.

When it reached his armpits, the phone rang again. Drat, now he'd have to dry himself. "All right, all right." He set the bottle on the concrete. Water poured from his arms as he reached over the edge for the towel and snatched up the phone.

"Hello? Hello?"

No answer again. Same number as before, too.

"What is this? Talk to me!"

Again, he pressed the phone to his ear and waited. For sure that was somebody breathing on the other end. Clear as could be.

So who was it? He squinted his eyes. "This is Vinnie. Now what do you want?"

The breathing lasted for several seconds. Then the caller disconnected.

Vinnie banged on the keys, redialing. "What kind of game are you trying to play, buddy?"

A mechanical voice answered after a series of rings. "Please leave a message."

Vinnie hung up. His thoughts darted like a pinball machine. Think fast. This might not be a new client after all. Who do you not want to hear from? Esposito? The angry car dealer?

What about Dougie. Or Freckles or Pony Tail? Worst case scenario, any one of those. But after all these years? The phone sat black and silent in his trembling hand.

Could be. Maybe the three of them had gotten together, after all this time. Decided to talk, maybe go to the police. No statute of limitations on murder, right? Vinnie had a lot to lose.

Up to his chest in water, he cast his eyes around the patio's perimeter. Nobody could watch him through those hedges. Too thick. And no one could climb over the pointed tips of his ten foot iron fence, for sure. A shudder rippled through his chest. He glanced back at the electric gate. Nah, he would hear that if it opened.

His gun.

Gripping the phone and the towel, he emerged from the pool. Tempted to run, he walked as fast as he dared to the back door. No need to please his enemies by breaking his neck on a wet pool deck, eh?

Water coursed down his legs as he jerked the French door open. He stopped short. Lusmila's purse sat on the table inside. When had she come in?

Vinnie secured the towel around his waist and crept down the hall into his bedroom. Silently, with his chest pounding, he slid open the drawer of his nightstand. Took out the revolver. Yep, loaded. He'd keep it handy until he got this little matter cleared up.

On tiptoe, with the phone in one hand and the gun in the other, he returned to the back doors.

"Mr. Vinnie, I didn't know you are home."

He whirled to see Lusmila's round face peering out through the kitchen door. Of course, he probably looked like a possum in the headlights. Too late to fix that.

Her gaze lowered to the gun in his hand, and her mouth fell open. "Why you have a gun?"

Vinnie lowered the gun beside his leg. "Oh, nothing. Just playing around. Nothing to worry about." He didn't want to sound like a scaredy cat getting hyped up over some dumb phone call. After all, the caller could be miles away.

"Mr. Vinnie. Why you sneak around? You making me worry."

Come to think of it, the call could have been a wrong number. Or some dumb kid playing a practical joke. A baby holding a phone. Good grief.

On the other hand, with his barrelful of enemies, someone could be trying to rattle him. Threaten him. But which one?

The phone rang in his hand He jerked it up and stared at the screen. *Same number. Let it ring.*

"Mr. Vinnie, you scaring me too. What is happening?"

Another ring. He squeezed the phone as if he could choke the caller. Maybe they were trying to scope out the house, see if he was home. Rob the place. Shoot him up. The phone rang again.

"Mr. Vinnie, you going to answer?"

He stared at the blue screen behind his fingers. It could be the Cuban mob. That Esposito—he had nasty connections.

"Please, Mr. Vinnie. Tell me what's wrong."

A couple more rings, and the phone fell silent. Vinnie must look like a crazed idiot to Lusmila. "Some people don't like me, and…" No. Don't bring her into this.

Lusmila stepped through the doorway. "Here, Mr. Vinnie, you sit down at the table. Right here. I get you a coffee." She pulled out the chair, and Vinnie sat, placing the phone and gun in front of him.

"Nobody going to hurt you."

Vinnie leaned his face into his hands. Maybe he was being paranoid.

In a few minutes, Lusmila returned with the steaming mug. With his body wet and chilled he shivered now from the air-conditioning, and was glad to wrap his hands around the mug. Funny how he felt like a child now in his grandmother's kitchen, the only person who never slapped him around.

112

"May I sit, Mr. Vinnie? I want to say something." She sat before he could answer.

He nodded without looking up. When he finally turned, her warm black eyes looked into his. "Mr. Vinnie, I see how you not answering the phone. You are too good a man. If someone is treating you wrong, we need to call the police. You don't deserve to suffer this way."

Sure. Him call the police? She meant well. Let her talk.

"I don't know your business. But long ago, when you invite me, an old widow, into your beautiful home, I see you are a good man. I know this."

Vinnie dipped his head. She had no clue.

"Nobody should get away with treating you bad. You like a hard loaf of bread. Crust on the outside. Soft on the inside. And you treat me so good. I never forget this, Mr. Vinnie. No more work in the bar. You bring me here with my Teresita." She gave his arm a little shake. "With *Teresita*. A *dog*. You are a good man. Why don't we call the police?"

If she only knew. "No, Lusmila. It's not what you think."

"Let's call the police. Get the bad guy locked up."

He turned his shoulders to face her. "No!"

Lusmila jerked back with a blink.

A flurry of sparks swirled inside Vinnie's head. He slid the gun under the fold of his towel and walked back to the French door again. He turned back.

He shouldn't have screamed at her.

"You don't understand, Lusmila. I can't call the police."

Chapter 16

At the nursing home, Tony passed the visitor's desk and waved his notebook at the receptionist. "Morning." He marched to the end of the long hall, where the south-wing nurses' station bustled. readying for shift changes. Perfect timing.

"Hi, ladies."

"Yay, Tony's here," one of the nurses said.

Half a dozen faces turned.

"Here's my order," she said, pulling a small brown envelope out of her pocket. Several others handed over their own.

"Thanks, everyone, for putting your name on your envelopes. Saves a lot of time."

"Thank you." They kept a menu behind the desk.

A hefty head nurse circled the desk with a clipboard. She pulled her reading glasses down with a scowl and flipped through her papers. "How come we only see you during the summer?"

He grinned. "You know I go to school the rest of the year, Miss Leticia." She was always trying to get a reaction out of him.

"Here," she said, after locating her envelope. "Put me down for chicken alfredo, hon. And some sweet tea."

"Large tea, mind you. Cain't function without that sweet tea."

Three more nurses shoved their envelopes across the counter at him. More orders than ever. The nurses were a loyal group.

"Thank you very much. Y'all are great. I'll be back as quick as I can."

He stuffed all the envelopes inside a larger one. Hopefully somebody had their bike down at Larry's today.

As he turned, Eve emerged down the hall to his left, pushing the wheelchair of a male patient. Before he could break away to speak, she disappeared through the sunny doors of the dining room.

The buzzing of an automatic door sounded and the patio door swung open. Tony squinted as sunlight filled the room. A man stepped through the automatic doors. And he carried a violin case.

Tony nearly dropped his envelope. The guy from the train station. "What's he doing down here?" He spoke to no one in particular.

The hefty nurse poked her neighbor. "Quick. Your 12 o'clock. Check him out."

What a bunch of man-watchers.

The man returned the nurses' gazes with a friendly wave then strode into the bright dining room as if he belonged here.

He'd probably been out on the patio the whole time Tony had been here.

Tony finally turned away. What rotten timing. The nurses' lunch orders, business which a few minutes ago had been a positive, now stood between him and discovering what this guy was up to.

As Tony opened the front door, violin music started up. Good music. Beautiful. But he tore himself away and raced across the parking lot. If he stalled now with the nurses' orders, it would run him out of business. He'd have to ask Freckles, correction, *Eve*, about the stranger later.

A hit man who played music. What was going on? Right here where Freckles worked. What was the connection? Did she know him? Were all his friends in danger?

Just because he played music didn't make him safe.

Chapter 17

Monday, 11:10 AM

Eve entered the sunny dining room pushing Mr. Shay's wheelchair. As she positioned him at a table, a man entered through the opposite door and stood in front of the windows. She could hardly make out his features for the brilliance behind him. Some aides liked to shut the blinds but not her. Her patients needed all the daylight they could get. So did she, today.

Thank God, her medicine had knocked out the headache quick this time, or the blinding sun would be turning her brain inside-out with pain right now.

She squinted at the tall, dark, handsome visitor. He seemed well-built, strong, with a lean facial profile and broad shoulders. But she'd never seen him before. Whose relative was he?

The man leaned over and lifted up a violin bow. He adjusted a knob at one end, brought the violin up to his chin, and tuned up. Then, with the sun glinting off his instrument, he began to play—the most angelic song she had ever heard. She leaned over the table and cut Mr. Shay's meat, but the music wrapped itself around her and carried her away, making the small task nearly impossible.

Mr. Shay rested his hands in his lap, in no hurry to eat. He ignored the food, even after she finished, and stared at the violinist with the most peaceful expression on his face. Were those little tears in his eyes? He seemed to feel the music too. Speechless nurses gathered in the doorways, obviously ignoring their duties. No sound like this had ever flowed through these shiny hallways before.

The man quit playing after only a few songs. It didn't seem fair. He smiled and put away his violin as patients and nurses clapped. He offered no encore.

"Is that all, sonny?" an ancient woman said from a table nearby. Murmurs of agreement rose from the rest of the diners.

Instead of answering, he bent at the waist, took the little old lady's hand, and gave it a kiss. She pulled her hand back, surprised, but clearly pleased.

After a little bow to the clustered group, he stepped out to the nearest nurses' station. Eve emerged from the other door in time to see him lay a handful of business cards on the desk. Then he disappeared through the automatic patio doors.

She'd have to get one of them. Who was this guy?

Back in the dining room, she circulated among the patients. Mr. Shay finished up and signaled for her. "Honey, could you take me to my room for my nap?"

"Sure, Mr. Shay." She unlocked his wheelchair and disengaged him from the table, pushing him instead toward the nurses' station. This detour would only take a second. "You didn't eat very much. Are you okay?"

At the counter, the cards lay face down.

Eve stared down at them. One card had handwriting on the back. She blinked and reached for it. Did it say what she thought it said? Nah, it couldn't.

She picked it up and handed it to Mr. Shay as she wheeled him away.

"Would you hold this for me?"

"What's this?" Mr. Shay said, taking the card and looking it over.

118

"Read it out loud to me."

"Come to The Rock on Wednesday at 7:00 PM." Then he flipped it over. "It's got something written on the back, though. Some kind of note, I guess."

"I saw that. Read it to me." What were the odds that word would be on the back of a business card like this? "Hang on, Mr. Shay, okay?" she said, and wheeled him back to the station.

"Excuse me, ladies," she said to the two nurses huddled over their work. "Please, did you notice someone writing on these cards?"

They shrugged and looked back at her with blank expressions.

Eve shuffled the remaining cards around on the desk. The rest were all blank. She took the card from Mr. Shay's hand and studied the precise handwriting again.

Her hand shook.

Freckles.

This had to be a coincidence. Only a few people knew that nickname.

Chapter 18

Tony burst through the back screen door of Larry's Restaurant and handed off his orders to John. "These are all for the nursing home. To go."

John gave him a strange look, and Tony thought about what he had said. "Well, right, what *else* would they be but *to go*?"

Tony plopped down on the barstool closest to the kitchen to wait for the orders. He drummed, twiddled, and tried to kill some time. His good friend Mike, one of the servers, passed by with an empty tray. He frapped it against Tony's leg and kept moving.

"Hey, Mike; wait." Mike was one of his luckier classmates who'd found a pretty good summer job.

"Say, you think I could borrow your bike for my nursing home run? I need to carry a basket today. Lots of cargo."

"Sure, just bring it back with a full tank." he said, and disappeared through the swinging door of the kitchen. Mike always said that.

Lucky Mike. His dad had bought him the bike and just handed it over. A gift with no strings. Too bad Tony's dad couldn't do that. Vinnie had the money, after all. But, no, he had to go make life hard, even impossible. Dad knew how hard Tony worked, and he wouldn't even give him a leg up. Well, Tony was no slacker. He might not have an actual job, but he would show him how hard he was working. He'd save his money and buy his own. He'd prove his worth.

Tony's gaze followed the mahogany bar to the man seated six feet away. Doug, a downtown accountant, was a regular who ate lunch here nearly every day. Probably so he could visit with Sue on the other side of the lunch counter. They had to be an item now.

Tony thought of offering Dad's standard message, "Dad sends his regards," but decided against it. In fact, maybe he would just forget Dad's, or rather Vinnie's, instructions from now on.

Doug's face seemed a little haggard today. Better leave him alone. Doug could be edgy at times. Instead, Tony feigned indifference and turned away, tapping his fingers on the shiny wood and studying other customers in the mirror. Once again, Larry had forgotten to turn on the music track, and Tony couldn't help but overhear Doug and Sue.

Every adult in town knew about the car accident a couple of years ago; the intersection on Route 200 that claimed Doug's young wife and left him with two daughters to raise. They had to be around eight and nine years old now. Even though Doug kept his voice low, Tony couldn't help picking up bits and pieces about the girls.

Doug shook his head, exasperated. "Both girls are waking up in the middle of the night, screaming and crying. I'm going nuts trying to settle them down."

One screaming child was bad enough, but two? No wonder poor old Doug looked bad.

Sue refilled Doug's iced tea. "They haven't been watching any scary movies or upsetting newscasts have they?"

Doug shook his head. "That's not my style, Sue. You know it."

"Don't snap at me. Just trying to help you figure it out. I know you're tired and worn out."

Sue walked away and waited on other customers. When she came back Doug set his fork down.

"We set up the grill, cooked a few burgers. And set up the foun—" The man's voice choked.

Tony watched for Sue's reaction.

"The one that was in the car when she...?" Her gaze softened.

"Yeah." The word came out hoarse.

Tony turned away. Give the man some privacy.

"We put it together on the patio. Got the pump going. And the girls were happy about it, excited. There's nothing there that would give them nightmares."

"Can your mother come stay a few days? Would that calm them down? They'll still be in their own environment."

The speakers burst to life and drowned out Doug and Sue's voices. Larry had finally remembered the music. That was the end of Tony's eavesdropping.

Tony stood to stretch, but a commotion out on Larry's front patio caught his eye. He craned his neck to peer around Doug and Sue. Everyone outside had turned to see whatever it was to the left. Tony stepped away from the counter for a better view.

There at the end of the patio stood the same guy he'd just seen at the nursing home. Boy, Mafia-guy sure got around fast.

The man lifted his violin to his chin, its wood gleamed reddish brown in the sunlight.

Just then, someone bumped Tony on the shoulder. It was Mike with Tony's crate of lunch orders. "Hot food. Get going."

Tony leaped up and grabbed hold of it. "Thanks, Mike. And thanks for letting me borrow the bike." Dad had told him long ago that bikes were for sissies. Just because Dad never had one. Of course they weren't for sissies. What about those triathletes passing through town all the time? They were plenty macho looking. And so what? If you needed wheels, you needed wheels. It'd be a long time before Tony'd have a car. He hadn't even taken drivers ed yet.

Tony blasted out the back door and hooked the crate on the front of the bike with a bungee cord.

If he hurried he could get back to Larry's and hear this guy play.

But wait, Doug was on that list too.

This was no coincidence. What was about to happen?

Chapter 19

Eve rolled Mr. Shay's wheelchair toward his room. "What do you think of the little invitation, Mr. Shay?"

"You ought to go. Come to The Rock on Wednesday at 7:00 PM, simple enough. If I were a little younger, I'd drive you down there myself and go hear him play that violin again. He was magnificent."

She laughed. "You would, huh?"

"I've traveled to big cities, been to all kinds of concerts, mixed with the pros, and I'm convinced. I know what I'm talking about."

Eve guided Mr. Shay's chair through his doorway. "That young man is one of the best." She pulled his bedrail down and folded back the cotton covers for his daily nap. The sun, almost overhead, allowed only a little sunlight upon a small portion of the windowsill. "What else can I get you?"

"Just raise the top of my bed up so I can read and hand me that Bible."

Eve reached for the well-worn book and handed it over.

He pulled a folded paper out of it. "This is my prayer list. I wanted you to see it." Mr. Shay opened it up and his thin gnarled finger trailed down the names and stopped in the middle. There were so many. "There's your name, and there's Billy's."

"You're praying for us?" She and Billy weren't as alone as she'd thought. Imagine, someone actually cared enough to pray for them. She cleared her throat and blinked back the burning moisture in her eyes. "Well, thank you, Mr. Shay. I appreciate it. We sure need all the prayer we can get." She sniffled. Why did she feel like bawling all of a sudden?

"Are you comfortable, Mr. Shay? Do you need anything else?"

Mr. Shay was so good, kind, and different than most. This was the first she'd heard about the prayer list. She hadn't minded Mr. Shay asking about her boyfriends or giving her advice. But she had no idea he was praying for her. He wasn't so much worried about himself as interested in the welfare of the nurses and other patients.

And not one solitary visitor came to see him. Such a shame. She would be proud to have a father like him. If she could just adopt him. Maybe the head nurse would let her take him home for a visit. She could serve him a nice meal on those new red dishes, and he would be the first person to use them. She'd better wait and ask, though. No need to disappoint him.

"I think you should go," Mr. Shay said, bringing her back to the present. He reached over and squeezed her hand. Then he gave her a smile and a wink.

"Go?" How strange he would say that. "You want me to *leave*?"

"No, honey." He laughed. "I'm talking about the meeting on the little card. I have a good feeling about it."

"Oh, the meeting. My mind was a million miles away. I'll think about it, Mr. Shay." She patted his shoulder. "Have a good nap."

As she turned back at the door, he was already reading his Bible. Maybe going to the meeting was good advice, coming from someone like him. She'd definitely give it some more thought.

What harm could it be?

Chapter 20

Monday, 12:15 PM

Out of breath after his mad dash back to Larry's, Tony rolled Mike's bike against the ferns growing out of the brick wall and locked the chain. He jerked open the back screen door and passed by the bar inside. Just in time. The notes of violin music still drifted in from out front. And Larry had propped open the front door. *Way to go, Larry.*

After a few really good measures, the music stopped. Larry's patrons clapped. Was the guy done already? He sure hadn't played very long.

"Tony." It was Larry, standing between the kitchen's swinging doors. In his hands, he held another crate with a pair of bagged hot lunches. "Got another delivery for you. Someone at the courthouse just called in an order."

He reached for the lunches. "Thanks, Larry."

The music started up again outside. *Rats,* just when he had a minute to finally hear the guy. *But good,* regarding the orders. The courthouse was only blocks away. Maybe he could get back in time. He'd have to pedal fast.

Tony stumbled out the back door with the crate, unlocked the bike, and circled around front in time to catch a few more bars, as well as the violinist's eye. The man actually smiled at him, but then turned back to his audience.

By the time Tony returned to Larry's, the violinist had disappeared. Vamoosed.

Not again.

126

Tony parked the bike and went inside. He plopped down on his favorite barstool again and stood a menu up beside his elbow. He slid his tips out onto the counter. No need to advertise his profits.

Mike tapped him on the shoulder again. "Hey, someone in the kitchen made a cheese and turkey by mistake. Want it?"

"Sure do. I'm starved."

Doug, two seats down, finally stood up to leave. It was obvious that Doug liked Sue the way he smiled at her. He acknowledged Tony with a nod and headed out.

Mike returned with the sandwich, and Tony tipped him a dollar. The sandwich would be free, after all.

"Hey, thanks, man." Tony took a bite as Mike pointed a thumb at the front window. "Should have heard that guy play just now."

Tony nodded. He covered his mouth with a napkin, "I wish. Who is he?"

"Don't know," said Mike, "Didn't say much."

Just then, Doug returned from outside and slid a small card across to Sue. "I need to get back to work, but the music guy left some of these on the table. Think you'd like to go? Maybe there's a little concert."

Sue leaned over and read the front of the card as she dried her hands. "Come to The Rock on Wednesday at 7:00? What's this? Where's The Rock?" She picked up the card and looked at the back. Her face took on an odd expression as she showed it to Doug. "D'you write that?"

He scowled. "Now that's weird. I just picked it up like that."

"Why would somebody write *Dougie* on the back?"

"Dougie? Not Doug? That's weird," he told her, taking the card and looking it over.

Why did Doug and Sue look so upset by a name on the back of the card?

Doug approached Tony on the barstool. He flipped the card around so Tony could see the handwriting on the back.

He leaned into Tony's face with his teeth clenched. "Know anything about this?"

Tony held his hands up. "Don't look at me. I don't know anything about it."

He snapped the card around in his fingers but kept his eye on Tony. "You'd better not. And neither had Vinnie. I've had enough of this kind of thing."

Nothing made sense. One thing for sure, the weird way things were going, Tony hoped Doug packed a pistol.

Monday, 5:15 PM

Upstairs Emily pushed the vacuum cleaner back and forth in her room near the window. The rugs up here stayed pretty clean, and she only vacuumed them every now and then. As she unplugged the cord below the window, a movement down on the sidewalk caught her eye.

It was him. The bearded guy. Probably heading home down there where she'd seen him with Grandma. She stepped behind the edge of the window with a shiver and watched until he disappeared.

At least now she knew what time in the afternoon to avoid him.

Monday, 5:15 PM

As he passed by the big house the bearded man resisted

the temptation to turn his head. He was getting much better at looking sideways—checking things out from behind the sunglasses—appearing to not watch at all. No need to scare her.

He'd caught her movement upstairs. From what was probably her bedroom. Yes, it was her. And she had stepped back to look.

But that boy she hung out with. He'd have to check into that.

Chapter 21

Vinnie sat up in the pool chaise and held the phone away from his ear. Tony stood about 10 feet away. "Hey, can you be a little quieter?" he yelled. "Clean that pool cartridge somewhere else. I'm on the phone."

Tony turned off the hose and moved the cartridge a few more feet away. "Sorry, Dad, I didn't hear it ring."

"Pay more attention. Pay more attention." Vinnie turned his back to Tony and pressed the phone against his ear. "So, now what were you saying, Esposito?" Vinnie listened and shook his head. "No, I'm not going to give you back the black statue. Don't care if you do have the money." Vinnie shook his head again. "Sorry. We made a deal, and you paid me. I've got this new statue, and you won a handful of money at the races. It's all good. Why don't you just leave it alone? Enjoy your money." Vinnie applied his ear again and shrugged. "I haven't got time for this. Just go buy another statue and leave mine alone. I'm having family time right now. Good-bye."

Flipping onto his stomach, Vinnie stretched out on his chaise, and tried to relax. He couldn't help but notice Tony. What was the kid doing? He yelled again. "Tony!"

Tony turned off the hose.

"Look, don't you remember anything? Change it out. Just change it out, clean that old filter, but change it out. Don't leave it disconnected. Go look in the pool equipment. Get the replacement cartridge."

"I thought I was cleaning it."

"You're rinsing it. Go soak the thing in cleaner. Look in there," he said, pointing toward the equipment room. "Think. Think." The boy needed to pay more attention, learn more responsibility. Tony should know, he'd watched Vinnie clean plenty of filters before.

"Sorry, Dad."

"Yeah, come here a minute. I want to talk to you. Sit down."

Tony sat on the edge of the other chaise, facing him.

"Now, I don't want you to think I've been snooping in your room or anything."

Tony glanced at the concrete then back at Vinnie. "You were in my room?"

"It's my house, ain't it?"

Tony didn't answer.

"So, I'm passin' by the room, okay? Just passin' by."

Tony blew through pursed lips and studied the pool deck.

"You had money on the dresser, folded up love notes, some poems, or something..."

"Dad, you read my stuff?"

"I didn't read anything. Just opened it up and shut it back, okay?"

"No, Dad. It's not okay. It's personal. Personal."

"I didn't read it. Now back to what I was saying." Vinnie reached down and grabbed his beer, took a long swig and forced out a big burp. "It looked like the room of an irresponsible child."

Tony lifted his hands. "I'm not irresponsible. Look around, Dad, look at me working, earning money, taking care of things here."

"Let me finish."

131

Tony leaned forward.

"I think in order to be more responsible you ought to go ahead and start paying part of your keep."

"But, Dad, you said when I was 18 that would happen. I'm 15."

"Not much, you pay me a percentage. Get used to paying bills. I think that would help you be more responsible."

Tony jumped to his feet. "Okay, fine. How much do you want? Just don't read my personal stuff. It's mine, okay?"

"And you don't need to be wasting your time on poems and such. You can't be in love with…"

"You did read it."

"No, I just saw the name."

"That's my stuff."

"Emily is your mother's music student, not your girlfriend."

Tony's face turned red. "My girlfriend is who I want her to be."

Vinnie leaned back against the chaise and touched the bottle to his lips. He paused and gave it a sniff. "What is that stink? I smell it again."

"Okay, how much do you want? Just say it."

"I think ten percent would be fine." Yeah, and Tony would be thanking him years later when he knew how to manage his affairs.

Tyrant drooled behind Vinnie's chaise. He shoved Callous away from Vinnie's ear. He laughed. "He smells you, you rancid stink-bag."

"You're no bouquet of roses."

"Enough outta you already. Shut it up."

Callous gave him a one-fingered salute. He hissed and blew spit out between his broken teeth. It landed on his partner. "You wart-covered idiot. You think you did that job just now? That was all my work. *I* did it. *I* told him what to say."

"You talk too much, stupid." Tyrant raised double fists and knocked the snot out of Callous.

Callous snarled and came back biting.

Tyrant raised another double fisted hammer blow.

They rolled off into the corner, clawing and tearing until their smelly green mucus made them too slippery to continue.

Chapter 22

Eve crossed her legs on the white leather sofa and jingled her car keys. "Hurry, Billy. It's time for me to go to work. Brush a little faster." The water in the bathroom trickled on. Billy was diligent with those teeth. That was for sure.

"I'm glad I went in yesterday, Billy." She spoke loud enough so he could hear. "The boss is going to keep me on a daytime schedule now. What do you think of that? Now we can spend more time together. Won't you like that?

No response, just trickling water. "You hear me?"

Billy popped around the corner with foam all over his mouth, and nodded happily before vanishing again.

Eve grinned. Her gaze drifted up to her painting over the television. Her one and only creation. Well, aside from things in her school art class. She remembered painting it, too. It wasn't half bad. That branch of orange blossoms could use a little better detail, though. She studied the pocket knife, and the piece of notebook paper torn into the shape of a heart. And those initials. That day was so sharp in her memory it could have been yesterday. The sun shined through the bedroom window. Her curtains billowed, stirring the perfume and pollen that drifted in from the trees outside. And she could still recall the scent of those waxy white blooms. So divine.

A few years ago, she'd finally revealed the secret of those initials to her sister Pony Tail. Her sister had smiled and said, "Yeah, I knew all along."

"Billy, aren't you done yet?" Again, just the sound of running water. "You're going to brush all the enamel off, sweetie."

Her picture was a prize-winner according to Pony Tail. Why had she stopped painting after just one? Oh, well, one day, far off in the future, when she retired she'd pick up the hobby again. Right now, who had time? And who had money for new paints?

Besides, what was there to paint? A picture needed purpose.

Silence from the other room. The faucet's trickle had stopped. "Let's go, Billy."

Eve raised her fingers in mid-air as if holding a paintbrush. She swished left and right, twisted her wrist up and down, swerved and dabbed as if painting over a canvas. At times she did feel that urge to pick up a brush. The itch to paint. There might be some talent deep within her somewhere.

But still, that would all have to wait.

Eve walked to her knickknack shelf beside the front door and picked up the pocket knife. She dusted it against her leg, then compared it to the painting. It really wasn't so bad for a beginning art student. Was it?

She could have returned the knife to Robert's father. But when she got up the courage to visit, the migrants had moved to a new camp.

Robert's poor parents. To lose a child in such a horrible way. Eve sighed and replaced the knife.

Poor child. And Vinnie! *The wretch*. What could she or Pony Tail or Dougie even say now to the law this many years later. Forget it. Those migrants were gone without a trace.

Billy stood in the doorway. "Ready mommy," he said, and wiped his mouth on his sleeve.

At the nursing home, Eve kissed Billy at the nursery door. "Bye now. I've got to go clock in. You be a good boy." Before she turned around, Billy had already skipped away to play. Thank goodness he liked this place.

Outside the cafeteria, Mr. Shay seemed to be expecting her. "No concert today?" he said, unlocking the wheels of his chair and nodding toward the window. "I'm kind of sorry about that."

"Guess there won't be," Eve said, searching the room for yesterday's guest. "Here, let's put you next to a table so you can eat lunch. Which group of friends will it be today?"

"I like to change things up, so how about table nine today?" he said, pointing to the left.

"I wish he'd come back today, too, Mr. Shay. That was some kind of beautiful music, wasn't it?"

"Good lookin' guy, too, huh?" The old man grinned. "Well, you remember what I told you?"

Eve felt herself blush. "I do, and I'm thinking it over too."

After lunch had been served and Eve had circulated several times, Mr. Shay laid his fork down. "Psst." He motioned Eve to him with a twinkle in his eye.

"What are you up to now?"

He fumbled around in the side pocket of his chair and came up with a gardenia. "See this flower?" he whispered.

"I thought it smelled good over here."

"I picked it a little while ago. Out on the patio." He pushed it into her hand. "Take it. I want you to do something."

"Well..."

"See that grumpy nurse's aide over there? That's the one I told you about."

In fact, the aide had a horrible chip on her shoulder, and Eve could never get a smile out of her. "Yeah?"

136

He grinned and pointed at the flower. "Sneak that onto her clipboard. He fished around in his seat and pulled out a small card with a picture of a kitten, like the kind the Veterans send out. "Put this little note on there with it."

She glanced at the shaky handwriting inside. *From your secret admirer.*

"Well, aren't you the stinker, Mr. Shay."

He winked and got back to his lunch. "Don't forget now."

Eve collected the flower with a chuckle and set off down the hall to do her rounds. The old guy was full of surprises.

An hour later, Eve found Mr. Shay in the game room with two buddies. "Who's winning, there?"

"Undetermined, honey, undetermined. I spilled the cards all over the floor a while ago. Messed everything up and we had to start over."

"You weren't behind, were you?"

His buddies roared at that and poked Mr. Shay.

"You ready for your nap or not?"

"Okay, let's go," he said, and pushed away from the table. "Guys, I'll see you after a while. Don't stray too far." He gave them a salute as Eve pushed him back toward his room

Eve smiled down at his bald head. "I delivered your gardenia. And your message."

"Oh, yes, thank you. We've got work to do on that girl. We'll wear her down with niceness."

Eve laughed. "You sure can come up with some doozies. By the way, Sammy is out of the picture."

He nodded and said nothing until they arrived at the room. "So, what happened, Eve?"

"Boys just don't have time for sick girlfriends. No patience for it. There's no *till death do you part* for them. It's all so superficial."

137

"Can't be real love then. You're not missing anything with that Sammy, Yammy, or whatever his name is."

She pushed Mr. Shay into the room and sat in a chair beside him. "I've got all these pretty things at my apartment, new plates, beautiful new furniture. But there's nobody to share it with. Mom's gone."

Mr. Shay said nothing, just listened with a thoughtful expression on his face.

"Sorry, I'm whining. You don't need to be bothered with all this."

"But are you sick? You don't seem to be."

Eve explained about the migraines and how she'd lost several jobs over them.

"There's no family?"

"Oh, yes, but I can't socialize with my sister. She smokes like a diesel truck, and it sets off my headaches. I just have to keep away. But Billy needs family, an aunt, an uncle, all those normal things, not to speak of a father."

"Well, honey, there's no problem too big for God. Have you prayed?"

"No, I guess I haven't thought of that. But I've worried about it a lot."

Mr. Shay took her hand in his. "That worry won't get you very far." He bowed his head and she did too. "Heavenly Father, we lift this lovely young lady up to You. You've heard the desires of her heart. Now I ask You to grant her those things according to Your will. Line her heart up with what You want for her, and draw her unto you. Provide for all of her needs, heal her sickness, give her little boy a daddy, and let this family come together. Watch over them both, Father, in Jesus name. Amen."

Eve wiped her eyes and gave Mr. Shay's hand a squeeze. Her voice cracked. "I don't think anyone has ever done that before. I mean, prayed for me. Thank you, Mr. Shay. It was beautiful, so beautiful. It made me feel so good."

"Now you just pray that when you think of it, and trust that God is going to find a way for you. Try not to worry. Turn it over to Him."

"I will." She stood and as he sat on his bed she helped him out of his shoes.

"I was pretty tired just now. Thanks for stopping by."

"Want your Bible?"

"Yes, thank you."

She hesitated before handing it to him. "May I hug you?"

"Why sure, honey. Just don't break my old bones."

Eve laughed as she embraced him. "Thanks for everything, Mr. Shay."

"Anytime, honey."

Maybe she should ask him about that red Buddha, and what the woman in the store had said.

"Do you believe statues can have magic?"

He raised his eyebrows and shook his head. "Oh, no, honey. treating a statue like it's alive, like it has powers, that's idolatry. You don't want to mess with that. God is a jealous God, and He's got no patience for that. Why do you ask?"

"Oh, nothing, just something somebody said. You sleep tight now, and don't let the bedbugs bite."

Mr. Shay had so much wisdom. If she could just be around him more and hear what he had to say. Soon. She would do that soon. And Billy would love every minute of it too.

Chapter 23

T ony dumped his brown envelope of the day's tips onto the bar. He separated the coins, sliding them around on the shiny wood. $4.65 He scooped it all back into the envelope.

The weight of the coins was too heavy for his pockets. He needed Sue to trade it out for bills.

Yes, the tips were adding up. But now that Dad had helped himself to Tony's money, he wouldn't have enough to finish paying for Emily's birthday dog by Saturday. Forget the surprise.

Tony turned on the barstool and peered past the foil-lettered windows to the patio. There were umbrellas, tables, and people, but not a sign of yesterday's violin player. Just his luck.

The phone in his pocket vibrated. He fished it out and checked the screen. *Mom.* "Hi, Mom."

While Mom talked, he stepped over to Sue with the envelope, and laid it on the counter. "Sue, would you mind trading these in for paper? I'd appreciate it." He pointed to his phone then leaned his back against the bar. Sue could always use more change at the lunch bar.

Mom had kept right on talking.

"Forget it, Mom. I can't do choir. I sound like a dying frog, and you know it."

Tony studied the bricks and mortar of the restaurant's wall as Mom chattered on. She wouldn't let go of the subject. Not until he said yes. That's how Mom was.

"You *what?* You invited Emily?" Mom knew all the tricks. He expelled a chest full of air. "Well, I guess I'll go along. But just don't expect me to sing." He paused as she continued. "Okay, sundaes afterward, that'd be great. Better than staying home with Dad—I mean Vinnie."

Sue tapped him on the shoulder and handed him the cash. He nodded his thanks as Mom fussed at him about his attitude toward Dad.

"Okay, I'm sorry. I know. Honor your parents and all that. But you can understand how I feel. I've gotta go, now. Talk to you later. No, I don't blame you for the birthday disaster. I saw how it was. I love you, Mom."

No, this whole mess was Vinnie's doing, not Mom's.

If Dad would just act like a dad instead of a bully, things would be better. Just act nice toward him. Stop trying to take advantage.

Tony stepped out the front door of Larry's and glanced around. So where was his stranger today? What would he be doing?

Tony wandered toward Starbucks. As he stepped over the curb, a familiar figure emerged from Leonardo's across the street, the other nice restaurant on the square. Tony stepped behind a light pole next to Starbucks and watched. Vinnie crossed the square and strolled past an ice cream kiosk. Where the two walkways met, Dad stopped to speak to a Hispanic man, probably one of his workers. The small boy at his side could have been a first or second-grader. Dad and the man chatted then shook hands.

Dad tousled the little boy's hair and took out his wallet. He seemed to be asking the man's permission for something. The man nodded gratefully, and Dad handed the little boy some paper money and pointed him to the ice cream kiosk.

The child scampered away. His dad followed, and Tony's dad headed around the block on the other side. Probably to the parking lot.

Tony gritted his teeth and kicked the light pole. So Dad had all the money in the world to hand out to other peoples' kids on the street.

But when it came to Tony, he had to pay a stupid ten percent income tax. And Dad couldn't even help Tony with a bicycle to ride for his deliveries. It wasn't fair.

Chapter 24

Tuesday 3:00 PM

In the kitchen Emily bounced up and down. She hugged her mom's neck. Mom had just hung up the phone. She had won the new attendance clerk job at the local elementary school.

"Congratulations," Emily squealed. "I'm so happy!"

Mom beamed and Emily let go to return to her cheese-toast snack at the table. "It's the perfect job. Now all our holidays will match," she said, stuffing in a bite.

Mom took a spoon from the dish rack and ran it through the icing in Grandma's bowl by the sink. Grandma fake-swatted her hand as Mom held the chocolate glob toward Emily like a peace-offering.

The grin hadn't left Mom's face. "So how about you call Tony and we drive out to Citra and see the old place?"

Emily's jaw dropped. Had she heard right? "You're kidding," she said, and accepted the spoon. "Sure."

"But keep in mind. I'm not getting out. No hanging around. No visiting. Nothing. Clear?"

Grandma stood behind Mom. She winked at Emily as if to say *Well that worked out like we hoped.*

Emily licked the chocolate icing off the spoon. "You want to go, Grandma?"

Grandma shook her head. "I've got things to do here. Y'all run on."

Emily finished up her toast, grabbed her phone, and raced out to the front porch swing to make the call. But at the door she stopped short, glancing around to make sure the bearded man was nowhere around. Nope. Too early. She plopped on the swing and dialed Tony.

Within minutes she and Mom were off in the car and had swung by to pick up Tony. On the way out of town Mom picked up hot-fudge sundaes from McDonalds and headed north to Citra. After that awful time at the Suwannee Emily could definitely use some extra calories.

The row of tiny cabins where Emily used to live were part of a now defunct sports-fishing camp. Years of drought had dried up its boating access and run it out of business, just like all the other fish camps around the lake. The dock, though still upright, had dropped several of its boards into the mucky dollar-weeds below. In front of the office an *Open* sign dangled from a broken lamp-post. Peeling plywood, most likely from last-year's hurricane, covered the office windows. The camp hadn't looked this bad when she and her mom had moved out a year and a half ago.

The cheap make-do cabins across the street from the office had long since evolved into low-rent housing. They'd initially been constructed for overnight fisherman. Old and run down now, their paper-thin walls hardly repelled the winter chill or the broiling summer heat.

Emily knew from experience.

"This is it?" Tony said.

Emily nodded. She opened the car door and fixed her eyes on the middle cabin. Her heart sank. It did look abandoned.

So did all the others where her friends had lived.

She and Tony crossed the street. Mom stayed in the car.

"Watch for moccasins," Emily said. "This is Orange Lake. It's riddled with them. Gators, too—all that stuff."

A thick black snake slithered across the grass in front of them.

"Whoa," Tony shot his arm across Emily to stop her as the snake disappeared through the weeds.

"As I was saying..."

Tony said nothing, just stepped higher, and kept his eyes on the grass.

She crept around the side of the one-room cabin and peered in through the open window. "Just like I imagined." Bean cans and mouse-droppings littered the table. And across the room above the sink her mom's once-cleaned and starched curtains hung out the window. Brown stains marred their hems.

Tony stood beside Emily and stared inside.

She nudged him toward the street again. "Come on. I've got to look for his boat." She had to make sure Dad wasn't out on the lake. *If the boat was gone...* She shuddered. That meant anything could have happened.

Tony followed her across the street to the broken-down dock. The murky lake, despite recent years of abundant rain, hadn't yet recovered from its post-drought conditions.

"He keeps it out here," she said, stepping carefully to avoid the more rotten planks. She stopped at the end and stared into the shallow water, the only place from which anyone could even remotely hope to launch a boat.

And there leaned Dad's old wooden boat, half-sunk in the shallows. A solid mat of undisturbed water hyacinths and duckweed covered the surface in and around it.

Emily gazed past it toward the canal's end. The willows had nearly choked it off from the lake.

"Well," Tony said, "At least he's not out on the lake somewhere." He seemed to understand.

145

Emily turned, realizing she hadn't heard those pit bulls barking. They must be gone too.

"His clothes, his stuff. It's all missing." Tony said. "He's been gone a long long time."

Mom called out from the car. "We need to get going, guys. Choir practice is tonight. And I'm joining."

Emily trudged back to the car.

The old place was just like she'd imagined. And Dad must had been gone a while. Judging by the condition of the boat, he'd probably left about the time she and her mother had moved out.

Abandoning the old house was like abandoning them.

Was God even listening to her prayers?

Tuesday 5:15 PM

On the way home Emily's Mom took the long way through town. Downtown's rush hour traffic filled the one-way streets. Emily, still daydreaming of the place in Citra, snapped to attention. "Mom, what are you doing? Tony lives back that way."

"Sorry, guys, I had my mind on other things," she said, slowing near Barner's Insurance Agency and turning left. "Heading back to your place, now, Tony."

As they rounded the corner Emily grabbed Tony's arm. "There! Did you see him? He just walked in that door."

Tony turned. Shrugged. "I saw his elbow. And a door shutting. But that's about it."

"Mom, could you go around the block? I need to read the sign on that door."

"I can't, Emily. I'll be late…"

"It's okay, ma'am. Emily and I can come back some other time," Tony said.

Emily poked him with her elbow.

He pointed a teasing finger at her to settle down, and added, "Would you like to drop Emily off at my house? Mom and I can take her to choir practice."

Emily wasn't in the choir, but this was fine with her. Hanging out with Tony was the goal.

Mom hadn't answered, so Emily helped her out as if she had. "Thank you, Mom."

Tony frowned at Emily with an expression that meant *What are you doing?*

"And really, Mom. Thank you for taking us out to Citra."

Tuesday, 6:20 PM

Tony, along with Emily, was the last to leave the dinner table. Holding his empty plate, he stood. "We'll help you, Lusmila," he said, and began stacking the dirty dinner dishes. Emily followed suit, collecting the silverware. In the other room, Mom was already changing clothes for the meeting tonight. Dad had taken off outside.

"Tony, Emily, thank you, *mijos,* but I can do this," Lusmila said. She took the handful of knives and forks away from Emily and shooed them away. "Go, go, Tony. You have company."

"Don't you want us to help you so you can get ready?"

Lusmila re-entered the kitchen with a shake of her head. "I get ready in a minute. These dishes are just going in the dishwasher. Go."

Tony shrugged.

"Hey, Tony," Emily whispered. "Why don't we take a peek at your violin?"

"I don't know." His insides were a little mixed up about that violin right now. Should he be happy or sad or what? He'd climbed out of bed one morning as Tony Vinetti, and then, at the end of the day went to bed as someone different. Should he love or hate the instrument?

"Come on, it belonged to your grandfather."

Tony stuck his thumbs in his back pockets and turned. "Come on then."

Teresita followed behind them, her toenails clicking against the marble floor.

"I can't really deal with this whole new identity thing right now," Tony said. "So let's just make it quick." He flopped down on the bedroom floor and pulled the case out from under the bed.

Emily grabbed a wadded-up t-shirt off the floor and wiped the dust from the case. "It's pretty dried and cracked. How old do you think it is?" Emily said.

He raised the rusty clasps and eased the lid open. "It has to be a hundred years old." In the bottom rested the instrument. He ran a fingertip across the deep pile of its velvet lining. Spots had faded from its original brown to gold. Or was it gold to brown? Hard to say. A small pocket attached to the lid held one end of the bow and a curved metal clamp the other.

"It's beautiful," Emily whispered, caressing its varnish. "Like dark red honey."

Tony said nothing, but trailed his own thumb across its surface.

"I can imagine your grandfather touching it like that."

Emily watched as he lifted it out, supporting its neck and body with both hands.

Scattered beneath it were a smattering of yellowed papers and a small envelope containing thin rolled up wire.

Emily felt of the envelope and laid it back down. "Strings, I guess."

He placed the instrument on his lap as Emily reached for the compartment at the end of the case. "What do you think's in there?"

"Open it," he said.

Inside was a cork covered cube of amber material with lettering on its side. She held it up so Tony could read it too. "Resin. Pretty." She lowered her hand. "It's well used, anyway," she said, eyeing its worn half-inch groove.

Tony said nothing, just pulled aside the cleaning cloth. "What's the little silver flute doing in there?"

Neither one of them had any experience with violins or the things that went along with it.

"And, aww…" Emily picked up a little pillow with a strap across the back and held it up to her cheek. "It's so cute. What do you think this is for?"

The objects in the instrument case opened up a foreign world to him. It was too much. "Let's close it up, okay? That's enough for now."

He shut the instrument case, blocking out all but the violin on his lap.

Emily wrapped her arms around her knees. "I didn't mean to rush you."

He traced his hands over the violin one more time, and gently plucked its strings. The sound was dull and unmusical.

Emily sat by and watched.

"It feels like a dream touching this. I can't seem to get my teeth into the idea that I'm not really Tony Vinetti now. But

I'm the grandson of the owner of this instrument. Who does that make me? You know what I mean?"

She nodded.

"It's not so much who I'm *not* any more. And don't take it wrong. I'm glad I'm not blood relation to Dad. Vinnie, rather. It's more about who I am now. Who I really am."

Emily took a deep breath and said nothing. Just kept her eyes on his.

"I'm meeting my heritage, my real self, for the first time—whoever that is." He gazed at the instrument. "When my fingers touch this wood, they're touching the truth." He pressed the violin against his nose and inhaled the sweet scent of its wood.

"My life won't be a lie anymore."

Emily remained quiet.

"What's hard to grip is the fact that I had no idea I was even living a lie. No clue. Not one."

"It must feel like a dream."

"Then bam! No warning. Something wakes me up. 'Surprise, Tony. You're someone else.'"

"I hope you don't think of me as part of that lie," Emily said. "I'm as real as ever."

"I know. I don't mean that."

Emily pointed to his heart. "And in here," she said, "you are still the same. The only thing new are the missing pages of your history and your new label. Nothing else is different."

Tony looked hard at her. "The history, though. It changes perspective. That's what's messed up. And now I can get a hold of the truth for once." He leaned against the desk leg, and stared at the instrument. "Enough of that."

Emily said nothing.

Tony held the violin over his left elbow. "I don't even know how to hold this thing." He laid it back in his lap and found the bow. "Let's see what it sounds like with this."

Emily leaned forward and helped him unclip it from the inside of the lid. "These hair-things look kind of loose."

"I'd be loose too, if I'd been sitting around for years." He held the instrument over his arm again and dragged the bow over the strings. It produced an ugly scratching noise. "Man. That's terrible. Worse than bad. How do people get music out of one of these things?"

"Maybe you should take it to Tweedle's Music Store. They could help you. I've been in there looking for CDs. It's just off the square. Who knows? Maybe he gives lessons."

Tony replaced the violin in the case. "Let's just put it away for now. If we don't get going Mom's gonna be late, and I know Lusmila wants to go to her church too. It's on the way to ours."

"So, what next?"

Tony gripped the bottom end of the bow with his fingers and leaned forward with a scowl. "I don't know. I guess I really want to find out more about my real parents and my grandfather." He tapped the other end of the bow against the carpet. "It's hard to explain how this feels, Emily, but it's like a black hole has opened up behind me and swallowed everything up. What's down there?"

A muffled snap rose from the bow. It had split lengthwise. One spear-like half lay on the floor, and the other, still connected by the pale horsehairs, dangled from Tony's hand. "Oh, man." His gaze met Emily's. "I can't believe I just did that. I barely tapped it on the carpet."

"We definitely need to go to Tweedle's now."

Tony blew out a breath. "I wonder how much this will cost."

"Well, at least you've been earning some money all summer. That should help."

Tony closed his eyes. "Yeah."

And if he spent his money on the violin, what about Emily's dog? What about a bike?

Chapter 25

Tuesday, 7:00 PM at Choir Practice

After Mom dropped Lusmila off at her own church, Tony found himself slouched beside Emily in the back pew of the darkened sanctuary. They were far enough away from the lit-up stage, yet close enough to enjoy the choir's music. He wouldn't even be here if Mom hadn't invited Emily. She knew he wasn't going to miss out on that.

"My stomach's growling," he said. "All I can think about is the ice cream we're going to eat later. I envision a big banana split."

"Tony, stop talking so loud. The choir director will chase us out."

That would be a great idea. He grinned and gave a vigorous nod.

She gave his shoulder a shove.

"Come on, Emily. What are you having?"

"I don't know. But it's nice of your mom take us out."

"Answer the question."

"All right. Something drowning in chocolate syrup. A hot-fudge sundae."

"Okay, good. Gotcha covered. Now about the violin tomorrow. When do you want to meet over at Tweedle's?"

Onstage, the piano kicked into high gear as the song bridged. "Listen to your mom play. I hope to play like that one day. She's so great."

Great, yes. Unlike her husband. "Tell me this—and yes, I

153

agree about the piano playing—but why would someone like Mom marry someone like Vinnie?"

Emily shot him an exasperated look.

"Never mind."

"Tony, you shouldn't disrespect your dad like that."

"I know. But guess what. He's not my dad."

Emily bit her lip. Tony'd better shut up. She was getting irritated.

Onstage, the orchestra bloomed into high instrumental sound, with a flute, cello, several violins, trumpets, and drums accompanying the choir.

"I can't play anything but a radio," Tony said.

"Well, whatever they play, everybody starts somewhere. Look at me. I'm just starting out. I hardly know anything at all. But I'm learning. And practicing. And this time next year I'll be farther along."

"Can you believe Mom tried to get me to join the choir? I can see the choir now, breaking ranks to hunt down the howling wolf among the pews."

Emily laughed and dug through her bag. "Want some gum?"

"Sure, thanks." He took a stick from the package she offered.

"Your mom asked me the same thing. You think I should join?"

He hadn't thought of that. If Emily joined the choir, he might consider it too. But *only* then. They could always give him the silent parts.

The song ended, and the director paused while members located another piece of sheet music from their folders. After a minute, he lifted his baton. The beginning strains of "You Are My Hiding Place," began to rise. Tony held up one finger so Emily would listen and nodded toward the choir. "This song is one of my favorites."

"The orchestra loves it too. You can tell."

"Wait, listen to that. That's a different…"

From the front left corner of the sanctuary came the purest notes he'd ever heard. They curled up like gold thread, so beautiful and clear he wanted to cry.

Tony climbed out of the pew and stood in the aisle. He adjusted his eyes and focused on the lone figure standing in the left front corner of the sanctuary. It had to be the stranger. His Mafia-guy. Wow.

Tendrils, like musical vines, entered Tony's ears. They wanted to become part of him, wrap around his head, spiral out through the roof, wrap and embellish the building, transport him to heaven.

His body wanted to race down front. But he resisted. What would he say? What good would that do? Instead, he stared, slack-jawed, absorbing every note.

Only an angel could play like that.

Emily tried to whisper, to question him, but Tony held up his hand. He didn't want to miss a single note of this.

Choir members and musicians played on, but heads shifted and eyes darted about in search of the player. The director, still moving his baton, peered over his left shoulder. He located the tattered violinist in the front pew and nodded, smiling. He dipped his knees as if to say, *Don't stop. Don't stop. Keep on playing!*

Tony had finally heard the man play a whole song.

No hit man, no beggar, and certainly no bum would be able to play like this.

But who in the world was he? And what was his connection with Vinnie and his friends?

155

Chapter 26

Tony stood frozen in place until the song ended. The man lowered his violin and approached the choir director, who immediately stepped down. They whispered together. The choir director patted him on the shoulder, and they shook hands. The violinist handed the director some small business cards, to which the director nodded gratefully and placed them on the edge of the platform. The stranger exited on the left, and the director announced that members should be sure to pick up a card at the end of the practice.

The practice ended, and Tony grabbed Emily's hand, and hurried her down front where choir members gathered up their music and belongings.

"Mom, did you hear that?"

"Yes. I nearly fainted. I'm just as amazed as you seem to be."

"I've seen that guy all around town. Emily and I are trying to figure out who he is."

"*You* are," Emily said.

He turned her way. "You're in on it now, too, aren't you?"

Emily smiled and gave a half-shrug.

"Let me get packed up," Mom said. "Why don't you step over to the edge of the stage and pick up one of those cards the man left?"

They trotted over. "Beat ya!" Emily said, reaching the cards first. They lay face down. "Look, Tony." She picked one up. "It's your dad's name."

156

Tony furrowed his brow and sure enough, on the back it said *Vinnie.* "I don't get this. There's nothing on the rest of them."

"Why would your Dad's name be on one? What's *that* all about?"

Tony shook his head. Dad didn't have any church connections. This card probably had to do with some *other* Vinnie in town.

But then, there was the man's list—with Freckles, Pony Tail, and Dougie.

Chapter 27

In the back seat of the car, Tony studied the card again. He tapped it against his leg and leaned forward. "Mom, what *is* The Rock? You know where it is?"

"Sure I do. It's got a little history too."

Beside him, Emily mouthed the word, "History?"

Tony held up one finger. First things first. "Is it close by? I'd like to scope it out and maybe go to this guy's concert, whatever it is."

"Actually, it's just a few blocks away."

"Really?" Perfect. "You think we could drive by, take a little peek? Before we head over to the ice cream shop?"

"Please, Miss Nancy?" Emily said. "I'd like to see it too."

"Well, if you all insist. I'd like to hear more from the guy too. He was pretty amazing."

Tony grinned at Emily who leaned back against the seat. Mom made a three-point turn at the nearest driveway and slowed a few blocks away as they approached a single-storied frame house.

"Right there on the corner," she said.

Emily craned her neck. "That's it? It's gotta be a hundred years old."

Tony put his window down. The loud bleeping of frogs from the nearby Tuscawilla pond filled the car. He'd been all over the place in this neighborhood. But never on this particular street.

"Go slower, Mom. I want to get a good look." Bugs flickered through the beams of the corner streetlamp illuminating twin sago palms and a wall of brown shingles. A wooden sign with the carved words "The Rock" hung from the front porch eaves. "Looks like some old vacant house to me," he said.

"Creepy." Emily said, staring at its black curtainless windows. "Looks deserted to me."

"Nah," Nancy said. "It's just dark." She coasted by its wide cement steps. Empty concrete planters sat atop its stone banisters.

"Slow down a little, Mom."

"I'm practically stopped already, Tony. I can't go any slower. He'll think we're stalking him."

"Right. Only no one's home," said Tony. "I wonder where he stays?"

As they eased past the corner, Tony glanced back.

Was it just a blip of his peripheral vision, or had something moved inside that window?

He snapped off his seatbelt and twisted around in his seat, driving his gaze into the black holes that served as windows. He stared until the building passed out of sight.

Nothing moved. Had it simply been his imagination? Was this where the man was staying? He had to learn more.

One thing for sure, there was more to this stranger than met the eye.

Chapter 28

Tuesday, 8:30 PM After Choir Practice

Tony licked the last drops of chocolate from his empty cone. "So, Mom, what about that history of The Rock?"

"There's not a whole lot to tell, son. When I finished high school the Jesus Movement was going full-force, and it dragged me right in along with all my friends. It was the time of the hippies, flower power, and all that."

"You were a hippie?"

Mom laughed. "No, I was a teenager during those times. I had friends who dressed like hippies. But we weren't real hippies."

"I didn't know the hippies and the Jesus movement had anything to do with each other."

"Hippies, drug addicts, and flower people were getting saved by the droves and joining the Jesus Movement. Now they were ex-hippies."

"Okay. Good to know that."

Emily spoke up. "My mom goes on and on about the Jesus Movement. She tells everybody it was the greatest thing ever. I thought she was just exaggerating."

"Oh, no. It was really big news at the time. Even Newsweek ran some feature stories on the subject."

"Your mom visited The Rock sometimes, Emily. We made a lot of happy memories and friendships. Some marriages too."

"What do you mean, happy memories?" Tony asked.

"Well, there was just a lot of camaraderie."

"What's camaraderie?"

"Friends. Like you and Emily."

Tony could feel the color rising in his cheeks.

"I don't get it," said Emily. "How'd it give you strong relationships?"

"It's a little hard to explain. See, back in the day, as you say, many of our parents brought us up in mainline churches, proper Sunday dresses, gloves, hats at Easter, suits and ties for the little boys…Nothing wrong with that, though."

"Aw, that sounds so sweet," Emily said.

"I'm glad I don't have to dress up. I hate ties."

Emily grinned at him.

"We were the Presbyterians, Methodists, Baptists. We all believed in Jesus, in getting baptized, and in joining the church."

"Isn't that the idea?"

"No, it's not about joining a church, it's about being born again—getting saved."

"The new crowd was getting saved then sharing Jesus person to person, telling people that they can be guided by God's Holy Spirit, minute by minute, and have a personal relationship with God.

"Teens would walk right up to strangers and share Jesus. In the square. In their blue jeans. People weren't used to that kind of openness."

Tony frowned and tried to imagine him and his friends doing that.

"That sounds really good," Emily said.

"It was. Kids ate it up. Parents didn't know what to think and resisted, which unified the teenagers."

Emily looked up from the last bite of her cone. "You got saved, too?"

"At 15."

Tony glanced at Emily. She seemed enthralled with what Mom was saying.

"Word just spread. Only later did we realize it was a nation-wide phenomenon."

"If you weren't in the churches, where did you hold your meetings?"

"There were adults who agreed with the movement—some held home groups."

"What was that like?" Emily said.

Tony interrupted. "Okay, what does all that have to do with The Rock?"

"They needed a meeting place."

"So the kids bought The Rock?"

Mom laughed.

"Well who did?"

"It's an ongoing mystery. Some anonymous adult. We've never figured it out, even after all these years."

"I don't understand."

"A real estate agent, hired as a go-between, ensured that The Rock would only be used as a Christian meeting place—forever, and for free."

"How would the violinist get hold of it?"

"That I don't know."

Emily wiped the crumbs off the table with a crumpled napkin. "I wish I knew who paid for it."

"You're not the only one. This mystery gets deeper and deeper," Tony said.

Now there was no way he would miss that meeting. And of all the people in town, how come it was Tony who had seen him first and followed him around town?

Chapter 29

Tuesday, 9:00 PM

Darkness settled over Vinnie's pool as the crickets in the bushes came back to noisy life.

"Crickets, little crickety-crickets." Vinnie's favorite night-time music. "I even like the sound of the word *crickets*."

With Teresita at his heels, and an icy beer in his grip, he stepped to the pool-deck wall and flipped on the switch. Lights blazed into glorious service under the water and around the patio. He wrapped his towel around his waist and dragged his lounge chair over into the shadows.

Teresita stared up at him.

"Oh, so you don't like it over here in the shadows? Sorry about that. This is my spot, kiddo."

He straddled the chaise and shoved the towel-wrapped gun under his seat where it would be handy. Just in case that caller decided to make good on his threat. But then, how many days had it been since the caller? Could have been a bunch of hot air.

On the other hand...

He leaned back in the chaise.

Teresita jumped up on his lap. He massaged her tiny ears. "That's a good dog. Don't tell Lusmila. She'll be jealous."

Night traffic beyond the hedges had thinned to an occasional slow-moving car. Weekday evening business around here was nonexistent, especially on Tuesdays when even the trains seemed to disappear.

Trains. Vinnie'd be happy if he never heard another train. Ever.

He should have thought about that idiot train station when he bought this place. What a stupid move—stupid, stupid. It wasn't a decision he could reverse quickly either. Vinnie hadn't been just plain vanilla stupid, but big fat chocolate-with-a-cherry-on-top stupid. He took a big swig, shook his head, and stared across the pool. Pretty soon he drifted off into a half-sleep, lulled by the sing-song rhythm of the bugs and Teresita's light noises. A distant horn roused him and he jostled the dog. "Stop snoring, Teresita."

She opened her eyes but closed them right back and continued as before.

Close by, the purr of a diesel vehicle eased up close on the quiet street beyond the fence. Nothing unusual.

But the sound of the crickets stopped.

A vehicle door closed. Too quietly. Abnormally quiet.

Vinnie sat up. Who did he know with a diesel engine? He held his breath waiting for the vehicle to leave, to pull away. But its engine purred on.

Who was out there?

Callous and Tyrant cowered in their corner near the pool. They always took a back seat when Fear arrived. The serpent slithered toward them like a purple-black ribbon and raised its head like a cobra. Yellow eyes bored into them as his forked tongue flicked in and out.

They backed into the corner, trembling.

"*Sssss!*" the serpent whispered. His lower parts whipped around their feet. "*Sssss!*"

164

Just as quickly he glided away beneath Vinnie's chair.

He slipped up and around the man's legs, thighs, and finally came to rest around his chest.

He met the dog's gaze. *"Ssssss!"*

Teresita tucked her head under her paw and whimpered.

Vinnie froze.

The hang-up caller!

He turned his ear to pick up more sound. What no-good thing were they up to out there?

His heart pounded like a jackhammer.

Teresita growled and struggled to escape his grip.

He tightened his arm around her. "Shh! Quiet!" he whispered.

Teresita growled.

He swatted her tiny back end. "Shh!"

Vinnie placed her on the concrete and stood to his feet. Straining to catch even the slightest movement beyond the eight-foot bushes, he crept backwards, and felt for the wall. He switched off the lights.

Teresita paced around his feet.

His chest tightened. Veins came alive. His eyes bored into the shrubbery. Minutes ticked by. A twitch. Over there in the leaves. Behind the black statue. Or was it his imagination? He squinted harder. But the foliage, as still as the sculptures, remained quiet.

A rustle. Then silence. But where?

A minute ticked by, and another. Nothing else stirred.

The dark walls of his home stood mute behind him. It would be nice to have his family around right now.

Where had Nancy and Tony gone, anyway? Choir. That was it. Where was Lusmila?

Vinnie narrowed his gaze.

He could stand here all night like a statue. Clever as an Indian, he was. He'd wait these guys out. Beat them at their own game.

He expanded his lungs and released a slow breath through his mouth. But his throbbing pulse still filled his ears.

He scanned the hedges. If he could just see past those limbs.

A flutter behind the statue. No more than a tremor. Vinnie blinked. Cleared his eyes.

Idiots. Someone was definitely outside that fence. He felt it. He sensed it.

The low purr of a diesel engine filled the air. Vinnie blinked again. His eyes burned now from all the staring. The towel under the chaise reminded him of his gun.

A full 10 feet away.

Right now the prowler probably didn't know Vinnie was even out here. If he went for the gun, they'd see him. A lot of good it was doing him over there. Another stupid move.

Vinnie tensed his knees, trying to get the shakes out.

A twig snapped behind the statue. They were out there!

Vinnie flipped on the lights and squinted at the sudden brightness. The bushes behind the statue quivered. A flurry of fading footsteps beat a quick retreat down the sidewalk outside. A vehicle door slammed and the once-idling diesel engine roared to life and sped down the street.

Motion lights kicked in and lit up the driveway to his left. The electric gate jerked and began cranking open. With his heart still hammering, Vinnie shut off the pool lights and backed against the wall. Sweat prickled over his torso. Was there more than one out there? Who?

The sound of tires rolled into the driveway. He peered around the wall.

A sharp breath escaped his lips. He pressed his head against the wall and closed his eyes.

Nancy.

Just his Nancy woman. *Thank goodness.*

Vinnie hung back in the shadows while Nancy and Tony entered through the side door. They didn't need to see him in this shape. Besides, he had a little job to do before seeing them.

All he needed was dirt.

And then, by golly, he'd catch himself a sneak.

He eyed the caladium pot next to the Mary statue near his chaise. Squatting down beside the concrete container, he gave it a tug and tipped it over. The roots of the plant held tight, but there was more than one way to skin this cat.

He rolled the pot across the concrete, spread a towel over a small patch of grass next to the automatic gate post and half dug, half dumped out the bulbs. He pounded the soil off the roots, gathered it on the towel, and tossed the bulbs aside.

Dirt. That's all he needed.

Vinnie pulled the corners of the towel together and lugged his load over to the place where he'd seen the bushes move. Then, with his bare hands, he flung the soil through to the other side of the fence until there was a smooth dirt-patch beneath the hedges.

"Now, Mr. Smart Guy. Step right up there in the dirt. Leave your footprints. Then I'll…"

What would he do? Would he call the police? He'd have to think that one over.

Chapter 30

Tuesday, 11:00 PM

Upstairs in her bedroom, Emily brushed her hair in front of the mirror. Maybe tonight she'd finally get a good night's sleep. Hanging out with Tony at choir practice had been fun and all, but there was that big hole in her heart. Dad was gone. Where? How could he desert them? That's what hurt the worst.

She placed her brush beside her clock. Above it hung the African woman's prayer-sash. What did she need that thing for, anyway? What difference had all that binding and praying made? Dad was gone. He'd abandoned them, lock, stock, and barrel.

She yanked the thing down and dropped it into the wastebasket.

Tuesday, 12:00 Midnight

Midnight hung still and black over Gaskille. Tony padded along the sidewalk beside Tuscawilla Pond, a glassy puddle of ink. His sneakers cut a stealthy path through the muggy air. His stealth seem wasted, silly even, with all these crickets and frogs. The park was as loud as a gym.

He brushed at the squadron of mosquitoes attacking his exposed legs. *Dumb choice of clothes, these khaki shorts.* A mosquito buzzed and settled on his neck, and he swatted it against the unbuttoned shirt collar. Vinnie's shirt. Straight out of Lusmila's ironing basket.

He tightened the garment around his neck. It swallowed him up, hiding his t-shirt. Which was all part of the plan, of course. Make it count for something. But his plan hadn't included the mosquitoes. Tony chuckled. Vinnie would wonder about the mystery blood on his collar.

Tony pulled Vinnie's baseball cap lower. Tony hated caps, especially one with Vinnie's sweat on it. But incognito counted tonight.

Streetlights glimmered across the pond. In front of him lay a circle of light below a street lamp. He stepped around it and through the shadows where nobody could see him.

He wasn't stupid enough to think he was alone. Above all, he needed to stay alert. Homeless guys slept in the park's bushes.

He approached a clump of hedges. Nothing to worry about there. The scraggly trunks were too skinny to hide a person. But he circled wide around a dense cluster of palmettos. He should have brought a big stick, *just in case.*

Of course it was dumb sneaking out of the house like this, but he had to get answers, even if it was the middle of the night.

Houses nestled dark and still on the surrounding streets. A dog barked across the water. It hadn't noticed him, of course. Or had it? Its master's porch light came on. Tony's pace quickened. Could residents shoot guns in the city limits?

A quiet *clack, clack, clacking* approached behind him. An engine of some type. He didn't turn. It grew louder. Slow tires rolled over the gritty asphalt.

Okay. What was that? He twisted around.

Electricity shot through his limbs. *What in the...?*

An ancient car with a cockeyed grill coasted along behind him with its lights off. Huge. Some kind of old Cadillac.

169

Why would some old beater be following him? Just what he needed, to get mugged and then rolled down into the cattails and moccasins of Tuscawilla Pond. What could they want with him?

Tony stepped through the next circle of light beneath a street lamp. This placed a wimpy trash can and the trunk of a small tree between him and the occupants of the car. Some protection. The car pulled up even with him and paused. He held his breath, tense, ready to bolt in the opposite direction

The doors remained shut. What were they doing? Inspecting him?

The car finally drifted away.

He blew out a breath. The pulse in his neck felt like it would explode. Oh, great. He should have run after all. What if they'd had a gun in there? And what if they came back for him?

A siren wailed briefly in the distance then faded. Maybe this wasn't the best path. Maybe the whole idiot plan wasn't the best plan.

He glanced around. Who else was out here? With all the noises at the pond, he'd never hear some weirdo jumping out of the bushes.

Tony picked up his pace. Jogged.

Maybe his whole plan stunk. Too late to go back, though.

As he passed Timucuan Feed Store's mailbox, a loud rasp emanated from the nearby bushes. He sprinted away with his heart slamming. Who cared what the noise was? Cutting left across the next corner, he headed full speed toward The Rock.

Answers. What had moved inside that window tonight?

One look and he'd head back home. Back to bed. Forget this prowling-in-the-middle-of-the-night thing.

The Rock, two blocks ahead, filled the street-corner. Its roof extended up into the arms of a giant oak. Except for the black rectangular holes of its curtainless windows, its shingled north side glowed bright under the streetlight. Tony slowed next to a large bush, trying to gain control of his breathing and his pulse.

An old battered Jeep was parked beside the curb across the street from the house, offering a perfect cover from which to view The Rock. Beyond the vehicle sat a two-story house with its own dark windows.

Tony crossed the street in front of the Jeep. He tried to act natural. Straightening his posture like a casual stroller, he eased into the Jeep's shadow by its back window.

A brief ripple of girlish laughter floated up from a street to the south, and Tony held his breath, searching for pedestrians. The street remained empty.

The smell of four-o'clocks tickled his nose. Without thinking, he turned to find its source. The blooms, yellow or white, he couldn't tell which, hung over a retaining wall, completely visible in the dark. One glance at his own light-colored shirt pointed out more of his bad planning. His clothes stuck out like a sore thumb in the dark. He should have dressed in black. But with the neighbors in bed right now, it might not matter.

Did standing out here in the dark make him a peeping Tom? Nah, he'd call it a stake-out.

A sudden violent slapping vibrated the inside of the Jeep's back window. Tony jerked away. He stared through the murky vinyl, unable to make out more than a lump of rags. Was it a dog?

"Get away, man." A male voice yelled. "What are you doin' lookin' in here?"

"Sorry,"Tony whispered, stepping to the left with his heart in his throat again. Forget about the Jeep. He'd never expected to run into a sleeping person in there. People were everywhere out here at night.

Without thinking, he crossed the street to The Rock and took cover behind the smooth twisted trunk of a crepe myrtle.

Behind him, The Rock's next-door-neighbor's house loomed dark and silent. He rested his hand on the tree's flaking bark as he studied The Rock, its empty parking spaces, and its deserted front porch. Not one sign of life. The black windows revealed nothing.

Maybe he could learn something around back.

He placed his foot in the tall grass. A twig snapped. He froze. Listened for a dog.

The odor of cigarette smoke reached his nostrils. His peripheral vision caught a moving speck of red. The neighbor's porch. The red glow held still. Had to be a cigarette.

"Stay right there."The voice was deep, husky.

Tony strained to make out a figure behind the screen. The red embers brightened as the person took a drag. "Thought you could get away with it, huh?"

"What are you talking about?"

"Don't play dumb with me. I hear you running the water. Every night. You think I'm deaf?"

"What?"

"You ain't usin' my spigot, you vagrant. You hear?"

"Sir, I'm not using your spigot."

Something on the porch clicked. Was it a gun?

"It's ma'am, you little twit. Stay right there while I call the police."

Tony dove to the right, beyond the porch, out of range

of the man-woman's gun, he hoped. *Bam!* A shot rang out.

Was she really trying to kill him?

His sneakers found traction. Pounded through the grass. Pummeled the sidewalk. Signs blurred by. Buildings. Bushes. He reached the street. Cut to the right. Forget Tuscawilla. Tony raced, pumping and gasping, fumbling for the string under his shirt. His key. One more block.

Up there. Closer... *closer... home!*

He fumbled with the key. Thrust in the lock. *C'mon, c'mon.* He gave it a twist.

Pushed the door.

Slipped in. Pulled it shut.

Locked!

He leaned over. *Gasp.* Never. *Gasp.* Again.

Gasp. Idiot. *Gasp.* What. *Gasp.* Were you thinking?

Nevermore. *Gasp.* No more prowling in the middle of the night.

Chapter 31

Tony waited inside the recessed doorway at Tweedle's Downtown Band and Music Store. Last night's fiasco was so fresh on his mind his hands still shook. He set the case down and shoved them into his pockets. Emily approached via the steep incline from the south. Watching her there on the sidewalk eased the sting.

She turned. Waved at someone inside a store. Sunshine blazed off her wavy hair. He drew in a sharp breath. Prettiest hair in town. Prettiest girl in town. Prettiest girl he'd ever met. The sight of her was like a drink of icy Coke on a hot day.

She shielded her eyes briefly and proceeded uphill. Amazing how her company put a new spin on his world.

A shudder rippled though him. What a dumb move last night. He never should have gone prowling around Tuscawilla at midnight. Good thing he hadn't met any thugs—well, maybe he had. But there were no dogs.

Speaking of dogs—he'd have to talk Emily's Grandma out of buying that poodle. Who would have guessed she'd get her a dog for her birthday?

But what if she wouldn't listen to him?

He'd already paid for the Australian shepherd. A hundred dollars so far.

Dad—*Vinnie*—sure wouldn't let him keep it. Not with Lusmila's poodle in the house. How'd that ever happen anyway? Besides, Tony wouldn't want to keep a dog that

Emily pined for and couldn't have. What a cruel twist that would be.

He'd get no refunds, either. The goat-cheese man had told him that up front. The only thing left to do would be forget the dog and let the man keep the money. Might as well flush the money down the toilet if he did that.

Or Tony could take the dog and try to sell it. Ha! Yeah, that was something Dad would do, not him.

What a betrayal that would be, and Emily would hate him for it. Imagine him buying a dog she loved, then selling it out from under her.

Emily stood in front of him. "Hi, Tony. You all right? What's that yucky look on your face?"

"Oh, nothing." He picked up the violin case, "Well, you ready? Let's go see the experts."

Inside the music store, Tony and Emily stood beside the counter as they waited for the elderly Mr. Tweedle to get off the phone. The case lay open with the broken bow beside it.

Tony leaned against the countertop and drummed his fingers lightly on the glass as he peered through its scratched surface to the clutter inside. Yellowed harmonica boxes, reeds, mouthpieces, drumsticks, and curling invoices filled the case. He whispered, "Mr. Tweedle hasn't dusted this thing in 20 years. Think he'll hire me to straighten and clean?"

Emily shrugged. "I don't really think he cares much, and probably not enough to pay."

He traced his palms along the counter's antique wooden frame. "Look at this old thing. How many thousands of oily hands and forearms do you think it took to burnish the wood like this?"

Emily coasted away. "You can look at the counter. I'm going back here, to look at the music books."

He leaned his back against the case. Morning light seeped through the grimy front door and back-lit Emily as if in a movie. He took a deep breath as she shifted her purse and traded a grin with him. So good to have her back from that stupid trip she'd taken. And she'd called him when she got back. He couldn't get over that. She'd actually kept his number.

On shelves above Emily's head perched an assortment of silver and brass instruments, just waiting for the right student to lift them up and set them free. Below them hung guitars of every color and type waiting for their own adoption. A musician's paradise.

He inhaled the aroma of instrument polish and printed music. It was similar to the smells of his own school's band house. Not that he took band class. No way. He'd only delivered a batch of papers down there for the school office.

Talk about uncomfortable. Those music geeks, like the computer nerds with their specially-wired brains, had stared at him like he was a space alien.

He'd had no business there. He had no business in Tweedle's store, either, but he had to tend to the violin. Okay, maybe he did have a right to be here. But he knew diddly about music.

Across the room, Emily showed him a CD of violin music, and he gave her a quick thumbs-up. They could spend more time looking at those later.

Mr. Tweedle finally hung up the phone.

Tony turned as the man rose from his broken-down chair and limped over to the counter. His bald head flashed briefly as he stepped through a ray of sunlight that sliced in through the gaping front door. Little wonder Mr. Tweedle had dust in here with that door hanging open.

Breathless from the exertion, the man raised his eyebrows. "I'm sorry, Tony, for that little interruption." He pushed the two broken pieces of the bow across the glass from where he had examined it earlier. "Here, you better just hang onto this. There's no fixing your bow. It has to be replaced. You say it was your grandfathers?"

Tony nodded.

"I'm sorry, son." The old man reached behind him for a fat dog-eared catalogue. He heaved it off his paper-strewn desk and then across to the glass beside the violin case. A few loose papers fluttered to the floor. Mr. Tweedle ignored them. Thumbing through, he pressed a page open in front of Tony, then grasped the counter, working to catch his breath. "Here are all the violin bows," he said, and pushed a stubby finger down the column of numbers. "I can't tell you what to do. There are lots of prices, lots of qualities. You have to decide whether you're going to be a fiddler or a violinist. What was your grandfather?"

"Concert violinist."

Mr. Tweedle raised one palm, as if to say, "There you go."

"Thank you, Mr. Tweedle." Tony swept his eyes down the prices in the right-hand column. It would be a while before he could raise enough money for a bow. "I guess I have to think about it. I don't know the first thing about playing. I don't even know if there's a teacher in town."

"Just remember," the man said, spreading his fingers on the glass. His eyes, large and watery like poached eggs, looked over his reading glasses. "It boils down to the sound you want. Get as much bow as you can afford. There's cheap, not so cheap, and really fine. The price goes up along with the sound quality."

"Well," said Tony, with his finger pressed against the jagged end of the bow. "Anything's better than this one."

"For what it's worth, the sound of a good bow is a great encouragement to someone starting out. Get the best you can buy."

"Could you still take a look at the violin? Check it out?"

"Sure. My background is band. But my colleague with orchestra experience can check the sound posts, the bridge, the sound, and listen to the strings." He pushed his glasses up and squinted. "Are you wanting new strings if they're needed? Multiple grades of those as well."

"If it needs them. I'll have to look at all the prices and think about it, and just to be clear, Mr. Tweedle, I'll have to earn some money before I can do anything."

"That's certainly understandable." The man straightened and held one stubby finger in the air. "Same as the bow, Tony. Don't get the cheapest strings. Get a good set. It makes a tremendous difference. That's something I think your grandfather would have wanted to tell you."

Something his grandfather would have wanted to tell him? It hadn't crossed Tony's mind that his grandfather would have had advice for him. Even if it did come through this man.

Get a good set. He'd do just that. As soon as he could.

"Thank you, Mr. Tweedle. I appreciate your advice."

"Take your time looking through the catalogue," he said.

Emily sidled up as Tony thumbed through the worn pages. She gave him a little kick on the ankle.

Tony ignored it and focused on the page. "Man, bows and

strings are expensive." He glanced at the intact strings on his instrument. "I know what you said, Mr. Tweedle, but on my budget, as much as I don't like to, I'll have to get a cheap bow right now. He pointed to one in the middle of the page. "This one will do. Since I already have strings, and they're not broken, I guess they'll can wait a while."

"I understand."

"Go ahead and give it that checkup it needs. Do you know how much it'll be?"

Mr. Tweedle closed the violin case. "It depends on my colleague, but not much. The main thing is the bow. Let's do it this way. How much can you pay a week?"

"How about ten dollars? If I can do more, I will."

"Perfect. Checkup now, and when you gather the money you can take the bow home." Mr. Tweedle turned the handle up so that he could carry the case. "On the other hand, once you pay it off, if you decide to upgrade, we can return the bow and order a better one."

Tony nodded.

"Why don't you come back in an hour? I'll try to have it checked by then." Mr. Tweedle waved his hand and headed down the dimly lit hallway to where his real office was in the back of the store.

"I'll do that. Thank you." Tony returned his attention to the better bows in the catalogue. Some were hundreds of dollars. Some were more.

Emily nudged him, but he didn't look up. How could he increase his earnings before summer's end?

A door at the other end of the hall opened briefly then shut again.

Emily jabbed him in the arm. "Tony!"

He finally tore his eyes away from the catalog. "Ow, Emily. Why are you beating on me?"

"You didn't see him?"

"See who?"

"I was trying to tell you. The guy with the violin. He just came out of that office and went outside. How could you miss him?"

"Our Mafia-guy?"

Emily leaned her head back in exasperation and looked at the ceiling. "No, silly. *Your* Mafia-guy."

Tony bolted for the front door. "I'll be back. I've got to figure out where he's headed." He grabbed the doorframe and turned around. "Emily, please, I've got to find out. Don't be mad."

"I thought you were going to the square with me. To the craft fair."

"Emily, please, I've got to follow him. You know something's up. Remember those names on the list?"

She followed him to the door. "I'm not hanging around then."

"What do you mean?"

"Maybe I'll just go by myself. Or go home. You're spending way too much time following this guy around."

"Emily, I promise I'll see you in a little while. I have to do this."

She crossed her arms. "I'm very upset with you, Tony."

He glanced at her sandals and smiled. "I know the truth, Emily."

"What?"

He pointed at her feet. "If you had on tennis shoes you'd go with me. Busted."

She kicked her foot at him and grinned. "You're nuts."

"Be nice to me," he said, pointing at her and backing out the door. "You're going to want all the juicy details."

Wednesday, 9:30 AM

At the kiddie-art booth the young man stood behind the table. Here came that honey-blonde. *His* honey blonde. Only she wasn't heading over to the craft side of the table to make a treasure chest with him, she was heading over to his aunt's side.

He sidled up to his aunt and whispered. "Trade sides with me."

Aunt Beth frowned.

"It's a girl," he whispered, jerking his head toward the honey-blonde. "A *girl.*"

Aunt Beth raised her eyebrows, gave him a knowing nod. She took over his table where a herd of kids worked on their dried-noodle projects.

As his honey-blonde stepped up, the young man laid a large sheet of drawing paper on the table with a flourish. He bowed at the waist. "At your service, ma'am," he said, with exaggerated courtesy. The girl blushed. She liked his charm, of course.

And she had on those ruffled shorts. He eyed his phone lying behind him next to his aunt's paints.

"And what would you like to draw, Miss...?" He left the sentence open for her to fill in her name.

"It's Emily," she said and pointed to the figurine collection. "I don't really have much time, but I'd like to try that bull-dog."

Hmm. She did look like an Emily. With another flourish he presented the small figurine and set it front and center of her paper.

He left her alone to get acquainted with the paper and pencils and reached for his phone. "Got to answer a text," he said. "You okay for now?"

She smiled and focused on her picture.

He swiped up his camera and shot away at different angles, making sure to capture her long legs in those ruffled shorts.

Other kids came along to draw and he had to put the phone away. He'd make prints and pin them to his wall at home.

After situating the newcomers with their own figurines he pulled up a stool in front of Emily.

"Say, didn't I see you walking down the street near here? Let's see now, it was...." He applied his thinking face, but he'd no more seen her walking down the street than he'd seen a jack-a-lope.

She barely raised her eyes. "Have you been in the historic district?"

Uh, huh, a local, just like he figured. He moved back to the newcomers and interacted with them a bit. No need to crowd her.

But the next time she glanced up he caught her eye and grinned. His dimples always pulled the girls in.

She grinned right back. Bingo. There it was. She liked him, he could tell.

"Maybe that's where I saw you," he said. "Over in the historic district. I bet it's that big stone house with the round turret in front."

She shook her head, and kept on drawing.

He turned and eyed the metal container that held his aunt's professional drawing pencils. "Wait," he said, and reached for the sharpest one. "Let me see your pencil."

She eyed him with a puzzled look.

"It's okay, I'll trade you." He took hers and instead of handing her the other, placed it in her palm and wrapped her fingers around it.

Color rose in her cheeks, but she quickly recovered.

"It's a professional pencil. Try it and let me know what you think."

"Thank you," she said, and focused once again on the bulldog figurine and her drawing. She started to say something else, and he gave her the dimple treatment again.

"It's good."

Of course she was falling for him. But he wished she would open up and talk more. Time was passing. He couldn't let her leave without another clue as to where she lived.

"Wait, I think I know where I saw you," he lied. "It was in front of that three-story white house on 8th Avenue. Was that it?"

She raised her eyebrows and kept on working. "That's a little too big," she said.

"The two-story blue one with the fountain?"

"Warmer," Emily said. "But no. Right size, though. By the way. I haven't seen you around here. You don't go to our school. I know everybody. It's your turn to tell me about you."

"I'm new. Staying with my mom and helping out my aunt. Dad lives at the beach."

"I see," Emily said.

His aunt glanced over and gave them a smile that said, *aren't y'all so sweet?*

"What about school?" Emily said.

"School? I graduated last year," he lied, making sure his aunt couldn't hear him, since she highly disapproved of his quitting school and poor academic past.

He didn't like answering questions, but he laid on another dose of dimples.

"So what will you do now? Now that you're done?"

Hmm. What should he say? "I'll get my degree and go on to med school," he said. Sweat prickled on his skin. All of a sudden he was feeling hemmed in, cornered.

Emily laid down her pencil and rolled up her paper.

"Here's a tube for your work," he said. "Keep it safe."

She fished a dollar out of her purse and laid it on the table. "I'm going to have to go. It was nice meeting you..." She left the sentence open so he could give her his name. He shifted his eyes to his aunt.

He couldn't tell Emily his real name of course. "It's uh, Eric," he said. "Nice to meet you, too." He hated getting cornered. It happened every time. People asking questions. He liked to be the one asking all the questions. At least he had the photos.

He'd keep an eye open and find out where she lived—in her little ruffled shorts. And he'd grab some shots of her at the house, too.

His eye followed the flounce of her ruffles as she strolled away.

Chapter 32

O ut of breath, and with an icy Coke in his hand, Tony flopped down on the bench in the middle of the square's craft fair. He needed to catch his breath. He drained the soda and filled his mouth with crushed ice. Heat radiated off his face and chest. Sweat dripped down his neck. His wild goose chase had sent him all over downtown and eaten up time, all with no glimpse of the guy. He'd flat out vanished. How could a person disappear so easily?

If Tony hadn't stopped in the doorway of Tweedle's Music Store before he took off looking, he might have intercepted his Mafia bum coming out of the alley. Then there was the issue of Emily, who might still be half-mad at him.

A pair of laughing, racing kids flew by in front of him and nearly tripped over Tony's shoes. Popcorn spilled all over the sidewalk. Blackbirds swooped in for a party around his feet.

Tony tipped more crushed ice into his mouth and chewed, his arms splayed across the back of the bench as he took in the noisy craft fair crowd. What a great free-for-all. No wonder Emily wanted to be here. He should call her and apologize.

He'd passed the kiddie-crafters, finger-painters, plaster-crafters, bead-workers, and puppet-makers. Behind him were booths for the older children and adults. Several Saturday vendors had returned for another piece of the action. Even the goat-cheese man was back, but that was no help to Tony right now. Sure, he could make another small payment.

But thanks to Vinnie's greed, he couldn't pay off the dog yet. Emily's gift would be late. He hated that. If he could even give it to her at all.

The phone in his pocket vibrated. He fished it out and checked the screen. A smile crept over his face. Emily. She couldn't be too mad at him.

He hit the green button. "Hi, Emily. Sorry I had to run away like that."

A soft mass bopped him on the back of the head. He brushed his hand across the spot and turned around. A grinning Emily stood there balancing her phone, a drink, and the white paper bag she'd clubbed him with.

I knew you'd be back by now. Looks like you're all worn out."

He hung up his phone with a laugh and pushed it into his pocket. "What's that delicious smell?" he said, eyeing the bag.

"Big juicy Reuben. Courtesy of Grandma and her gift of $5.00 this morning," she said, circling the bench. "Want to share?"

"Oh, yeah. Come on over. And I'll fill you in," he said, making room for her. "I thought you went home mad."

"Nope." Emily pulled out two sandwich halves and placed them on her flattened bag between them.

"Thank you. I was starving."

"It's not even lunchtime."

"I'm always hungry. So what have you been up to, besides buying a Reuben?"

"Art. Don't you know?" she said, handing him a napkin. "I'm a budding artist. They've got a kiddie-art booth back there with crafts and little statues of dogs, horses, ballerinas, whatever you can imagine to draw—and a real artist lady on duty—for people who need help."

"Good. Now I won't feel so guilty for leaving you."

"Still, though, it didn't excuse the fact that you ditched me to go hunt for that homeless guy."

"Sorry, Emily. I apologize for leaving you behind. You know I wasn't trying to abandon you."

"Forget it. You would have hated the art stuff." She pointed to the sandwich. "Eat. I'm still mad at you, though. You owe me."

"So where is it?" he said, taking a huge bite and ignoring the mad part.

"What?"

"Your art work," he said with his mouth cram-packed.

"Oh. At Mr. Tweedle's. I went looking for you and asked him to hold it until we got back. He's a sweet little man."

Tony managed to swallow. Too bad he'd finished off his Coke already, Emily's was way too small to share. He'd get water from a fountain. "Thanks for the picnic. This is the best Reuben. Where'd you get it?" he said, stuffing his mouth again.

Emily chewed and grinned. Without looking up, she used her elbow to point to a booth behind her and about 15 feet away. The banner on its awning said Riley's Reubens.

As he chewed, Tony scanned the line of people standing below the sign. He tapped Emily's shoe with his and pointed. There stood Mafia-guy, ordering a sandwich. Tony wiped his mouth with the back of his wrist and grabbed a napkin. "Let's watch him. If he goes somewhere..."

A bearded man in a mechanic's outfit stepped up behind Mafia-guy.

Emily, tapped Tony's arm. "The mechanic. That's him. Now do you believe me?"

Mafia-guy turned and spoke with the mechanic. After

they'd both ordered they spoke again, and Mafia-guy handed the man a card. They shook hands and went their separate ways.

Wait. An electric bolt shot through Tony. That mechanic was the same guy that he'd caught staring at Emily. And them talking together shed a whole new light on things. Were they connected?

Tony wadded his trash and tossed it in a nearby can.

"You go left, and I'll go right. Act casual."

"I'm not chasing that guy with the beard!"

"Forget the bearded guy. One dude at a time. We can't follow both of them, anyway. Go! We'll split up and take opposite sides of the square."

Emily froze, a frightened look on her face.

"Look, think about the bearded man's clothes. He's dressed for work. He'll probably go back to work. Don't worry about him right now. If we find out more about the Mafia-guy we'll know more about your guy. Right?"

She didn't budge.

"Look, we're going north and south. He went east. He didn't even see us. If you get scared, go back to Tweedle's. Okay?"

She finally moved off to the left.

Tony scanned the area. *Drat.* Too many people milling around. He couldn't see a thing. After a few minutes he dialed Emily's phone. "Has he come your way?"

"Nothing."

"Walk farther to the left. Go to the end of the block. He's got to come out somewhere. Give him a minute." Just then Tony spotted Mafia-guy on the west side of the next block with a white Riley's Reubens bag. "Skip it. I found him."

"Wait for me."

"Take it slow. Don't be obvious."

With long strides, the man was headed away from the square. He hit the traffic light just right and crossed without pausing. He passed Gaskille's Favorite Coffee Shop and descended the hill.

Tony raced behind with the phone pressed against his ear. But the red light stopped him. The traffic, slow and thick around the square, crept forward. No way could he get through. Across the tops of the cars he saw no sign of the man. He punched the traffic button three times.

Emily arrived at his side.

"Come on," he said. "He's disappeared."

With no cars in sight, they plowed forward, disregarding the *do not walk* signal. Out of nowhere a lifted Jeep appeared. It's horn blared like a train's.

"Look out!" Tony pulled Emily back out of the way.

She stumbled and yelped, but Tony caught her by the arm. "Careful, there." Her sandwich and Coke had spilled in the gutter. "You okay? I shouldn't have hurried you like that. I'm sorry."

She wiped mustard off her cheek. "My poor sandwich!"

"We'll get another one. Come on. Let's get a look down the hill."

"What'll we do if we find him?"

Good question. "I don't know. Investigate. Find out more about him. See what he's up to."

They stopped at the corner, and Tony stared down the hill. The only people in sight were a couple of young mothers with baby strollers. The man couldn't have vanished into thin air. He couldn't have reached the next corner that quick. He had to have gone into a building. Tony slapped the light pole. "This is driving me crazy."

189

Emily pointed to the alley behind Tweedle's. "Could he be back there?"

Tony darted over, slowed at the corner and peeked around. He leaned against the wall with a grin.

"What?" she said. "What did you see?"

Tony put his finger to his lips and motioned for her to look too. "Halfway down the alley. See the shoes sticking out from behind that dumpster?"

Emily backed away with a squeak. "It's him."

"Let's walk on by as if we're just passing through the alley."

They stepped through the opening, dodging a wide puddle of soapsuds behind the coffee shop. He and Emily tiptoed along the wall where ferns grew between the mossy bricks. "He's eating," Tony mouthed as the light sound of rustling paper came from the other side of the dumpster. His finger rose to his lips.

Emily pulled at his arm. "I can't do this."

"Shh. Yes you can. Come on."

The odor of garbage thickened as they approached the dumpster. Tony's heart thumped like a jackhammer. "Wait." He swung around, grabbed Emily's hand and led her back to where they had entered.

"What are you doing?" she whispered. Once again they stood in the bright sunshine.

"We can't sneak up on him. We have to talk. Act normal. What if he's crazy?"

"You're scaring me, Tony. Maybe he's dangerous."

"I don't really think so. Let's try again, but no whispering. Just talk. Like normal."

Emily's eyes grew big, but Tony pulled her into the alley by the hand. "So, tell me about your drawing class." His words came out a little too loud.

Emily's voice quavered. "Well, I drew a boxer dog."

"Yeah? What did it look like?" This had to be the lousiest acting he'd ever done.

Close to the dumpster, Emily stood still. "Mmm. A boxer, I guess. Dark, velvety jaws, pretty brown face. Want to see the picture later?"

"Yeah, really, I do." Tony pulled her along, keeping her just behind him, as he edged along the dumpster. "They're one of my favorite d…" He reached the spot where the skinny sockless feet jutted out. He peered around the corner.

"One of my favorite dogs."

The man on the ground jumped. He clutched his Reuben sandwich to his chest as if Tony might snatch it away. His long stringy hair and vacant saggy eyes were nothing like the Mafia stranger that Tony'd seen around town.

"Uh…" It took a second for Tony to recover his voice. "Sorry, sir. Didn't mean to interrupt your lunch. We're just passing through here."

Emily offered a tiny polite wave and clung to Tony as they scrambled toward the exit at the other end of the alley. Out in the sunlight he moaned and slapped his hands against the brick wall. "I just *knew* we'd found him."

"So, where did he go?"

Tony turned. "Maybe the store?" It was time to check on his violin again, anyway. "All I know is he passed through here, and he's as fast as a moccasin. Come on. Let's go," he said, ascending the sloped sidewalk.

Emily trotted to catch up. "Really, Tony, I should kick your shins for dragging me through that alley. What if that guy had attacked us?"

"How could he do that when he's sitting down behind

a dumpster? Besides, you told me I'd better not leave you again. Make up your mind," he said as they turned left in the direction of Tweedle's store again. The sunny spot that lay across Tweedle's floor had now shortened, and glowed closer to the door. Inside, Mr. Tweedle stood at the glass counter. He held the silver mouthpiece of a disassembled trumpet and a polishing rag. "Hi, Mr. Tweedle."

"Well, if it's not my little friends again."

Tony scanned the street. If the guy was in the store, he had to be hiding in the back. Tony settled against the counter to watch Mr. Tweedle. Outside, a young couple walked by with a baby stroller. Tony returned his attention to Mr. Tweedle's polishing rag.

"Tony, the violin's taking a little longer than I thought. A little delay with my orchestra connection."

Mr. Tweedle reached down beside his desk and handed Emily her cardboard tube of art then went right back to polishing.

"Thanks for keeping my picture, Mr. Tweedle," Emily said.

"Sure, honey. No problem."

"Come back in another hour, Tony?"

"That'll be fine, thanks."

The back door opened at the other end of Tweedle's hallway, and Tony stepped sideways to see who it was. Too late.

Whoever it was had shut the door again.

It had to be their violin guy.

Wednesday 11:30 AM

The young man at the kiddie-art booth helped his last little artist glue on his final noodle. The boy's mother paid up. Before leaving she promised they'd return after lunch to finish the project.

The young man sighed and flopped into his chair. His booth was now empty, and he could look forward to another lunch with his aunt and her boring lectures. He closed his eyes and imagined Emily's long hair and ruffled shorts.

Emily was his girl now. She'd fallen for him—hook, line, and sinker. He knew it by the way she smiled and asked questions. He raised his fingers and touched the deep creases of his cheeks.

He grinned. That was it. She liked him for his dimples.

But all those questions she asked. He hated questions. Questions cornered him. They bothered him. Questions made his heart pound in a bad way.

He leaned back in his fold-up chair and reviewed his mental image of Emily. The picture that refused to leave. And that was fine. He didn't want it to.

Wait—*the pencil*—that professional one Emily had used. He sat up and scrounged around on his aunt's knick-knack table until he found it. *There.* He'd lost track of the other one.

He sat back again, rolled it up and down against his cheek and under his nose. Felt it. Smelled it. Its black paint was forever changed. Her hands had touched it. He gave it a kiss and laid it back on the table. Once he got the money, and the pictures printed, he'd tape the pencil on the wall beside them—if his aunt ever actually paid him.

He glanced over at his aunt. He was tired of all her talk about an honest day's work. At least at *juvey* he didn't have to work. He stretched his arms behind his neck and glanced across the square.

Whoa. He dropped his arms again.

Here she came, his honey-blonde girl friend, and that fake boyfriend of hers. The one that didn't deserve to be around her.

He did, though.

Over by the bench she said something to the imposter boyfriend and took off walking by herself. Her boyfriend took off in the opposite direction.

The young man pulled off his apron. "Aunt Beth, I've—I've got to go do a little something. I'll be back in a few minutes."

He didn't give her a chance to answer before he'd squeezed between the tables and melted into the crowd.

She sputtered and hollered. "Don't you stay gone."

If he didn't follow Emily home he'd never find out where she lived.

Wednesday 11:40 AM

Emily's stomach growled. Time to get home. Her snack had long since worn off. She headed down the street toward the historic district and Grandma's house.

So much had happened this morning. With Tony it was always an adventure, even if that mafia-guy was probably no big deal at all. At least Tony was a barrel of fun to hang out with. He had imagination, that was for sure.

The kiddie-art booth had been fun, too. And that new guy was nice. Cute even. And well-dressed.

As she reached her street she stepped over all the cracks in the sidewalk. At Grandma's she lingered along the end of the front walk to pick a handful of daylilies.

Grandma always loved a bowl of fresh flowers.

And come to think of it, that new guy did look like a doctor-type.

Chapter 33

Wednesday, 2:15 PM

Emily used her toe to push the front porch swing back and forth as she waited for Tony to come by. He'd be here any minute. The chain squeaked as if to say *Pray for Dad, Pray for Dad.* Had she even thought to pray for him today? Or last night? *Okay, Lord bless him,* she whispered. There wasn't time for much more than that right now. Tony'd be here any second.

Besides, God wasn't listening to her prayers, much less answering them right now. Dad had deserted them, and she'd probably never even see him again. He could be as far away as Alaska or Canada. The old drunk. What a disappointment. It might serve him right to get eaten alive by a grizzly.

But bless him, Lord.

There, she'd done it. She'd prayed for him.

She glanced toward the sidewalk out front as Tony strode past the azaleas down by the street. He had mentioned she shouldn't go out alone considering the strange bearded man who kept showing up. Especially now that Tony'd actually *seen* the man. It irritated her that he hadn't seemed to believe her before. She yelled through the screen door to her mom. "Tony's here now. Be back in a little bit." She trotted out to the sidewalk where Tony reached for her hand. They'd planned to go check out that mystery door.

"I know we're going the other way," Emily said, nodding toward town. "But if you've got time there's something I want to show you down the hill."

Tony shot her a curious look. "That bearded guy—he came around again?"

She pointed down the street. "No, but the other morning he came from that direction. It's a clue, that's all."

"There's nothing much down there," Tony said. But he was already tugging her in that direction.

She pointed out the sign at Eleventh Street. "Right there's where he came out."

Without slowing, Tony turned left and headed up the side-walk along Eleventh, a dead end. There were few houses along the way. Toys littered the front walk of the first old house and an old lady swept the sidewalk in front of the second. At the end, one small duplex backed up to a paper-mulberry woods. "There's nothing past those trees," Tony said. "Nothing but a big ditch Dad used to play in as a kid. They called it Forty-Foot back then—and there's a railroad track above it. It's a climb, not a shortcut. So whoever the guy is, he's not cutting through here—he lives here."

"I'm guessing the duplex."

"Wanna peek in?"

Emily drew back. "Are you kidding?"

"Nobody's home," he said, and led the way behind the first unit. He peeked in through the kitchen window.

Emily stood back. "This gives me the creeps," she said. It was too much like peeking in the back window of that garage at the Suwannee where she and Mom nearly lost their lives. She wanted to forget that. "Tony, I don't think this is legal."

"It's just plants and lots of books," he said. A cat appeared in the window and rubbed up against the lacy curtains over the sink. "And a cat." Like the other apartment, the curtains over their double glass doors were shut. "I think a woman lives here."

"Hurry up, Tony, let's go. This makes me nervous."

He shielded his face and peeked into the other apartment. "Whoa. This is bare. Really bare. I mean somebody lives here. But there's not much going on. Hardly any furnishings. A chair, a table with folded clothes. Some lined up papers. A couple of dishes draining on a towel by the sink. That's it."

The sound of a car told them someone was pulling up in the front driveway. "They're home. I told you I don't like this." This was way too much like her nightmare at the Suwannee.

She stepped forward and grabbed Tony by the wrist. "Let's go," she said. "Let's go now."

A car door slammed. She backed up by the wall next to Tony and listened. One of the front doors opened and shut again.

"Come on," Tony said. He took her by hand and led her along the side of the building. The street was empty now. The woman with the broom had disappeared. They headed down the sidewalk toward the intersection.

"Whew," Emily said, and shook her hands as if purging them of nervousness. "Glad that's over with." She tucked them under her armpits. "And just so you know—I'm not going with you next time if you're going to peek in windows."

Tony ignored the remark. "Well, whoever the guy is, he travels light, and he's neat and tidy."

"*If* that's his apartment."

"Hmm," Tony said, thinking things over. "Why would someone do that? Travel light, I mean."

"Maybe he's a criminal, like fresh out of jail. Or running from the law. Like you'll be if you got caught looking in windows again. Anyway," she said, picking up her pace, "let's just get off this street. It gives me the willies. What if he shows up while we're here?"

197

"Emily..." He raced to catch up as she jog-walked away. "What if that was him back there?"

The insurance building was halfway to downtown. The big gray door Tony'd seen around the side of the insurance agency was unmarked. Just a doorknob with a keyhole. He stepped into Barner's Insurance on the front side of the building and asked the receptionist about the door around the side of the building. Did it belong to the insurance agency?

The woman gave them a curious look. But she refrained from nosing into their business. "That's not ours, hon," she said. "That door leads to the second floor. Somebody else rents that."

They thanked her and left. "We could watch the door, see who goes in," Tony said to Emily. "Let's go get a soda and sit in the shade over there." He pointed to the shady sidewalk beside the *Antique Boutique* across the street. "If anybody goes in the door I can ask them—whatever."

Eventually an ancient silver Mercury Marquis pulled into one of the diagonal spaces facing the gray door. Tony leaped up. "Here goes nothing." A red-faced man with big jowls and protruding gut stepped out of the vehicle.

Tony waited until the man approached, and called out. "Sir. sir!"

The man stopped, turned, as with great effort, and raised his eyebrows. Tony jogged across the street with his soda. In the meantime, two other cars pulled into nearby spaces.

"Um, do you—would you mind, sir—could you tell me who rents this space? I mean upstairs."

The man studied Tony, scowled across the street at Emily, then turned his back and stepped toward the door.

"It ain't none yer bidness, young man, none a'tall."

Heat crept over Tony's face as he crossed the street again. "Well, that was awkward." They both giggled. He took Emily by the hand and helped her up.

They'd wasted a whole hour and he needed to get back home for chores. They headed back Emily's house.

Wednesday, 2:15 PM

In Eve's apartment, two invisible imps perched on her shoulders and dug fat fingers inside her skull. "Wait till you feel the heartbeat," Leftie said. "One, two, three…" He nodded at Rightie standing ready for the signal. His mouth opened in a grin. "Now!"

He and Rightie, both minions of Subjugation, kneaded Eve's brain in rhythm with each beat. Leftie snorted and reached down through her body to palpate her stomach. "Watch this. She'll get all pukey, now."

Eve leaned her elbows onto the placemat and pulled the hot compress away from her eyes. Once again she checked the clock.

Rightie squealed like a teapot and squeezed harder. "How'd you know when to start again?"

"I'm the smart one, stupid. Didn't you hear? Her next dose is in 15 minutes. Put your ears on. Oh, I forgot, you don't have ears. You're deficient."

"I heard, dummy. She said she'd drive over to the retirement home to collect her paycheck. She didn't say anything about the medicine."

"Idiot. You only half listen. But hey," the gremlin snickered, "it's only going to be a small check this time with all her little sick days off. A little more work on our part, and she'll lose this job."

He guffawed and threw his foot up for a high-five with a squealing Rightie. "Teamwork! Whooo! I haven't had this much fun in a while."

Minutes ticked by. Eve heated her cloth in the microwave and replaced the compress over one eye. The imps backed off slightly. She looked around with the other eye. "Billy…"

"See how weak her voice is? That's just right," said Leftie. "It's working."

"Please pick up your toys now. Mommy's got to go. We'll be getting in the car in just a few minutes, right after I take my headache medicine."

Billy ambled over to her with a toy car pressed against his chest. He studied her face with his Caribbean blue eyes.

"I despise that kid's eyes. Look how pretty they are. Disgusting," Rightie said.

Billy's dimpled hand reached up and lightly caressed the waves of his mommy's long red hair. "I'm sorry it hurts, Mommy."

"Oh, gag." Leftie hissed, turning his back on the tender scene. He spat and growled. Rightie turned with a squeak and spat too. In an instant, they swung back around.

Now the woman's eyes had tears in them.

"Oh, sick, she's getting sentimental."

"Thank you, Billy," Eve said, smiling. "Mommy's going to be okay. Thank you for being such a good boy."

Rightie jerked his hand up and slapped Leftie's naked rump. "I can't help it. This brings out the slaps in me. I just want to hit and kick and pinch when I hear this mushy stuff."

Leftie roared and kicked him in his belly. "Stick to your

job, moron. Get your hands back in there and focus. And stop all that squealing."

"I can clean up good," Billy said.

"Thank you, honey. Go get your book bag for me and brush your teeth."

Billy pushed his toy crate into the coat closet then ran to the door with his blue and red Spider-Man bag. "All set, Mommy."

"Okay, good job! Now put the bag down and go make your teeth sparkly and white."

She rose slowly and eased into the kitchen.

"There, she's feeling pukey now. I can tell!"

Opening the refrigerator Eve pulled out a ginger ale.

Rightie glanced over at Leftie and put on a face of mock sympathy. "Aw, look, ginger ale again. Poor little thing, feeling bad now."

They bent over, slapping their legs and howling with laughter.

"Move *gingerly* or throw up. Move *gingerly* or feel more pain," Leftie said.

She closed the refrigerator and pressed the cold can against her cheek.

"Make her drop it," Leftie said.

Rightie pulled back his fist. "Shut up, and don't tell me what to do."

With a lightning swing, Leftie punched him in his warty lips. A pointed yellow tooth flew out and twirled across the floor.

Rightie's foot landed full-on in Leftie's face. "I'll kill you."

By now, Eve had popped the lid and thrown the pills into her mouth.

Leftie elbowed Rightie and peered around into the woman's face as she took another swallow.

"She's looking at it. She's looking!"

Eve's gaze settled near the front door where the red marble Buddha stood on a table with its arms stretched up. "Woo, hoo! I'm watching those eyes. There she goes!"

Eve hesitated, studying the statue's round shape. Leftie nodded. "Don't you know, the red's what caught her attention in the first place?"

"Does marble actually come in that color?"

Leftie grinned, "It's fake, you dingo."

"I love fake. Fake diamonds, fake money. Wheee!"

Leftie slapped the other gremlin in the face. "Pipe down and feel for a pulse again. One, two, three… now!"

Eve grimaced.

"Billy? Are you ready?"

"Hear it? She can hardly talk. Happy dance. Happy dance."

Billy came around the corner, his cheeks smeared with toothpaste. Eve reached for a table napkin and gave him a swipe. "Let's go get in the car."

The gremlins rode her shoulders out to the vehicle where she buckled Billy in the car seat.

"Hang on tight. She's going back inside."

"I predict she'll turn out the lamp beside the Buddha."

"Too easy, gumbo-brain. I predict she'll *touch* the Buddha."

Back inside, Eve flicked off the lamp. She grabbed her purse and paused by the statue.

Leftie danced on her shoulder. "Dig in, dig your fingers in. Palpate now, stupid, really hard. Squeeze. Stop. Squeeze. Stop. Keep it up."

"She's looking at it. See her eyes?"

"Give it a try, girl. Give it a try," Leftie said, palpating as hard as he could.

In the darkness, Eve reached out a fingertip and gave the image's red belly a rub.

Leftie screamed. "Stop your squeezing. Stop now! She did it. Make her think it's the touch."

Rightie pulled his hands out of her skull then swung his knuckles into Leftie's eye with a screech. "You aren't the boss. Quit telling me what to do."

Leftie grabbed his neck. "I could kill you."

"Yeah? Prove it."

"Wow." Eve said.

"Shut up, now. She's talking."

"That's interesting," Eve said, frowning at her reflection in the mirror. She touched her forehead. "It did seem to help."

She bent to pick up Billy's bag and the imps plunged their hands into her brain again, giving it a giant throb.

Leftie leaped down, hitting the back of her knee with both feet.

"Whoa!" Rightie jumped off her shoulder as Eve fell. Her head cracked against the doorframe with a loud thump.

Leftie danced a happy-jig. Then, just for fun, he twirled around and heel-smacked Rightie on the back of his head. More teeth flew out.

"Hey!"

"Yes, I am the boss, you idiot."

Chapter 34

"Hold my hand in the parking lot, Billy." Eve held his hand as they walked into the Summit Nursing Home.

"You going to get paid today?"

"Such as it is, Billy. It's going to be a mighty small check. I could do so much better without these headaches."

Inside the double glass doors, she peeked through the crack in the office door. Patricia, the head of the nursing home, sat at her desk studying her computer screen. When she saw them, she picked up Eve's white envelope and came around the desk to meet them.

"Hi, Eve," she said, smiling. Her eyes lit on Eve's goose-egg, and her expression changed. "What in the world happened to your head?"

Eve touched the injury. "Oh, I tripped and fell against my doorframe. It'll be okay. It's just a bump."

"Let's get some ice on that. I'll be right back." Patricia took off down the hall, leaving them in the office. Eve took the opportunity to sit in a chair. Billy crawled up in her lap.

In a few minutes, Patricia returned with the ice pack. "Here, just touch this against it. It's awful purple. And pretty big. Do you need to lie down? Maybe we should check you for a concussion."

"No, no, it's all right. It hardly hurts anymore." But when Eve touched the ice pack to the bruise, she winced. "Ouch. Well, maybe it does still hurt a little."

STRANGER WITH A BLACK CASE

"Sit there and rest a minute." Patricia bent over and smoothed Billy's hair. "How are you, young man?"

Billy smiled and held out his new Spider-Man backpack.

"Are you staying today? I thought mommy was off."

"No, ma'am."

"He just likes to have his bag with him," Eve said. "Toy cars, snacks. To keep the good stuff handy."

Patricia made an approving face at Billy's backpack. "It's very nice, Billy." Then she straightened and looked at Eve. "I thought I'd better warn you, dear. Mr. Shay is gone."

Eve's mouth dropped open. "What?"

"His heart."

"But, but…" Eve clapped her hand to her mouth as her face contorted. She laid the ice pack down on Patricia's glass desktop. "Gone?" she said, choking on the word. "How could he, Patricia?" She stared up at the other woman before breaking into sobs. Patricia snatched up a handful of tissues and handed them to her.

"I'm so sorry, Eve. I know you really liked him."

"I saw him just yesterday. He was doing so—so well."

"Where is he gone, Mommy?"

Patricia answered for her as Eve wiped her eyes and blew her nose. "He passed away, Billy. He died. He went to Heaven. Mommy's upset because he was a good, good man, and she'll miss him. They were friends. Everyone will miss him."

"I know Mr. Shay. I like him, too."

Eve bawled into the tissues. "I remember now. He told me how tired he was when I put him down for his nap."

Billy wrapped his arm around Eve's neck. "Mommy, Mr. Shay can keep grandma and granddaddy company in Heaven."

Eve hugged him against her chest then turned away to

blow her nose into the tissues again. She sighed. Now the bump on her head really throbbed. "I know, Billy," Eve said, resting her cheek on top of his head. "I know Mr. Shay's going to be fine where he is now."

"And Grandma and Granddaddy won't be lonely up there anymore."

"I know, Billy, but we're going to miss Mr. Shay, so much. We're the ones who will be lonely."

"Don't be lonely, Mommy. I'll help you."

Patricia laid a gentle hand on Eve. "Now, you know what I'm going to say. We have to keep our professional distance."

"I know, Patricia. But he was just really, really special."

"Here, Eve." Patricia picked up the ice pack again. "Can you put this back on? And let me look at your eyes." She studied Eve's pupils. "Well, you seem to be okay. But why don't you sit here in my office for a few more minutes, anyway?" Patricia stepped over to the sofa and rearranged the pillows. "Better yet, come lie down over here instead. Put your feet up. But stay awake. I'll run Billy down to the nursery. Would you like to go play down there, Billy?"

After two hours of keeping an eye on Eve as she worked, Patricia brought Billy back to the office. Eve moved groggily to the door. "Thank you so much, Patricia. Thanks for caring about my head. I didn't mean to break down that way. It's just—It's like I'm turning and walking away from a void, now. A void where Mr. Shay should be."

Patricia gave her an understanding pat on the arm and a nod. She held out the tissue box again. "Take a handful. You just go home and get some rest, now. Let me know if you have any problems."

Billy clung to her hand as they walked to the car. He

chattered away, trying to cheer her up with all the fun things Mr. Shay, grandma, and granddaddy would be doing up in Heaven.

Mr. Shay's last words, what were they? He had a *good feeling* about that meeting at The Rock. And the magic touch thing with that red statue. That hadn't turned out so well, had it? She blew her nose again.

Billy looked up at her with a little frown and squeezed her hand.

She smiled down at him.

She'd go to The Rock. She would. Just for Mr. Shay.

Chapter 35

Finally finished with his chores, Tony stepped along the tidy row of black parking meters then veered across the street toward Mr. Tweedle's. His payment on the dog at the square would have to wait a few minutes.

Tony's biggest regret was not being able to pay off the dog today, even though it was first on his list.

Gathering orders for Larry's, racing to get the hot lunches back to the nurses—everything had taken so long today. Too much time. Especially the chores Dad had called him about.

He creased the bills in his pocket with his thumbnail. The old violin was now Tony's only connection to his true self. He had to pursue that too, now. Whatever the cost. Fixing up the violin was like an act of loyalty to his grandfather.

Grandpa was likely a good man. At least a smart man, and one with special abilities. Tony could be proud of that. Unlike some other people Tony knew.

Within seconds Tony swung around the doorpost of Mr. Tweedle's shop, now shady and cool with the sun on its far side. Mr. Tweedle, in jeweler's glasses, sat bent over something tiny on top of his desk. The phone book pages, weighed down by a disassembled flute, fluttered under the breeze of a ceiling fan. Mr. Tweedle had not noticed Tony.

Tony grinned and waved. "Hi, Mr. Tweedle."

"Hi, son. Just a minute," the man said, without looking up. "I don't want to mess this up."

Tony wandered over to the CD rack by the front window. "It's fine. I'll just look around."

Flipping through the bins, he searched for the violin CD that Emily had shown him earlier in the day. Buying music was last on his list, though.

After a while, muted voices drifted in from the rear office, reminding Tony of his real purpose for being here. Mr. Tweedle appeared in the back hallway with Tony's violin case in his hand. When had he slipped out? Pretty quiet for an old guy.

At the counter, Mr. Tweedle paused several seconds with his hands on the case as if he were catching his breath, and then he opened it up. He turned it so Tony could take a look. The violin seemed cleaner and shinier than before. "All fixed up with new strings. We adjusted some things, and you're good to go. Now we just have to order the bow." He turned the case back around and snapped it shut.

"But, Mr. Tweedle…"

"I know. This is on the house. You can pay for the bow."

He'd still have to hustle to scrape the money together before a bow came in. "Wow. Mr. Tweedle. It looks great. I don't know how to thank you." Too bad he couldn't hear the instrument without the bow. But even if he had one, who could play it? "This is fantastic. Thank you so much."

"It's all right." Mr. Tweedle set the case up straight. "Now, if you need anything else, you just let me know."

"Order the same bow I showed you before, Mr. Tweedle. I can't go up in price yet."

"It's a plan. I'll call you when it's in."

Tony carried the violin to the square where the last couple of craft-fair moms were busy rounding up tired, whiny kids. Artists, including two of his former art teachers, folded tents and loaded boxes into the backs of cars. Appearing in their empty places were the Wednesday afternoon fruit and vegetable stands, which would stay on the square until about seven to accommodate the nine-to-five crowd.

Tony fingered the $10's worth of tips he had collected today. It was more than he had started out with. As long as he didn't leave it laying around again for Vinnie to discover, he could make a little headway.

On the left a nurseryman hung a purple orchid in his tent. A woman set up potted petunias, and another arranged homemade soaps and lotions. Next to this, Mr. Wallaby arranged his tomatoes, yellow squash, and red and green peppers. At least at the square you could buy local produce. Wednesday afternoons seemed just as busy as Saturday mornings. Both markets brought people to the square, which the city fathers loved. Tony loved it too. He scanned the tents for the goat-cheese man, and finally located him adjusting his tent-poles southwest of the gazebo. The man needed a regular spot.

Tony drifted over to the tent. Its red streamers fluttered against Mr. Daniels' face as he shoved the frame in place.

Tony stepped close. "Hi, there."

"Howdy," the man said, reaching overhead to pop a tent-pole in place with his palm. "I've got the dog in the truck if you wanna look."

Tony pulled an envelope out of his waistband. With expenses adding up, he'd better keep back a ten. Even if he put it together with this, it wasn't quite enough, anyway. He thumped it against his other hand with a grin. "Got most of the money," he said. "Still working on the rest."

Mr. Daniels smiled and took the envelope. He shoved it in his pocket and continued adjusting the tent. "Just give me a few minutes here. I'll be right over." He tossed Tony the key. "If you want to get his water and bowl out, I was getting ready to set him up here beside me."

Tony caught the key ring and made a beeline across the grass to the man's shiny red truck with its windows part-way down. The lucky guy had snagged the front-corner parking space. The dog lay curled up on the seat. Tony climbed into the driver's side and set the violin case in the floorboard. The dog yawned and sat up.

"Hey, there, pooch. Not going to bark at me? Think you know me already, huh?" Tony lowered the driver's window the rest of the way. "Gets hot pretty quick, huh?" The dog wagged his tail as Tony smoothed his warm side. "Emily's going to be surprised."

The dog laid its head over the console with his nose close to Tony. His eyes closed again, soaking up Tony's touch.

"That's a good dog." Tony combed his fingers over the silky speckled hair. His gaze turned back to the square. He straightened. The now familiar silhouette of Mafia-guy approached along the north leg of the sidewalk. He seemed oblivious to the bustle around the square and strolled with his hands behind his back and his eyes on the sidewalk. His lips moved slightly as he approached the red truck. His shoulder almost brushed the big rearview mirror. Tony could have reached out and grabbed his arm. Instead, Tony shuddered. Could be the guy was nuts. Or he had a Bluetooth. Or a hidden microphone. That was it. A spy. In the rearview mirror, the man's image diminished as he slipped away and disappeared around the east corner. Tony turned and gave the dog another rub.

Someone poked Tony's shoulder, and he jumped. Mr.

Daniels, at the driver's side door, laughed. "Mighty nervous today, kiddo." Tony climbed back out as Mr. Daniels fished in the console for a receipt book and pen.

Tony, still distracted by the bum's activities, kept his eyes on the square. Mr. Daniels chattered on as he used the driver's seat as a table to count out the contents of the envelope and fill out the receipt.

Tony peered through the crowd, and after a bit the top of Mafia-guy's head came back into view. He seemed to be circling the block again. Sure enough, in a few seconds the bum approached along the west side again. It couldn't be Tony's imagination. Why would the guy walk around and around the square? Weird. But, then, maybe he was just exercising.

Mr. Daniels snapped the receipt off the pad. "Here's your paperwork, young man, a pleasure doing business with you." Then he reached under the seat and brought out a new leather leash, "Here, hook this thing on. Law says you'll have to keep him on it around town."

"Thank you, sir, but I can't…" First the violin, now a new leash. The expenses were piling up quick. What a dumb oversight. Of course the dog had to have a leash. And a collar. Maybe Tony needed to sit down and write out a list.

"No, the leash is on me. Let's just say I admire what you're doing. Let me know how the young lady likes her surprise, now."

"You mean, you want me to…?"

"Go ahead, take the dog. Today. Give it to your girl."

"I'll get you the rest of the money as soon as I can."

"We'll call it even. How's that?" Mr. Daniels reached in the side pocket and pulled out a plastic shopping bag. He dropped the dog's water and food dishes in it as well as a zip-lock bag of dog food, and handed it to Tony. "Take this too."

"Wow. Mr. Daniels. I can't thank you enough. She is going to love this dog. You saw how she reacted. She's in love with it already." Tony reached across the cluttered console and snapped on the leash.

In two bounds, the dog stood wagging on the sidewalk as if he understood the sale. "Thank you again, sir." Tony shook the man's hand, leaned back inside and retrieved his violin. He nodded good-bye and then jogged east on the sidewalk before turning south. Forget going through that crowd. The dog cooperated as if he were used to it. Thank goodness for that. He had to get the dog over to Emily's.

A block away from the square, Tony paused beside a light pole. He turned around and scanned the crowd for Mafia-guy. Sure enough, there he was, leaving the square, probably heading toward The Rock. And now Tony couldn't even follow. Of all the lousy timing.

Chapter 36

Tony raced up the worn concrete steps at Emily's house. Or rather, her grandmother's house. The Australian shepherd's toenails tapped across the pale blue planks. He wagged as if he realized something was up.

A dog exactly like this one had saved Emily's life, and she wanted another one.

Tony leaned over and nudged the dog next to the wall where Emily couldn't see him. It would be like a dream come true for her.

"I hope you're home, Emily," Tony said. He pressed the bell. From deep inside the house the three notes of the chime sounded loudly enough to be heard at the front door. He glanced around the porch, which surrounded the house on three sides. The place was wide enough to sleep the Confederate Army. He'd have to ask her grandma how old it was.

A three-person swing dangled from chains on the far left. Tony shuddered. Emily had mentioned that her stepfather repaired it once. Tony wasn't sure what the man had done to Emily, but whatever it was, they'd locked him up for it.

The porch boards vibrated. On the other side of the door's oval window, Emily appeared with a brush in her hand. She swung the door open. Her blondish-brown hair rippled over her shoulders, just like the special angel his mother always put on top of the Christmas tree. She must have just blown it dry. "Tony!" she said, unlatching the screen door.

A cloud of fragrance drifted out around him.

"Hi!"

Wait till she sees the dog.

Tony smiled and tugged the dog toward the door so she could see him. Emily glanced down. The surprise on her face was all Tony needed. Her hands flew up to her mouth, and she burst out through the screen door. "Tony! What are you—how did you?" She dropped to the floor and threw her arms around the dog. "Hey, there, you little precious."

The dog licked her all over the face.

"What are you doing here, little dog?"

Tony squatted on the other side of the dog. "He's yours, Emily. Happy birthday."

"No way," she said, staring over at him. "No way. I can't believe you did this! Ohhh!" she squealed, but not so loud as to scare the dog.

Then, before Tony realized what she was doing, Emily grabbed his face and kissed him right on the cheek. The dog stuck his nose in the middle of it, knocking them both on the floor laughing. He danced back and forth, licking them both.

After an appropriate pause, Tony stood, dizzy from what had just happened.

"I hope it's all right for you to have a dog."

"Are you kidding? Grandma will absolutely love him. Mom too."

Had she really just kissed him?

Not sure how to proceed, Tony fumbled a good-bye and sprinted back toward the other side of town… to The Rock.

Now that she'd kissed him, how should he act? What did that mean?

His brain frothed like a shaken soda.

Emily *more* than loved the dog. That's what he'd hoped for.

But had she really kissed him? It was more than his mind could grasp. The thoughts kept him from focusing on his next problem: his approach to the old building. He had to shake out the carbonation and get his brain on straight.

Racing full speed, he closed in on the real estate office along the boulevard. His heart thumped a million miles an hour as he bent over at the stop sign to catch his breath and peer around. To passing motorists, he would appear to be just another winded jogger. A single car exited the side street where he was headed. Besides that, the street appeared empty of pedestrians.

He pivoted left and jogged slowly toward The Rock. The third house down was the house where he'd been shot at. It showed no signs of habitation. Good. Good fat riddance. They must be at work. No signs of life at The Rock's front door either. Tony slowed to a walk, which he continued around the side of the building through tall Saint Augustine grass. All the while, he studied The Rock's dark, curtainless windows for signs of habitation.

A light west wind rustled the trees, cooling him and bringing the scent of cooking bacon from somewhere nearby. He took a deep breath and glanced around at the neighbors' windows. Nothing.

Eyes back to The Rock. How could there be a meeting tonight? The building showed no signs of activity at all. Shouldn't someone be in there getting it ready?

Except for the bacon-cooker, the entire neighborhood seemed dead. He eyed the screen porch of the cigarette-woman's house, hoping for a glimpse of the telltale bullet hole, but turned away quickly. Maybe another time. He hung close to The Rock's wall, moving slowly, and trying to act natural. If the bacon-person spotted him out here they might just call the cops. Have him arrested for prowling. Which, come to think of it, he really was doing. But he had to satisfy his curiosity.

In the back of The Rock was a three-foot stoop. The door at the top stood slightly ajar. Tony flattened himself against the wall and pressed a finger against the door. It squeaked inward about a foot. The drumming in his ears quickened, but not from the race over here. A breeze caught the door and pushed it wider. Sunlight and leafy shadows fluttered over the dusty floor. He stared at the footprints inside. Someone had definitely been in there. He leaped up on the platform and peered in. Musty air and silence filled the room. It contained no furniture other than neat racks of folded metal chairs and a couple of rectangular tables against the walls.

Near the front door on the other side, a stack of folded chairs almost blocked a kitchen entryway. Through its opening stood ancient yellow cabinets with a plastic dish rack on top. On the door to its left hung a restroom sign.

There couldn't possibly be a meeting here in three hours. So what was this whole deal with the business cards about? A planned massacre? Vinnie had a lot of enemies. Maybe this was something to do with that caller Dad was worried about.

Clinging to the walls, Tony crept in the direction of the kitchen. He stayed away from the middle of the floor where squeaks would be more likely. Near the kitchen he paused. Glanced back through the door he'd entered.

The craziness of what he was doing began to grip him. It would only take a few running steps to clear out of here.

But no, not yet. He took a few more shaky steps, inhaled

slowly and purposefully. He needed to finish the job, get it over with, before someone actually did come along. A quick glimpse into the kitchen would answer a lot. Just a little more information. Investigators didn't take off running when the situation got tight.

Without a sound, he tiptoed around the folded chairs. He leaned over. Peered into the kitchen.

And the sight made his blood run cold.

The bottoms of a man's shoes stared up at him from the kitchen floor. Shoes connected to legs. And a body.

A dead body?

Electricity pulsed up Tony's neck. He blew air out of his mouth and scanned the corpse. It was definitely Mafia-guy.

No wonder the building was not ready. The man's brown ponytail slumped to one side along his back. His arms sprawled above his head, hiding his face. But where was the blood?

Tony stepped through the kitchen door. He'd never seen a dead body before. He sank to one knee beside the body and fumbled in his pocket for his phone. He'd have to call 9-1-1. The skin on the man's hands looked normal, not gray like people said.

The phone trembled in Tony's hands. The man couldn't have been dead very long. The cops might blame Tony for killing him. They'd ask why he was in here in the first place. And that man—woman next door. She might identify his voice.

If he turned around and walked out now, nobody would know he was here.

But the dogs. Dogs would find his scent. He couldn't fool anyone. Not with all the CSI science they had out these days.

He stared at the body. He should never have come here in

the first place. Another dumb decision. The dumbest move of his entire life.

Then the body breathed.

Tony jerked back. His head slammed against the doorframe. He scrambled to his feet. Grabbed the back of his head. Stood.

The man turned his head and frowned. He rolled over and squinted up at Tony. One hand reached for a small paper, which must have been under him on the floor, and he folded it quickly, stuffing it in his jacket pocket.

A copy of the paper from the train station? A different paper? Addresses? Had to be.

"A-are you all right?" Tony stammered, moving backward. "I thought you might be dead in here. You were face down and all."

The man sat up, massaging his eyes with his thumb and forefinger.

"No, just praying," the man sighed. "I guess I fell asleep."

Praying? This didn't sound like a hit-list type of character.

The bum gripped the kitchen counter with both hands and pulled himself to his feet. Only then did Tony notice the scar running from the man's left cheekbone down to his chin.

Tony took one step backwards. "I... I'm sorry to drop in on you like this. The meeting is tonight, and I was checking things out. The door wasn't locked."

The man smiled. "It's okay. I needed to wake up." He reached for the light switch and turned it on. "Good! They finally got the lights on. Just in time. I've been waiting and waiting on that. He looked at Tony. "So you're coming to the meeting tonight?"

"Mmm, yeah."

"I've lost a little time here," he said, glancing at his watch. "Would you like to help me sweep and set up some chairs?

My helper hasn't shown up. I'm Rocky, by the way," the man said, and stuck out his hand.

"Uh, I'm Tony." He couldn't believe he was actually talking to Mafia-guy and shaking his hand. "Nice to meet you." Tony pointed to the man's violin case on a small kitchen table. "I've heard you play around town. You're really, I mean—you are *really* good."

"Thank you, Tony." Rocky reached into his coat again and pulled out a wallet. "Here's a little payment if you can hustle really fast," he said, and lifted out a $10.

Tony drew back with both hands in the air. He should be the one helping the guy. "I can't take your money."

"I insist. Take it. A workman is worthy of his hire." He pushed the bill into Tony's hand.

"Could I ask you about the meeting? Why are you in town and all that?"

"Well, let's just say," said Rocky, looking through the open back door with a pensive face, "let's just say it's a project."

This was more confusing than ever. What kind of project was it?

"Thanks for the money," Tony said, and stuffed the cash into his pants pocket. "Just tell me where you want everything."

A shadow darkened the door and both of them turned. Tony nearly choked as he saw who it was. It was the guy with the beard.

Rocky said something else, but it didn't register with Tony. All he could think about was punching the bearded man's face.

Rocky stepped forward. "Here's my helper. Eldon, meet Tony. Tony, Eldon. Thank you for coming."

Eldon nodded.

"His boss let him off a little early today, but he's only got about half an hour to help out. He's got to get back across town after that."

It was all Tony could do to stay civil. "Hello." He shook the man's hand but wanted to break it. Emily would be freaking out right now if she knew about this. And rightly so. What he really wanted to say was "Look, Bub if you stare at my girl again, I'll throttle you," but he didn't. He clammed up. Tight. Best to just let this play itself out and see what developed. Act like he didn't know the man. Wait and watch.

"Eldon's going to help you set up chairs."

Though Eldon shook hands, all he did was dip his head toward Tony and get to work. Tony kept an eye on him as the man worked. Steady and quick, the guy never spoke a word.

Rocky stepped out of the room. Tony watched Eldon as he swept the place up. When the older man set up chairs, Tony did the same. Then they took rags from an old bucket and dusted everything. Eldon glanced around as if making sure all was done, wiped his hands on his pants, gave Tony a nod and stepped outside.

Who was this creep?

Then something trivial and unrelated to Eldon, something that didn't add up, crept back into Tony's consciousness. That wallet of Rocky's. Rocky seemed like a pretty nice guy. But, violin or not, what was an expensive leather wallet like that doing in the hands of some homeless guy like him?

One thing for sure, Tony wasn't giving up until he got to the bottom of it all.

Wednesday 5:30 PM

The bearded man strolled through the historic district.

He neared the big house with the daylilies and started past it down the hill. But as he approached the driveway a car pulled across in front of him and up to the house. Dust flew up and formed a settling cloud. He adjusted his sunglasses and kept himself from turning.

Discretion. The last thing he wanted was for people to think was that he was stalking them.

It was the woman, though. Alone. He'd seen that much. But he was so far past the house he couldn't turn his head to satisfy his curiosity.

But what was that in the orange tree up ahead?

A small orange grove covered the half-block beyond the big house, and on its corner, closest to the street, a movement rustled a limb.

An animal?

On a breezeless day like today, all the limbs with their dark leaves and fruit should be hanging still and lifeless. And they all did. Except for that one.

The man kept his tread silent. He closed in on the tree and stepped close, out of sight of the house. No need to alarm the residents.

He waited. For whatever it was—whoever it was.

He edged around to the far side between it and the next tree.

And there he was. Some teenager with a phone taking pictures. Well, at least he was craning his idiot neck trying to get a shot of the car in the yard.

"The police know you're trying to take pictures of women in their front yard?"

The kid jumped. His phone flew out of his hand. It landed in the sand.

The man spread his elbows and opened his stance as the boy scrambled for his phone and brushed the dirt off.

"I didn't... I mean I..."

The man crept closer to the boy. Got in his face. The boy backed away. He shoulder-butted the kid. Knocked him down.

The boy scrambled up again.

The man with the beard kept his voice even. But serious. "Get off my street. It's mine."

The boy backed away. Turned and hustled back toward town, glancing back every so often over his shoulder.

"And stay off!"

Chapter 37

At the dinner table Tony leaned toward Dad. He waited for an answer.

Dad cut another bite of chicken Parmesan. Maybe he was finally thinking it over. Still damp from the pool, his gold Italian horn glimmered against his dark chest hairs as he chewed.

"Come on, Dad. Hire me like you hire those Mexican workers. They probably aren't even legal. And look at me. I'm a hard worker, as good as any of them."

"You ain't old enough, kid."

"Just try me, for the rest of the summer, anyway. I bet I have a lot more energy than those *muchachos*."

Dad ignored him and kept right on chewing. "It's good chicken, Lusmila."

Forget it. Why'd Tony even bother asking? Dad treated him more like a stranger than a son. And it wasn't like Dad—*Vinnie*—didn't have the money. He had plenty. So why was he so dead set against hiring Tony for a paying job?

On the other side of the open doorway, Lusmila scraped leftovers from a pan. "Thank you, Mr. Vinnie."

Mom picked up the small business card from beside her plate, the one she'd gotten from the violin player at choir practice.

"Whatcha got there?"

Vinnie shoveled in more food and chewed noisily while shooting a quick, darting glance at the card.

Mom hesitated.

"Well…"

Tony's cell phone chortled. Bad timing. He pulled it out of his pocket just far enough to view the source of the text. "Sorry. It's Emily."

"Put that phone away during dinner," Vinnie said. "Don't you know the art of conversation? What's wrong with you young people? Go! Drop it off in your room. I don't wanna see it in here no more."

When Tony returned, Mom picked up the card. "It's just that we heard a really remarkable violinist the other day, honey. He's going to play again."

"Dad," Tony said, "He was so—"

"Don't interrupt. I'm speaking with your mother."

Dad didn't care about Tony. He cared more about his workers. And now he wouldn't even let Tony join the family conversation.

He glared at his dad. Right. Some art of conversation. Tony stood, stalked into his bedroom and slammed the door.

Behind Vinnie, Callous and Tyrant slapped a high five and hovered closer.

"Yeah?" Vinnie, still chewing, ignored Tony's slammed door and propped his elbows on the table. His kid Tony—with that little routine of his—well it was just one more black mark of disrespect. Vinnie wasn't goin' to chase nobody down the hall.

He focused on Nancy with a look that said, *tell me more.* It was time he gave her a little more attention these days. After all, Nancy and Lusmila—they were about the only ones left who gave him any respect any more.

On the other hand, it was just like Nancy to go on and on about a topic. "The man was so good. With that one violin, he sounded like a whole orchestra playing. You had to have been there. Very unusual. Angelic even."

"Yeah, yeah?" Violins? Music? Inwardly, Vinnie rolled his eyes. Pretty boring stuff, actually.

"He's having a meeting tonight."

"A meeting?"

"And we're invited."

He snorted. "We? As in *me too*?"

She nodded.

"Invited by who?"

"The violinist."

Vinnie nodded. "That's nice." *Sure, like over my dead body.* Vinnie wasn't into meetings, and Nancy knew that. In his mind he was already slipping down into his pool's cool, blue water. He'd give her one more minute of his time and then he was out of here.

"On the back of the card, honey, it had your name."

An electric current buzzed through Vinnie's brain. Wait. *Vinnie's* name? On the back? Okay, now, maybe he'd better sit up and pay attention.

A black serpent of fear slithered through the French door and up Vinnie's legs. It curled around and around until it clenched his chest.

The pulse galloped in Vinnie's neck. He placed both wrists on the table and stared at Nancy. His name on the back? "W-w-*wait*. Say that again."

"Your name. It was on the back of the card."

What was wrong with Nancy, acting like this was nothing?

"Like what? Like I'm supposed to *know* this music-head

or somethin'? I don't know no violin player. Somethin' ain't right here."

Indeed something wasn't right. Nobody came around town lookin' for Vinnie. Not unless it was trouble.

This could be the caller.

Nancy shrugged. "Just passing on the invitation."

Vinnie scowled. This had to be a plan to get him cornered. Vinnie's insides raced in circles. His guts climbed the walls. They screamed an alarm. "Ain't no way on this messed-up planet I'm going to no meetin' just because some violinist leaves my name on the back of a stupid card." He swallowed a burp. "Sounds more like a *hit* appointment." He gazed into Nancy's clueless face. "You give him my name?"

"Honey, it's nothing like that. This was just choir practice and he was a very nice man. That's all."

"Better yet, did you get *his* name?" He pressed his fingers against the table and leaned toward her. "Whadda ya know about this guy?"

"Excuse me, Dad, I..." Tony was back. It wasn't enough he'd slammed the door, now he was back in the room interruptin'.

Vinnie raised his palm. "I'm speaking with your mother."

Tony bypassed the upraised palm. "I'm going with you, Mom."

Vinnie stood, and shoved the chair away with the side of his foot. He clamped his fingers over the top of his glass. He swung it in an arc. "Go, then. See what happens. I've warned you." He belched and narrowed his eyes at Tony then headed out to the pool.

The French door banged shut behind him and rattled its frame.

"Two of a kind," he muttered. "No sense. Get yourselves shot to pieces!" he yelled. "Keep it in mind, I told you so."

Huh, maybe that would scare 'em into stayin' home. Vinnie was no chump. There was nothin' good about this invitation.

Chapter 38

Wednesday, 7:00 PM

Eve parallel parked her car and walked a block to The Rock. She stepped up to the porch beside Doug who leaned against the front doorpost. "Waiting for the meeting to start?"

"This spot gives me a clear view through the building." He opened his coat to reveal his gun.

"Oh, Doug, I don't see a need for that."

"The whole setup is weird. Maybe Vinnie's behind it, but he hasn't shown up."

"You think…?" Eve glanced around.

"Maybe. But none of these folks seem to be from Vinnie's low-life crowd."

"I'll go on in then. Here, give me a hug."

Doug gave her a hug. "Good to see you." Though not a real brother, Doug could have been, given they'd known each other their whole lives.

"Where's Billy tonight?" he said.

"Babysitter next door. Where are your two cutie pies?"

Doug grinned. "Grandma's, of course."

She nodded, distracted by the beautiful music now floating out the door. "This guy's just so, so good… like velvet."

"Yeah." Doug thumped his chest. "You gotta admit it hits you right here."

Eve waved good-bye with her fingertips and stepped noiselessly through the hushed listeners.

She sat down front. The violinist, only a few feet away,

closed his eyes as he played "Holy, Holy, Holy." There was something different about the guy. As if he prayed each note. As if there were no ceiling, right up into heaven.

The chords cascaded upward, filling the air in the room, changing the atmosphere. They entered Eve's skin, her muscles. Eve placed her palm on her heart expecting to find herself changed, altered, her heart leaping with odd palpitations. But instead, it beat like normal.

She glanced around. Doug had finally come inside and taken a seat in the back. He leaned forward with his elbows on his knees as if mesmerized.

Eve turned back to the violinist. How could one instrument sound like a whole orchestra? She closed her eyes as the warm shaft of music lifted her, almost to heaven itself.

She shivered. Something more than just that one little violin played in the room. It couldn't be her imagination. Was that a cathedral full of angels singing along?

The song faded away, and the violinist bowed his head. "Let's pray." He prayed so quietly it seemed Jesus must have been standing next to him. She closed her eyes to join in, but after a few seconds, she had to peek to see if Jesus was actually standing there. Aside from Mr. Shay's prayer, she hadn't prayed in a long, long time. The man standing in front of her knew just how to do it.

She wanted that too.

"Jesus, I adore You. I worship You," he said with his eyes closed, completely unself-conscious about his audience.

Eve pressed her eyes closed too. She shouldn't be watching people pray.

"You are the mighty Son of God and You are worthy." He took his time. "You are so worthy, oh, so worthy, to receive honor and power and glory. Blessed is Your name, Holy Jesus. Thank You for Your love. Thank You for dying on that cross. Thank You for letting that blood run down, that sacrifice to redeem Your children. Thank You for adopting us into Your family, for giving us life. Thank You."

She glanced up at the man's raised arms. A fervency radiated from his face. "I worship You, Jesus. Thank You for forgiving me of all my sins." His cheeks were shiny with tears. "Blessed is Your holy name." He wiped his face, "Father give me the words to say to Your people."

After he said amen, the people lifted their heads. The chirps of crickets and evening birds drifted into the silent room from the open door behind the man.

Eve shot a quick look to her right. There sat Nancy and another woman beside Tony and his friend Emily. He and Emily were holding hands, no less.

In the back row near Doug, Claire sat next to her husband, Ted. Closer to the front and still wearing scrubs, sat Alfreda and Dorothy from the nursing home. Bravo for them, they had made it.

Eve turned back around. What else would this guy say? He'd already spoken volumes, at least to her. He had cleaned up rather nicely since the other day. So very nicely. A tremble passed through her as she studied the man's chiseled face, dark eyes, and back-lit hair in the ambering sun. Mid-thirties, maybe?

She sighed and forced herself not to stare, lowering her gaze to the long shadows that stretched from his chair to the audience.

Who was he?

Tony glanced down the front row. There at the other end sat Eve, totally engrossed in what Rocky said. She appeared to be a whole lot better than the other day when her boyfriend dumped her, a whole lot more relaxed.

Rocky laid the violin in its case on the floor and began to tell a story. Tony furrowed his brow, trying to catch every word as the man leaned in to the audience to make his points. Every now and then Rocky would stop his message and introduce a short piece of music whose notes illustrated that part.

He told the story of Joseph in the Bible, and how his jealous older brothers hated his guts. They stripped him and sold him as a slave to some Egyptian merchants.

After this part of the story, Rocky played a tune that painted a picture of the desert scene where Joseph, bound and heartbroken, stumbled across the desert away from his brothers. Tony's gut wrenched as Rocky's sad and arid notes laid Joseph's sorrow before the audience.

Rocky returned to the story. After several disastrous setbacks in Egypt, Joseph grew up to become one of the most powerful men in Egypt, second only to the pharaoh.

Many years later a famine occurred back in Joseph's homeland, Israel. Searching for sustenance, Joseph's brothers trekked south, all the way to Egypt, the only place with stored food. And all of the rations were under Joseph's command.

At first Joseph's brothers did not recognize their grown-up brother. But Joseph recognized them. When Joseph finally revealed his true identity to them, the brothers panicked. Would he have them put in prison? Have them killed?

Rocky's music at this point brought tears to Tony's eyes. Such passion and fear in those notes. He'd never heard anyone dramatize a story in such a way. Rocky had to have written the songs himself.

Joseph's story continued. Instead of killing his brothers, or enslaving them, Joseph helped them and forgave them, reuniting the entire family.

This time as Rocky played a joyous song, Tony felt like dancing out of his chair. What a range of emotions the man's instrument could bring. Whatever it took, Tony had to learn to play like this.

Rocky laid the instrument on his knees and looked into the eyes of his listeners. "Like Joseph, we may face horrible, catastrophic events. God can use it all to bring about good.

"I don't mean to excuse Joseph's brothers. No. But God took the situation and used it for a bigger purpose. To help all of Israel."

Rocky leaned back. "I ask you. Was Joseph right to forgive his brothers? Or should he have punished them? Tell me what you think."

Tony raised his hand. "He should have forgiven them. That's what families do."

A smile crept over Rocky's face and he nodded.

Tony gazed at the floor. What had he just said? And here he was, a kid who couldn't even forgive his own Dad. He despised him.

Dad deserved it, though, the way he treated him and Mom. Like the two of them didn't count for anything.

Tony lifted his eyes to find Rocky still smiling, as if he could read his thoughts.

"What the brothers did was wrong. But Joseph was the bigger man when he forgave his brothers."

Tony shifted in his chair. So it would make Tony the bigger

man if he forgave Dad? Hey, it wouldn't be so bad to say you were the bigger man, would it?

"Because Joseph forgave, God was able to help the entire nation of Israel.

"Why else do we forgive?" Rocky asked.

Emily's hand shot up. "Because Jesus forgave us."

"He did." Rocky's voice was gentle. "And he told us to do the same. According to the Bible, if we don't forgive, He can't forgive us."

Emily wove her arm around Tony's.

"It also says everyone has sinned and missed the mark," Rocky said. "Nobody's perfect. No matter how good a person tries to be."

Tony curled his fingers through Emily's. Him perfect? Tony was so far from perfect he stunk.

So who was this guy? It seemed like he could read Tony's mind.

"Jesus's blood ran down that cross as the payment for all our misses, and all our mistakes. No matter what they are. You and I could never pay for all our sins. But He loves us and paid for all of it so He could call us His own, adopt us into His family."

Tony shifted the other way. He'd tried to do right but messed up so many times he couldn't count. Especially with Dad. His insides were crusty black.

"The only catch," Rocky said, "is we've got to accept it. Ask for God's forgiveness. Just ask. That's all. And let Him take the lead as Lord of our life, instead of ourselves, from now on."

Tony'd never thought of asking God to forgive him. If that's all it took, that would be mighty good. A fresh start. Who wouldn't want a fresh start?

"Without forgiveness," Rocky said, "we go to hell when we die. All of us, no matter how sweet and nice we've been."

Tony squeezed Emily's arm. She was the sweet and nice one.

"If you want that forgiveness, to be adopted into God's family and have a fresh start in life, think about it for a minute. I'll play another song. If you decide you want it, you can pray along with me."

Tony bowed his head along with the rest of the people in the room. Around him a few people sniffled. Why wouldn't he want what Rocky was talking about? He'd heard about Jesus in church, of course.

But never once had he asked to be saved like this, asked God's forgiveness.

He'd never thought about being a child of God.

Adopted.

Since Dad couldn't do the job, Tony needed a Father. He might as well ask.

Tony prayed, repeating the words Rocky said, asking God to forgive him and live in his heart. When the prayer finished, Tony settled back to let the experience sink in. To feel the new lightness in his being.

High, bright notes of a new song filled the room. Behind him, Doug wiped his eyes across his shoulder. Must have affected him too.

How could Tony define the difference he felt? He hadn't noticed feeling heavy before, but an invisible weight, like a ton of bricks, had lifted away as he prayed just now. Tony closed his eyes and squeezed Emily's hand.

But, like a sticky-note stuck in his mind, there was something else from Rocky's message that clung to Tony, a concept he needed to digest. Something he had to do.

Forgive. Could he forgive Vinnie? For all his rotten antics, for keeping Tony's true identity secret? For never telling him he was an orphan? And popping it to him like that on his birthday? Treating him and Mom like no-accounts? Refusing to give him a job instead of his workers?

If we don't forgive we can't be forgiven. Wasn't that what had Rocky said?

This truth crawled around inside Tony's head like biting ants. Why hadn't Tony ever heard this before? It had to be dealt with.

Tony had enjoyed his resentment. Been proud of it. Now his crumpled trophy of shame had to go. But it would take a miracle.

I'm sorry, God. I don't know how to forgive him. Help me out here. Please.

Rocky prayed again as the meeting closed. After the prayer, Rocky raised one hand.

"Before you go tonight, I'd like to give a tiny homework assignment to those who plan on returning tomorrow night. I want you to read two little verses before you come. He reached in his pocket, pulled out a small stack of cards, and held them out to Tony. "Could you help me pass these around?"

Tony distributed the cards quickly. After a glance at their card, individuals tucked them away in purses and pants pockets.

Even Eldon, sitting back in the corner by himself. It was the first time Tony had noticed him. He'd better not mention it to Emily.

"On the front you'll see the verses, Deuteronomy 7:25-26. Once you have read the verses, ask God to tell you what it means. Then when you find the object or objects, bring them tomorrow night. We'll dispose of things in a burning pit out back. By the way, don't bring them in the building. Think of this as a first step in starting fresh."

Tony turned, but Eldon had disappeared.

After the service, Eve caught Claire and Ted before they wandered down front to speak to Rocky. "Claire! Ted!" With tears streaming down her face, Eve wrapped Claire in a big bear hug. She held her like this for several seconds.

"I'm so sorry," Eve said, letting go of her. "Can you forgive me? I've been wrong this whole time. I don't mean to cut you out of my life." She wiped her eyes with the back of her hand then opened her purse and pulled out some tissues. "Seems like I'm the tissue queen these days. I don't mean to blubber all over the place."

Claire gaped at her. "Oh, are you kidding? Of course I forgive you. I love you, Sis."

Eve blew into the Kleenex and peered over it with puffy eyes.

"Oh, my goodness, your eyes are so bloodshot."

"It's all this wonderful music. I've just never heard anything so beautiful. And the wonderful message. Speaking of red, I have these new red dishes," Eve said with a laugh. "I'd like you both to come over and try them out with Billy and me. They're just begging to warm up beneath a nice hot meal."

Claire grabbed her by the shoulders. "Don't worry about me smoking in your house. I'm trying to give that up, Sis."

Eve waved the Kleenex and puckered up for another cry. "It's...it's the headaches, Claire. The smoke. It just kills me. But it doesn't mean we can't be sisters. I'm so sorry I let it grow into something big. I've wasted part of our sisterhood with a stupid quibble." Eve wrapped her arms around Claire again. "And I want my sister back."

"Has it occurred to you that maybe this guy will pray for your headaches?" said Ted. "Maybe God will give you a miracle."

Eve stopped herself in mid-cry and stared at Ted. "I think that's a wonderful idea. Thank you." It would also give her a chance to meet the man.

After some time, the crowd thinned out and Tony ambled up front, leaving Emily and Mom talking to a few stragglers. Now he could chat with Rocky.

Rocky motioned him over. "Tony, I forgot to mention something during clean up, but I noticed you and your girl-friend the other day at the music store."

Tony felt the heat rise in his cheeks. People had noticed. He forced his attention back to Rocky.

"Would you like to bring your violin tomorrow night? I'd like to bless it."

"Bless it? What do you mean?"

"Objects can have blessing over them, Tony. They can bring good to those around you." He smiled. "The opposite is true too."

"A blessing? Sure, I'd like that. Thank you."

Emily and Mom approached from behind.

Tony swung around. Good thing Emily hadn't seen him blush just now.

"Oh. Uh, Rocky, this is Nancy, my mom, and my—my really good friend, Emily." That hot feeling crept up his neck even worse than before. He took a step sideways and out of Emily's line of sight. Maybe nobody had noticed the heat in his face.

Rocky nodded at them. "So glad you could come tonight."

Mom extended her hand. "I overheard what you said about the blessing. Then you said the *opposite* is true?"

"Right. I'll be answering your questions about that tomorrow night. Will you come?"

"Absolutely."

Emily tugged on Tony's hand and whispered that she wanted her own mother here tomorrow, too.

Eve, Claire, Ted, and a handful of others clustered around the musician to greet him and shake hands. But Tony wasn't finished yet.

He held up a card, one that Rocky had left at choir practice. "Could I ask a quick question?"

The violinist's eyes crinkled at the corners as he smiled. "I bet I know your question."

"The name on the card. Could you explain that?"

"I'm not trying to be coy, but could you wait until tomorrow night? That's another important thing I'll let you in on during the meeting. In fact, I won't even have to explain, a few will even figure it out themselves."

"You can't—you can't clue me in tonight?" Tony said, disappointment leaking into his voice.

"No, it's very important that I wait, and I appreciate your patience."

Tony gave in with a nod and stepped away. Of course he'd be back.

Rocky's attention turned to Eve, and he took her extended hand.

"I just want to say, Mr. Rocky, I don't know where you learned to play like that, but I've never heard anything so beautiful, like angels were singing with you. It made me cry."

"Thank you so much. What did you say your name was?" he said, finally letting go of her hand.

Eve blushed. "I'm sorry. It's Eve."

"Such a lovely name. Do you play an instrument?"

"No, no. Not a musical bone in me."

Rocky nodded. "That's all right. Everyone has different talents. Will you be back tomorrow?"

"I wouldn't miss it."

"I'm happy you came tonight. And I'll look forward to seeing you tomorrow."

Eve crossed the open doorway. The red flames of sunset lit up her hair like fire.

Tony had never met anyone else in the world with hair that color. He glanced at Rocky. A look of what could only be wistful admiration passed across the man's face as he gazed at Eve from across the room.

Judging by Eve's embarrassed reaction to the guy's hand-holding, Tony guessed the chemistry was probably mutual.

Most of the cars outside Rocky's building had driven away. Tony waited for the man inside the doorway as Mom and Emily headed out to the car. "Mr. Rocky, maybe you'll just tell me to come back tomorrow, but I do have one more question."

Rocky grinned. "Go ahead."

"Well, when you were walking around the square, it looked like you were talking. I didn't see a Bluetooth. What was that all about?"

"Well, I'm not crazy, Tony. I was praying for this town. And the meeting."

"Going around and around the square?"

"Seven times, like the Israelites walked around Jericho."

Tony couldn't remember that story. "Okay."

"Unlike the Israelites, I prayed for good things to happen to the people of this town. I prayed for the people to get saved."

"Okay, then. One more question."

"Go ahead."

"That note you carry. What is it?" Tony didn't mention the note he'd found.

"That one is going to have to wait until tomorrow." Rocky grinned and snapped his violin case shut.

Tony turned to leave.

"Wait, Tony, one question for you too. Think your dad would be interested in coming down to the meeting tomorrow?"

"I'll ask. But I really doubt it."

Tony waved and walked away, sure he caught a glimpse of disappointment in the man's face.

Rocky didn't even know Dad. Why would he ask about him? Probably just trying to get the whole family saved.

But then, there was the card with Vinnie's name and the note.

Of course the man knew Dad.

Chapter 39

Wednesday, 9:15 PM

Barefoot, in his t-shirt and red plaid boxers, Vinnie held the refrigerator open in the dark kitchen. He glanced at his watch. Nancy and Tony wouldn't be back home till about 10 o'clock. And Lusmila, off the clock now, sat reading her newspaper by lamplight at the opposite end of the kitchen.

Vinnie wrinkled his nose at the selections in front of him. Peach dumplings or banana pudding? Maybe he should have both.

As his dish touched the counter, the front doorbell rang.

Who could that be? With the front door right on the street, nobody ever approached the house from that side. No place to park out there except the sidewalk itself. Only the mailman ever did that. And never at 9:15 at night. Family and friends all used the side door.

So it had to be a stranger. Maybe the hang-up caller.

Vinnie poked his head around the corner. "Psst!" His voice came out in a loud whisper. "Lusmila! Go see who that is." He didn't care if she was off the clock right now.

"Who would...?"

"I don't know who it would be, but whatever you do, don't let anybody in. Just see who it is and get rid of them. I'm not home." He pointed a finger at her. "I'm *not home,* you hear? And keep the chain on the door."

"Yes, Mr. Vinnie." Lusmila slid her newspaper to the floor and stepped through the dining room into the wide foyer.

Fear, the purple-black serpent, glided like an invisible ribbon around Vinnie's slippers. Up, up, he slithered, along the man's legs, past his belly, and up around his chest. And there Fear tightened his grip and held on.

Vinnie fled down the hall to his room. Leaving the lights off, he shut the door behind himself. Pressed his back against it. He'd wait right here until Lusmila came back with her information.

It had to do with that card. No doubt about it.

Maybe now he'd find out who'd been toying with him. And solve the problem once and for all. Vinnie twisted the lock on the door and rested his hand on the doorknob. Just in case.

Last night they hadn't rung the doorbell. But then, maybe they had. How could he know? He'd been outside. Maybe they'd rung it; maybe they hadn't. They were coming for him.

His heart hammered in his ears. What did they want?

Over the years he'd made plenty of people mad. But they'd never followed him home. If that was the case, if they were that angry, they had guns.

The doorknob trembled under his fingers. He let it go. No need for Lusmila to hear his nervousness.

What he needed was his gun. Where had he left it? Oh, yeah. In the bathroom under that stack of towels. He whispered a curse. *Great.* But how could he have guessed the stupid idiot would come knocking at his door again in the middle of the night?

He put his ear against the door. But the pulse in his ears turned Lusmila's words at the front door to mush. He couldn't make heads or tails of them.

The *flip, flip, flip* of her slippers approached his room. He nearly leaped out of his skin when she tapped at the door.

"What?"

"Mr. Vinnie. I don't understand. He want to talk about an accident."

The other day when Vinnie almost hit the train? *That wasn't no accident.*

What could he be talk...?

Nooooo... not that accident with the migrant kid!

The serpent of fear grinned wide. It slithered up, encircling Vinnie's neck. It pressed against the hot, rapid pulse. It was time. After all these years, it was time. His orange tongue flicked in and out, and his yellow eyes peered into the man's round wide ones. *"Sssss! Gotcha gotcha gotcha,"* he taunted.

Vinnie's past had come full circle.

Vinnie sucked in a sharp breath.

Nobody knew about the train accident. No one but Dougie, Pony Tail, and Freckles. They must have teamed up.

His heart pounded as he stood listening behind the door. The seconds dragged out like minutes. His limbs felt numb like they didn't belong to his body.

"Mr. Vinnie?"

He rubbed spastic fingers over his face. He couldn't stop them from shaking.

She'd said *he.* It had to be Dougie. Had to be.

"What did he look like? The guy at the door."

"I look out through the peep hole, but I don't know. Grownup. Tall like you. I never see him before. He say to tell you that everything is okay now. He say not to worry anymore."

What kind of trick was this?

Icy blood exploded through Vinnie's neck, his arms, his

legs. It threatened to burst through his skin. His brain spun like a pinwheel.

"I tell him you not home. He walk away."

Thank goodness. Vinnie closed his eyes and listened to his own shallow breathing. Even with his eyes closed, the room dipped and swirled.

"Mr. Vinnie, you okay?"

Sick joke. The kid at the tracks was dead, even if the ambulance did come pick him up. Vinnie'd watched it through the bushes. And nothing about it could be okay now. Not then, not now. Never.

He slid to the floor. Dropped with his face in the rug. This could not be happening, not after all these years. He'd had those kids under his thumb. What had changed to make them turn on him?

Lusmila knocked again. "Mr. Vinnie. You okay?"

Vinnie managed a hoarse whisper. "Okay, thank you, Lusmila."

"He leave you an envelope."

An envelope? Vinnie opened his eyes. A crack of light seeped under the door. Shadows shifted. The door bumped as Lusmila slid the envelope underneath. The envelope touched his hand, and he jerked away. His mind went numb.

His body rocked in rhythm with each heartbeat.

The day had finally come. People knew.

The grin widened on Fear's scaly lips as he tightened his pythonic grip around Vinnie's chest. The man could barely breathe. *Good.* He flicked out his forked tongue and constricted the neck.

Vinnie raked his hands through his hair. Oh, God, what was he going to do?

He was going to prison.

Wednesday 9:30 PM

The man tossed his empty peanut butter jar in the trash. Waiting until bedtime to prepare tomorrow's lunch was a mistake. And now he'd have to pull on his shirt and double-time it over to the Buy It Less Grocery.

He glanced at the clock. They'd be closing in 30 minutes.

Again, darkness lay deep over the corner near the Buy It Less Grocery, the last store of the night to close. The manager locked the doors behind his last customer once again and the man trudged toward the street corner to cross the boulevard's eight lanes. In one arm he carried a cold gallon of orange juice and in the other an overstuffed brown bag filled with a half-gallon of milk, peanut butter, onions, Ramen noodles, bacon, bologna, and several cans of Vienna sausages. *Might as well get something tasty for once,* the man figured. He hoped to make it home before the bag burst at the seams. Come to think of it, he should have gotten one of those big plastic bags with a handle. But he was partial to brown bags somehow.

Once again, with his mind a million miles away, the man watched and waited for the signal with the little walking man. Last time a truck had nearly hit him. Above him the only good streetlamp within a quarter mile buzzed and faltered, still more off than on, and threatened to fail completely. Across the boulevard lay the wilderness of empty parking spots and a deserted plaza.

The signal changed. He glanced left and right. No zooming trucks tonight. He headed across boulevard and past the plaza to his street.

The brown bag pressed against the milk and began to dampen. Summer air brought out the condensation on all the cold items. He reminded himself to get the plastic bag next time.

He moved on, block by block.

Drat! He was only halfway to his house, and the bag was nearly worn through.

There weren't many bus benches in the historic district. But there was one in front of the big house with the daylilies. He'd park himself there and shift the stuff around in the bag. If he could.

Otherwise, he'd have to hide some of his goods in the weeds of the empty lot across the street from the daylilies and come back later for them.

The streets were empty. He'd barely reached the bus stop across from the big house when the bag split through. Vienna sausage cans dropped out and rolled over the bench and into the weeds.

Man, he wished he'd carried some plastic bags in his pocket. He sorted the groceries into two piles, those to take now, and those to come back for. Then he leaned forward to catch his breath. Thanks to all the recent walking he was doing much better. But he still needed to get in better shape.

He glanced over at his pack of bacon. Hmm. Well, maybe after this one he'd leave that off.

A noise, a movement, and a flash of light across the sidewalk drew his attention.

He raised his eyes. *Wha...?*

He hadn't even heard the guy walk up. And wasn't that the kid from the orange tree? Between his bench and the glow of the big house's upstairs window, the young man's silhouette stood out plain. *That punk. What's he doing out here in the middle of the night taking pictures of the girl's window?*

On quiet soles the man crept across the asphalt until the picture on the punk's cell phone became clear. No guesswork here. The kid was a peeping Tom.

Energy like the Hulk's roared up through his core and out through his hands. "What are you doin' on my street? I warned you, punk. This is my street."

The kid turned and the man busted his face with his fist.

The kid reeled and the bearded man stepped back to watch him stumble to the pavement. He whimpered, clutching his jaw. "Please don't hurt me." His phone lay on the concrete, its screen shining up at the black sky.

The man stood with his elbows out. His feet apart. "Shut up, you little wuss." He wanted to kill the little pervert, but he knew better. "You're lucky that's all you got."

Like a flash, he grabbed him by the hair and yanked him to his feet. "Stand up when a man speaks to you." He jerked his hand away. The kid was taller than him. It mattered not.

"Please don't hurt me," the kid whined again, fingering his damaged jaw.

The man whirled the kid around and gripped him in a head-lock. The punk grappled behind his head. He raked a long sharp nail down the right side of the bearded man's face. The man growled. He should have seen that coming.

He tightened his squeeze. "You're nothing but a perv, taking pictures through girls' windows at night." He gritted his teeth. "A pervert! You're lucky I don't pulverize you."

He twirled the kid around again and landed a fist in his gut, holding back just enough of his rage to keep from killing him.

The boy grunted.

"And that's for the cut on my face." He widened his stance again. "Wanna try it again?"

The kid leaned over, gasping. "Please, mister."

"You sound like a girl."

Once again he grabbed the shock of hair with his fist. "Listen here, kid." He jerked the kid's head back and waited. "A grown-up's talkin'. What are you supposed to say?"

"S-sir?"

He tightened his grip, wanting to pull the hair out, break the punk's neck, but held back.

Instead, he twisted the kid's head toward the sidewalk. "You see that there? I don't know where you live, but you get started. Go home, you stray dog. Git! And tomorrow you clear out of this town."

The boy gasped a few breaths.

The man held his grip. "I don't *hear* you."

"Y-yes sir."

"Now when I let go you don't turn around. I don't wanna see your face. And I'd better not see it in this town ever again. Ever. Or you'll get to see what I look like when I'm mad."

"Y-yes sir."

He let go. "Now git!"

The boy bent to grab his phone and the man stomped his fingers against it.

"Oww!" the kid wailed, pinned to the ground.

"Leave it."

"I'll go, I'll go."

The punk scrambled away on all fours. But not before the man planted a foot across the seat of his pants and sent him sprawling one more time.

"Now get up."

"Okay, okay, I'm going."

The man spread his elbows and waited. "Run," he said. "Run!"

The boy bolted and the man chased him half a block.

"Go, go! I'll boot you again!" The man paused at the corner and watched as the punk high-tailed it away.

"Don't let me see that ugly face here again, pervert!" the man yelled after him.

He brushed off his clothes, returned to the street, and picked up the phone. He'd take his hammer to it later.

Punk.

This was his street.

Chapter 40

Thursday, 6:30 PM

Rightie scowled across Eve's shoulders at the other imp. That dumb look on Leftie's hideous face told him his partner didn't know a thing more than he did.

This whole deal was looking bad.

Their woman sat there on the white leather couch reading those Bible verses over and over again and talking to herself.

She read aloud. "The graven images of their gods shall ye burn with fire: thou shalt not desire the silver or gold that is on them, nor take it unto thee, lest thou be snared therein: for it is an abomination to the Lord thy God. Neither shalt thou bring an abomination into thine house, lest thou be a cursed thing like it: but thou shalt utterly detest it, and thou shalt utterly abhor it: for it is a cursed thing."

Each time she read it, Rightie grabbed his belly and doubled over. "Ahhh! Stop the pain! I hate that Book!"

Leftie whirled in circles on her shoulder and screamed his own curses. They were in big trouble.

"Wow. It's right there." Eve said. "Burn them with fire."

"So, if they bring the cursed idols into their home they'll become cursed like the idols. It's an abomination to Him. Something God hates with a passion. Oh, dear," she said. "God, I'm so sorry."

"She's looking at the red Buddha again," Rightie said. "Not good, not good." He reached across the woman's head and clawed a hunk of meat out of Leftie's bristly jowl. Leftie hit back, launching them over the back of the white couch with Rightie kicking and scratching like a cat until they landed, scuffling, on the carpet behind it.

After a brief chat with her neighbor, Eve hung up the phone. The Bible verse left no doubt in her mind what she had to do. The neighbor would come in a minute to help lift the red abomination into the car.

A knock sounded on the door. Eve jumped off the couch a little too fast. She clutched her head, waiting for the pounding to subside.

She couldn't get that red statue out of her home soon enough. And to think she'd brought the thing into the house with her own child. How could she have been so foolish? But she hadn't known. *God forgive me.*

She peered out of the peephole and then swung the door open. "Hi, Mr. Martin. Thanks for coming. Sorry to have to bother you, but I was afraid I'd drop it on my toes or hurt my back. Let me get my keys. There's an empty box in the trunk."

"I don't mind at all, little lady. Is this it?" he said, turning toward the red marble statue. "Ain't that a beauty?"

Another pain shot through Eve's skull, and a white light flared behind her eyeballs. She winced and drew in a sharp breath. "Not so pretty if you get to know it," she mumbled, opening her purse and handing him the car keys.

In less than a minute, Mr. Martin had the statue shut up in the car's trunk. "That'll do it, young lady," he said, and brushed his hands together.

"Thank you so much. You're a mighty good neighbor." With her purse in hand, Eve locked the front door and climbed into the car. She started her engine and waved to Mr. Martin, who was already back in front of his own apartment. "Say hello to Mrs. Martin for me."

"You bet, honey. Take care!"

Could she make it to the meeting with this headache? Thank goodness Billy was at a friend's tonight. "Jesus," she whispered. She'd used His name several times since last night. Her foot pressed the brakes at the next red light, but pain blackened her vision. Was the light green yet? She couldn't tell. "Help me to see, Jesus. I have to see!" More than one angry car honked behind her. Of course, the light had to be green by now. She clutched the steering wheel as the vision slowly crept back into her eyes. She pushed the accelerator. Drivers stared hatefully as they passed. Several gestured, but she let it go. "So what? You have no idea. Go on around."

A vice-like tension gripped her head as she moved up Pine Street. Nausea burbled in her stomach.

"No, no, not now!" Thank goodness, Billy wasn't here.

Sometimes the headaches came on like this. All of a sudden. She fumbled behind the passenger seat for a plastic bag. There. Got it. Shaking the bag open she swerved into the right lane and then coasted up the slope into the Dairy Queen parking lot. Her foot hit the brakes as she leaned over the bag. Her stomach erupted.

Oh, God, please don't let this thing have a hole in it.

It was all she could do to get the vehicle in park. She fished around behind the seat again. Found a second bag to double with the first one, and some tissues.

She wiped her streaming tears. Tears not from crying, but from the strain of it all. She let out a sigh.

Oh gosh. Thank God for the lukewarm bottle of Aquafina

in the console. She rinsed her mouth and spat on the asphalt. *Sorry folks.* Hopefully, no one had noticed. Tossing a couple of Altoids into her mouth, she moved the car to the rear parking area. Just to pause and catch her breath. Maybe she'd be a little late, but nothing could stop her from going to that meeting tonight.

After checking her mirror to make sure no one could see her, she stepped out of the car and stuffed the disgusting trash into a receptacle. Preparedness had become her motto. There were plenty more bags behind that seat if she needed them. And more mints. And medicine. Hand sanitizer. Whatever she required.

But she *would* get to that meeting.

Eve backed out of the parking lot.

Two miles and a few minutes later, she parked on the street in front of The Rock. Doug and Sue had beat her there.

Doug greeted her as she popped open the trunk. "Need any help?" he said.

She smiled and gave him a thumbs-up instead of nodding. Anything to keep the headache from crushing her again. She pointed to the statue.

He grabbed hold, heaved the red statue over his shoulder, and hauled it around back where he dumped it into a rock-lined pit.

Eve slammed the trunk. "Wait a minute." She reached back in the car and detached her lucky rabbit foot from the rearview mirror. Doug came closer and she tossed it to him across the top of the car. "Throw that in there too. I'm done with these curses."

254

Leftie and Rightie, still scratching and clawing, chased the red Buddha into the pit. Rightie had to comment. "Now look. It's all your fault."

"No. You made me lose my grip on her."

"*Your* fault. *Your* fault. *Your* fault."

"No its *not!*" Leftie screamed. And the scratching, biting, and clawing continued down in the ashes. "I hate you," he said.

"I hate you more," the other said, and he clamped down, tearing out a hunk of leg with his teeth.

"And I hate you *more, more, more!*"

Chapter 41

"**M**om! Come in here and help me find the right things!" Tony stood in the middle of his room with a large paper bag opened beside him. In the bottom sat a Halloween mask.

Mom came to his door. "Okay, now look around. Think. What do you see that would be an idol or abomination? What hits you right off the bat?"

"I guess that weird group of games. I didn't like them anyway." He started grabbing titles off the shelf and pitching them in. Ejecting a disc from the computer, he examined the title then threw it in with the rest. "Zombies, living dead, and all that. Never should have bought these."

"What about those books up here? They've always bothered me."

Tony stared at the expensive leather bound books from Dad. Collectors' items. "Yeah. What do you think he'll say about it?"

Nancy walked out the door. "I'm not making that decision. You are."

"Thanks, Mom. You're a big help. I'm trying to turn over a new leaf, you know. I'm trying not to rile him up, okay?"

Mom stuck her head back in and gave him a frown. "I know."

He studied the titles. Witches, warlocks, and wizards. "Got a box?"

Tony set the last box on the table as his dad, dripping from a swim in the pool, stopped at the back door and dried himself. Dad took a long look at the dining room table through the half-open door. "What's all that in the box?"

"Just some books, Dad."

"Books I paid big money for? An arm and a leg for? What are you doin', getting rid of 'em?"

"Just—taking them somewhere, that's all."

"No, you're not. Put 'em back in the room. You wanna haul off some old clothes? Fine. But show some respect for what I've given you." Vinnie stepped back out cursing under his breath.

Mom came into the room. "Better put the books back. We'll take care of it some other way. Bring the other things though."

A Ouija board stuck out of the top of the bag. "Here, Mom," he said, lifting it out. "Why don't you carry this out, and I'll take the bag?"

Grabbing her purse, Mom locked the side door behind them. They threw the whole collection into the trunk and climbed in the car. As they backed out of the driveway, Tony caught a glimpse of Dad through the back gate. There he sat with his feet in the pool, pouring himself a glass of scotch.

"Stop. Wait a sec, Mom. I have something I need to do."

He leaped out and strode toward Dad. His last few steps faltered. How was he going to say this?

"Dad?"

Vinnie didn't look up. His voice was flat. "Whaddya want, Tony?"

Tony crossed his arms and shuffled his feet. He cleared his throat. "Dad, I love you."

No response.

Tony continued. "And I'm sorry for the way I've been to you."

Vinnie curled his fingers around the edge of the pool and nodded his head, still staring into the water. "I love you too, son. And I'm sorry too."

"Don't you want to go tonight?"

"No. Good-bye, son. I'll see you when you get back."

If Dad would just go listen to Rocky's words they could be a great family.

"Dad..."

Vinnie raised a hand for Tony to stop.

"See you when you get back, son."

Another time, then. Tony backed away.

"Bye, Dad. I do love you."

Chapter 42

Thursday, 6:55 PM

At The Rock Tony held Emily's hand and followed both their moms into the building. There sat Eldon by himself in the left back row again.

He caught the man's eye and Eldon nodded. Tony didn't return the nod, but blocked Emily from seeing him. Even if he was polite, the old geezer had stalked his girl friend. At least Tony could sit between the man's gaze and Emily.

Emily's mom headed for the front row on the far right. Good. They'd be as far away from old Eldon as possible. Emily would freak out if she saw the guy. Maybe after the service Eldon would clear out quick like last night. And Emily would never know he'd been there.

After that, if Tony saw him again, he'd give him a piece of his mind.

Thursday, 7:00 PM

For the second night in a row, Eve slipped into an empty front seat at The Rock, only this time they entered through the sunny back door along with Claire and some friends. Her heart raced. Why did she feel such a compulsion to be here tonight? It couldn't just be the idea of getting rid of the idols.

Despite the headaches and the episode on the way over, her heart felt light. Even before she'd read the verses, Eve hadn't felt this way since… since she was a kid.

Twisting backward, she spotted Claire and Ted, Doug and his girlfriend, all gravitating to their same seats in the back like last night. Tony and his girlfriend sat over to the right.

Consumed with dumping her Buddha statue in the pit outside and watching Doug beat it to pieces, she'd forgotten about their speaker until now. Where was Rocky?

A figure moved down the aisle, and she turned. It was Rocky. She inhaled sharply and whipped back around to face the front. She refused to stare at any man's good looks. But he'd certainly changed since the first time she saw him at the old folks' home. Her heart thrummed and she risked another peek. He strode to the front and sat down in his folding chair. The new stylish cut, expensive shoes and pants, the crisp shirt. He was hardly the same man, and even better than last night.

What was going on?

After the singing and the music, which were wonderful, Rocky reviewed his previous message on forgiveness. He invited his guests to dig deep and find if they had any roots of unforgiveness. He encouraged them to make God first in their lives and make Him Lord.

Eve shifted in her seat. What was wrong with her? Only half of the man's words were sinking in tonight.

This was ridiculous. She took a deep breath and willed herself to pay attention.

"Now, about your questions," Rocky said. "Before I answer them, I need to tell you a story." He set the violin down and leaned forward. "This is a true story, and if it hadn't happened, well, I'd likely be dead.

"Because of a horrible tragedy, a very good thing came to pass. But the good thing wouldn't have happened without the tragedy."

Tragedy leading to good? None of Eve's tragedies had ended well.

"Now I'm not smart enough to figure out all the angles on it," Rocky said. "But I do know that God loves each one of us, no matter how little or unimportant we appear to be in our own eyes or the world's eyes. And the people around us who seem to be the most evil and despicable—well, He loves them too."

Eve crossed her legs. She had to hear this. A handsome composed man like this couldn't have possibly suffered a tragedy. Sadness, sure. But not a tragedy.

The room grew silent as listeners focused in rapt attention.

Rocky paused and extended his legs out straight. "Please observe." He notched up both pants legs. The audience gasped. Metal rods extended from his shoes. The man had prosthetic legs.

The silence deepened. Rocky paused for a long minute before letting the pants drop back down into neat creases again.

Eve shuddered and squeezed her eyes shut against the red flashes inside her eyelids. Her brain spun dizzily. The memory that she'd wrapped in the fog of time and blocked out of her consciousness had rudely returned.

A roaring filled the space in her head.

But Rocky's next words shut it down.

"These legs are simply the evidence of a bad, bad accident."

The audience seemed to hold its breath.

Eve finally opened her wet eyes.

A sad smile lifted the side of Rocky's mouth as his eyes traveled from Doug, to Claire, then finally to her.

Wait. She wiped her eyes. *Why had he singled out the three of them?* Or had she imagined it?

261

To everyone else, *everyone* else, the looks he'd given to the three of them would seem random.

"It was a train vs. boy accident."

She gasped. Her heart flipped in her chest. Could it be? *No way.* She bit her lip and pressed her fingers against her mouth. No, she was stupid for even considering that.

She glanced over her shoulder at Claire and Doug. Doug was frowning in disbelief.

Robert couldn't have survived. Was Rocky a nickname for Robert? She turned and gazed into the man's face. Could it be *him?*

Rocky went on, "When the ambulance picked me up, my legs were in pieces."

A wave of dizziness worked its way through Eve's head.

Robert had died that day. He couldn't be alive.

She closed her eyes again.

"In the first hospital they called me a medical miracle."

"They pumped me full of other peoples' blood, then flew me to a university hospital. Days later, a farm accident took my parents. My family disappeared. But unlike Humpty Dumpty, the nurses and doctors put me back together, and the Catholic Church took me under its wing. Soon a child-less family adopted me. With the church's help, they made sure I had an education, music, and even two new legs. My new parents poured on me all of the things they would have given to their own children if they'd had them.

Eve's hand dropped across her lap. She stared at Rocky and his brown eyes. How could it not be him? The tips of her fingers tingled as if hot poison had finally drained out of them.

"So I learned the violin. Eventually the family moved to New York and dragged me right along with them. Through music lessons, they discovered a hidden talent in me, an anointing that only came from the Lord. One thing led to another, and after a time I found myself in the orchestra."

A pleased murmur fluttered through the crowd.

"Now, to make a long story short, I'm concert master of an international orchestra.

"Those music lessons that started as something to entertain a boy with no legs, ended up bringing me such great happiness. Now, like David in the Bible, I take my bow and strings and visit with God Himself, worship Him, and adore Him. And it gives pleasure to others."

A man in the back raised his hand. "You don't think any of this could have happened without the accident?"

"Not in a million years. I was a migrant farm kid with no future."

"But don't you blame God for all this pain you've endured?"

Rocky laughed. "God didn't cause this, but He was in control the whole time, turning something bad around and using it for good—giving us the science that provided me two nice legs.

He grinned and held up one palm. "Nobody suspected the fake legs. Right? And yes, it was painful." He shrugged and made a face. "I try not to think about that part."

Doug eased to his feet with Rocky's card in his hand. "Why the cards with the names?"

"My way of reuniting with three grown kids who witnessed the accident," Rocky said. "They needed closure."

Doug crumpled slowly into his seat. The realization had hit.

Rocky continued. "I had to share what God has done for me and let them know after all these years that I am all right. You see, years later, once I got over my howling self-pity and wondering why all this bad stuff had happened to me, I began to think of the other people at the scene. How it might have traumatized those three children.

"Did they think I had died? Were they okay? Were they messed up? I worried. And I'm glad to let them know I am all right. I think they are too."

Eve's cheeks ran hot with tears.

It was him.

Doug nodded, biting his lips, evaluating. "What about the low-life creep who did this to you?" A bitter tinge colored his voice.

"It took me years to forgive the boy. That's no lie."

"What about him, though?"

"I invited him tonight. He might be running scared. I tried to find a way to let him know that he was forgiven."

Doug shook his head. "Why would you even try to forgive him?"

"Think back to last night's teaching. Can I be forgiven if I don't forgive? Even science shows that unforgiveness is a deadly poison and leads to diseases of the soul and the body. It wasn't my job to hate. Not anymore. And when I let go, a weight dropped off my shoulders."

Doug looked down at his feet, still shaking his head.

Rocky continued, "I finally wrote him a letter. I told him he's forgiven. I've prayed hard for him and those three children who witnessed it. I don't know what else I could do for him."

Eve glanced at Tony. The boy had no clue about his father's past. Thank goodness none of them had ever told him. She eyed Claire again. Then Doug looked up and met both of their gazes. She would never tell Tony about Vinnie. Neither would they.

Eve stood up and moved toward Rocky. Her feet felt surreal, as if she were walking through a dream, and she could not stop herself. A sob burst out as she gripped Rocky's arm. "We thought you were dead!" was all she could whisper.

Claire and Doug crowded behind her. Robert stood as they wrapped him in a group hug, half crying half laughing. Eve glanced backward as the audience clustered around. The people had no idea.

After several minutes, Doug and Claire stepped back into the milling, chattering people.

Rocky turned to Eve as she sniffled and dabbed her cheeks with a tissue. "Eve, I hope I'm not out of line. But I want you to know that I have never forgotten anything about you through the years."

She blinked as she looked into those soft brown eyes. Hadn't forgotten? Lightheaded, she reached for the back of his chair.

He took her hands and steadied her. "There was one other important thing. A personal matter I couldn't mention in front of the whole group." His hands, strong and warm, enveloped hers.

The room swirled around her. Was this a dream?

"Eve, is it possible that I could... May I call you?"

She sucked in a ragged breath and then found her voice. "Y-yes. I would really like that."

After all these years?

Chapter 43

After the service Tony stood near Rocky at the fire pit in the back of the church. He held Emily's hand and stared down at the collection of crushed idols inside the low wall of stacked limerock: the shattered Buddha, the statue with all the arms, the masks, the head, someone's ripped apart Ouija board, and his own bag of stuff.

Emily, both their moms, Eve, Doug, Claire, Eldon, and several others gathered in the circle with them.

Doug gripped the sledgehammer which he'd used to smash the objects before the service and swung it a few more times, breaking the stones even further.

Emily tightened her grip on Tony's hand and gave it a jerk.

"Hmm?" he said, and glanced up. Emily had caught sight of Eldon and wanted to point him out.

"It's okay," Tony reassured her. "I'm here with you. He's not about to try anything. Ignore him for now. Here, stand on this side. He can't see you."

She switched sides but dug her fingers into his arm.

Eldon reached into his shirt and took out a half-empty whiskey bottle. Several in the crowd took a step back as he raised it up and pitched it into the pile of broken idols. It shattered, draining liquid over the mess.

Claire and a few others collected sticks and debris and tossed them over the mound as Ted poured on some lighter fluid.

"Let's pray," Rocky said. "Father, we come to You in

obedience, destroying those things that You hate. We declare that we love what You love and hate what You hate. You're a jealous God, and You'll have no other gods before You. Out of obedience and love for You we set these things ablaze in the name of Your only Son, Jesus, who saves us and loves us. Be Lord in our lives. We repent and make You first in our lives."

The demons cowered. A mighty angel—invisible to the humans, but so beautiful and bright the demons had to shield their eyes—raised his arm in their direction. "You are rejected. *Flee!* Flee to the pit! You've been ordered in the name of Jesus."

Wails of terror flew up as the demons backed away. They gnashed their teeth and screamed. Howls rose in a noisy cacophony, "*Nooo,* not back to hell. *Nooo.* Not there!"

"Go!"

Whump! Howl! With a swirling scream they were gone.

Tony focused his attention on Rocky as he fumbled around in his pocket and came out with a box of matches. Pulling one from the box, he struck it and threw it in. It ignited with a *whoosh,* and everyone stepped away.

The flames burned hot with the sound of beating sails. Tony wondered and frowned at the strange fire. It was black as melted coal. Nothing he'd ever seen could compare to it. The low flames rose like a dark lake and rippled with pale yellow crests. Gases that stank like rotting sardines and sulfur boiled up and rolled over the sides. A furious black smoke swirled from its center and rose rapidly through the tree limbs. Demonic moans burbled from under the heat and whistled up like screams from the smoke, finally disappearing as the smoke faded away. Tony held his breath as long as he could then turned away to catch a gulp of fresh air from behind him. Around him others did the same.

After several minutes, Rocky picked up his violin that he'd left over by the steps. The instant the man touched his bow against the strings, Tony shut his eyes and let the notes lift him away. The symphony filled his whole being as it curled up into the treetops, part of an invisible orchestra. How could that be? Tony squeezed his eyes shut. There was something else. Chords of angels hummed along with the notes. Tony breathed in the music, careful not to open his eyes, lest he destroy it.

Someone tapped him on the shoulder. Rocky. Tony frowned. How could Rocky play and be over here at the same time? Tony glanced around for the source of the music. Was it all in his mind?

"Did you bring that violin so I could bless it?"

Emily let go of his arm.

"I didn't forget." Tony said and stepped over to the car to bring it over.

He shook his head. The angel music had faded. But what had just happened?

Rocky, back near the fire pit, had waited for him. "Take it out so we can pray."

Tony set the case on the ground and lifted the instrument in front of him.

"I don't want you to drop it. Hold your violin against your heart and put your other hand on my violin."

Tony did as he said.

"That's it. This is not some formula, but I want you touching mine, because this is the way a man of God imparted a blessing to me in the beginning." Rocky placed his palm over Tony's hands. "Lord, I pray for this young man. Give him the same kind of anointing that You've given me. Give him the heart to do Your work. I bind this gift to him and I bind him to Your calling for him. Lead him and guide him every step of the way. Let him be jealous of this gift, to guard it and treasure it against an enemy that would want to use it for wrong. Use it only for Your glory. We speak a blessing over Tony and a blessing over this instrument in Jesus' name."

Tony swayed, suddenly dizzy. His knees had turned to jelly. "Whew. That—that was awesome," he said, stepping backward to regain his balance.

Rocky grinned and took his violin back. "That's just a little taste of God's power."

Tony placed his violin back in his case and began to shut the lid.

Rocky stopped him. "Wait. Not so quick."

"What?"

"Remember that day you came into the music store?"

"Right, you said you were there."

Emily came to stand at Tony's elbow.

"Yes, I was in and out that day. I saw your instrument. Mr. Tweedle asked me to evaluate it."

"What did you think?"

"It's a very nice instrument. Just fine. But did you ever read those papers?" There's something important in there.

"What papers?"

"One of them is a letter. It sounds like it's from your grandfather. You should read it."

Tony eyed the case. Emily and both mothers now crowded him.

"I've got to go." Rocky patted his pants pocket, "I have a 9:45 train to catch, so I need to get packed up, locked up, and put out those flames. Sorry to race away like this." He held out a card.

"If you need me, call me. I'll be happy to have you visit me in New York. Please come up. Anytime."

Tony tipped the card toward the streetlight and stared at it: New York International Symphony Orchestra, Robert Cavasos, concert master. *Wow.* "Thank you, Rocky. I... I don't know what to say." He glanced up. "I'll definitely be in touch with you. Wish you could stay."

"Duty calls."

"We want to thank you for everything," Mom said. "You've done so much good in this town."

Rocky shook hands with both mothers, Emily, and Tony, and backed away with a nod. "You take care now." He pointed a finger at Tony. "You probably haven't seen the last of me, Tony."

Tony grinned at Emily as they headed to their car out near the streetlight. "This calls for a celebration with ice cream."

Mom gave him a hug. "I can't wait to see what's in those papers."

Tony couldn't wait, either, but it had to be the right time and place, not out here in the street.

As Emily approached their car a voice called out. "Charlene, Emily." She turned at the familiar voice. It was the bearded man.

Mom grabbed Emily and pulled her behind her. Tony stepped in front of Emily.

"Eldon! What are you doing here? Are you stalking us? And what's this beard thing—this, this *get-up*?"

Emily's heart leaped. She stepped out from behind Mom. "Daddy?" How had she not recognized her own daddy?

"I'm sorry, Charlene." He glanced from Mom to Emily. "I... I wanted to know you were alright. Both of you. I've done some changing."

Mom was livid. "Go home. You have a whole lot more proving to do than—going to a church service. To *think!*" She pivoted with her hand on her forehead and then turned back to him. "And dressing in disguise?"

"It was the only way. I wanted to know you were okay. Know you were alright."

Emily flung her arms around him. "Daddy!"

He looked down at her. "Somebody must have been praying for me, Little Bit." She beamed as she met his smile and those crinkly eyes. Those same wonderful, kind, endearing eyes. Dad had never been one of those drunks who got angry and beat people. No, he'd always been the stupid, goofy drunk. The kind that might pet a growling dog or go fishing in a lightning storm. And no wonder he'd worn the sunglasses. Even with the beard she would have recognized those eyes.

"What happened to you, Daddy? Look at your face."

He touched his face, running his fingers along the bloody scratch stretching down his right cheek. "This? Ah, this— yeah. This is nothing."

"It's half your face. Don't we have some antibiotic in the car, Mom?"

"Let me tell you, Eldon," Mom interrupted. "I'll have to see a whole lot more out of you than this little one-time charade."

Mom had been hurt, Emily knew. And kids never seemed to know the half of it. But she wanted to believe her daddy.

"You'll see, honey, you'll see," he said to Mom. "I'm new at this, but I'm another man, now. A man with a nice job. I'm even going to AA. And I still love you. But. I'm leaving now. I'm not going to pester you." Dad gave Emily a big squeeze before turning away. He held Emily at arm's length and gave her a wink. "There's always hope, Little Bit. Always hope." He blew Mom a kiss and walked away into the dark.

Her mom looked over at Tony's mom. "I'm going to beg off our little get together if you don't mind. I think I need to go on home." She turned to Emily, still irritated. "What do you want to do?"

Before Emily could answer Tony stepped in. "We can bring her home if that's okay."

"By 11:00, please. Nancy, I'm sorry. I'm very frazzled right now. I'll see you all later." She flounced toward her car, flung it open and jumped in. The engine revved. Emily watched until her taillights disappeared.

Emily, unable to deal with the mixture of embarrassment, happiness, and disappointment at Mom's negative reaction, dropped her arms. She let out a big sigh. "Wow, sorry, y'all." Her voice cracked.

Tony wrapped an arm around her. "So. Your dad didn't run off and leave you after all, did he now?"

Tony. Always the encourager.

Tears surged up in her eyes as he wrapped his other arm around her. She leaned into his shoulder and bawled. "It's okay, Emily. It's okay. We all understand." He patted her back until she calmed down, then walked her to the car where they climbed in. Tony's mom handed back a box of tissues.

"I need to think," she said as Tony closed the door. And he gave her space without talking.

What had Dad said—*I'm new at this?* Maybe the baby in the diapers symbolized Dad being a baby Christian.

And there were other things. "Tony, remember what Dad said about AA?"

He nodded.

"You think it was an AA meeting behind that unmarked door?"

He nodded again. "That would explain the grumpy man's reaction."

Something else tickled the back of her brain, the African woman's words. *"You must speak to de devil, I bind you up, you spirit of alcohol. You spirit of unforgiveness. I bind you up in de name of Jesus. You have de authority."* Only it had come out like *ou-tor-itee.*

Emily had forgotten all about the unforgiveness part. But now she understood. She needed to pray for her Mom, too. Mom could at least give Dad a chance. He certainly had cleaned up.

The belt!

Lord, I'm sorry. Forgive me. You were listening all along. And you were answering. I just didn't understand.

Emily gave Tony's hand a squeeze. As soon as she got home—and spent a little time with her new dog—what was she going to name that little sweetie?—she'd go upstairs and dig that belt out of the trash. Then she'd get back to praying better. Enough of that wimpy *bless Daddy* kind of praying.

Chapter 44

Vinnie fingered the unopened envelope under his left thigh. His Scotch, diluted, sat untouched beside him as he stared down into the pool's blue water. The sounds of Nancy's car leaving and the electric gate still echoed in his ears from two hours ago. Now only the noise of the Thursday night traffic broke the stillness on the other side of his hedges.

If only he could ignore the letter and make it go away.

But things didn't work like that.

He had to read the letter. Figure out who was pulling his chain. That kid died under that train. No one could come along and say things were okay. No one. Someone was playing a mean game. And it had to be Dougie, Pony Tail, or Freckles.

Or all three.

They'd teamed up. Decided to fight him back. Send him to prison.

He hadn't wanted to do it this way, but now he'd have to get tough with them.

He pulled the letter out and slid his finger under the flap.

"Dear Vinnie," the first line said. Right. He rested the paper on his leg. If he could just make this go away. He picked it up with a groan and read some more.

"It's taken me many years to be able to say this. I do forgive you for the train accident so long ago. What you did to me was wrong."

"To *me*? That migrant kid couldn't have written this. He was dead."

The letter went on. "But you were just a kid, and I know in my heart that you didn't mean for it to get out of hand."

Vinnie laid the paper on his leg again. Okay, forget it. Forget it. Vinnie wasn't responsible for this dumb kid's train accident. The boy had stuck his *own* leg under the train, right? One of those three trailer park kids wrote this. Not that migrant kid.

What a joke. The kid had *not* survived.

He was dead. *Dead!*

Vinnie picked up the letter.

"Things got out of control for you, I know. Please understand. The accident is not important anymore. God took a bad thing and turned it into something good. My life as I know it would never have happened otherwise."

He wadded the paper and crushed it under his hand against the concrete. It was all he could do not to throw it in the pool. This was the sickest gag anybody'd ever pulled on him. He closed his eyes and roared into the sky, unaware of anything more than the cool water around his feet and the black sky above. If he could only make this nightmare disappear.

He squeezed the ball of paper and picked it back up. Maybe he ought to read it all. Unwadding it, he flattened and smoothed it against his leg.

He took a deep breath and lowered his eyes to its words.

"I do forgive you, and God can forgive you and help you start over. Would you like to have a clean start, a clean heart, and be forgiven? I would love to pray with you and tell you how this has all worked out for the best in my life. Then you will see that I am sincere. I'll contact you soon, Robert Cavasos."

No, you fool. Vinnie shook his head. *I'm not an idiot. Whoever you are I know what you're up to. You'll pretend you wanna talk then you'll pull out a gun. Or you'll turn me in to the police. I'll end up dead, or in prison. Forget it.*

Enough of this. Vinnie balled up the paper again and lifted his arm to aim it across the pool at the gargoyle. He'd walk around and pop it in the trash behind the bar when he got up.

In the shadows behind the gargoyle, a single branch quivered.

Vinnie froze and squinted his eyes. Then *Pap! Pap!* and his world went black.

Chapter 45

Thursday, 9:15 PM

Esposito balanced his half-burned cigarette on the black iron rail of the fence. His mood matched the black night around him. He reached for the gun in his interior holster. Screwed on the suppressor. Anyone glimpsing his dark-colored janitor suit and broom would think nothing of it. He leaned the broom on a post and set the five-gallon bucket down on the concrete. The words *City of Gaskille* marked its side. His get-up was clever, to say the least. Esposito squatted as if picking up trash. He was well-hidden by Vinnie's low-hanging bushes. He raised the gun between the iron bars of the fence and pointed it at Vinnie.

Vinnie, on the opposite side of the pool, dangled his feet in the water. Reflections of the underwater lighting fluttered over him as he grumbled out loud and read some kind of paper. He wadded it up. Then he changed his mind and flattened it on his knee to read again. Couldn't seem to make up his stupid mind.

He steadied his hand and sighted down the barrel at Vinnie. Esposito moved his lips silently. "You're not takin' advantage of me, Vinnie boy. Who do you think you are, taking my statue and hiding out behind these bushes? And I don't need to think twice about this deal tonight."

Esposito cut his eyes to where his diesel truck purred by the curb a half block away. His shapely young wife waited inside. He sighted down the barrel and settled his finger on the smooth trigger. Age hadn't drained away his manhood. Virile was the word. *Virile*. She'd see.

Across the pool Vinnie wadded the paper again. His arm lifted as if he would throw it toward Esposito. Wow, what a great shot.

He pulled back the trigger. *Pap! Pap!* The gun kicked. Vinnie dropped backward. His head thumped on the deck like a ripe melon. Perfect. But was he dead? Esposito stared at Vinnie's chest to discern a rise or fall. He couldn't tell a thing from here. Probably dead.

"Adios, Vinnie," he whispered. "We won't be missing you."

Esposito set the gun behind the bucket and reached inside his jumper for the rope. He pushed his arm as far as he could through the bushes and tossed his lasso. After four or five tries it landed around the gargoyle's black wing. Well, it wasn't the head, but close enough. He pulled. The dang thing didn't budge. He yanked again. cursed. *Nada.* Now what?

All he needed was to knock the image off its base. He jerked a little harder.

Yes! The statue tumbled. It crashed into the foliage with a whoosh and a thump. Branches snapped like toothpicks. It slammed against the concrete, the head inches from his knees. Right where he needed it. Lucky day, *amigo*.

Esposito placed the barrel against the ugly head, closed his eyes, and shot. *Pap! Pap! Pap!* Music to his ears. The figure shattered into a dozen rocky pieces. Esposito brushed its powder from his face and slipped on his rubber gloves. With his small flashlight in one hand he reached through the iron bars again, and raked through the debris. All he needed was the two red eyes. Bingo. He dropped the first one in his pocket. Where was the other one? His fingertips strained

278

to reach a likely chunk two feet away. He caught hold and flipped it over. Covering his eyes with his forearm, he blasted the rock apart. There it was, the second eye. He snickered as he plunked it into his pocket with the other. Stupid Vinnie. He had no idea about the rubies. The dummy sure liked the cheap concrete sculpture though, didn't he? Even thought it was marble.

Esposito reached up for his cigarette. He placed it in his mouth and took a long drag as he stood and coiled the rope then stuffed it in his jumper. He flicked the butt to the dirt and ground it in. With a wide smile he slipped the hot gun into his bucket and headed back to the truck. No one would ever know about their little deal gone bad.

Upstairs Lusmila leaned forward in her low, stuffed chair and closed her Bible. Maybe she would go to bed early tonight and say a few extra prayers. The poor family had so many problems. Little Tony finding out about his adoption. Mr. Vinnie and that letter that troubled him so. What could be in it?

So strange about that. The young man who left the letter seemed so nice, so polite. There was nothing scary or mean about him. Yet Mr. Vinnie had gone totally *loco* after that.

Maybe Mr. Vinnie was going *loco* for real.

Lusmila turned out the lamp and glanced toward the open window of her third floor room. The lights in the pool blazed so bright they reflected off her ceiling. Perhaps she should sew some curtains. Sleep would be hard tonight with all that brilliance.

Leaning toward the window, she gazed across the pool.

Her eyes narrowed. Could it really be? The black statue lay on the ground, busted in pieces. Uh-oh, Mr. Vinnie was not going to like that.

The sound of a diesel engine roared away from the street below.

Her eyes drifted to the near side of the pool. She clapped her hand over her mouth. Mr. Vinnie lay flat on his back. "Mr. Vinnie!" she screamed. "*Dios mio, dios mio.*"

She flung open the door and flew down the two flights of stairs. "Oh, Jesus mio, no," she moaned all the way down.

She jerked open the French doors, nearly tripping over Teresita. Teresita yelped and followed. Lusmila sank to her knees beside Vinnie.

Vinnie lay pale against the concrete. Blood pumped steadily from a black hole in his chest. "Mr. Vinnie," Lusmila wailed. She whispered now, inches from his face. "Please, please, you can't die."

Vinnie turned his wide eyes her way. "Help me, Lusmila," he whispered.

She gathered his shoulder and head and glanced down at his chest. "Anything, Mr. Vinnie."

The blood still bubbled from his chest. His voice gurgled. "I don't want to go to hell."

"You're a good man, Mr. Vinnie. So good to me. So good."

"No." His voice strained. His eyes grew wider, more exaggerated. "No. A killer. Help me. Don't let me go to hell, Lusmila."

She wrinkled her brow and stared into his eyes. She had to talk fast. "Pray, then. Pray Jesus save me. Jesus forgive me. That's how you do it."

"Jesus. Forgive. Me." The words left his lips, and his head rolled to the side.

Crack! The angel brought his gleaming sword down. It cut between the man and his demons. "Out! No more rights! *Flee!*" He commanded.

And with a mighty noise the demons darted like black bats into the sky—away from Vinnie's body.

Lusmila leaned across the dark puddle, sobbing—and clutching him to her chest. "Mr. Vinnie, Mr. Vinnie!"

Lusmila gripped the kitchen phone as if it still connected her to Miss Nancy. She waited in the dark. Numb. The noise of the 9-1-1 vehicles grew louder. Miss Nancy had called them.

Always, Miss Nancy knew what to do.

Help was coming. She glanced down at her white dress. Mr. Vinnie's blood was smeared across it. Poor Mr. Vinnie. After all these times she had tried to tell him about Jesus and faith and a beautiful life. But he had shooed her away. And here at the last minute…

Out by the pool, Mr. Vinnie lay like a child, alone. Asleep on the concrete. Beside him, lay the wadded letter. Like a ball it teetered on the edge of the pool. The letter. Did she dare look at it? It would certainly help her understand his trouble. She could give it to the police. To Miss Nancy. Explain how Mr. Vinnie was acting.

Why had the young man's letter bothered Mr. Vinnie so? Lusmila had to know.

Now or never, she had to save the letter from falling into the pool. Miss Nancy would be here any second.

281

Maybe Lusmila was wrong to do this, but she cared for Mr. Vinnie. She did care. He had done so much for her.

She might get arrested for touching it, but she had to read it. She stepped across the textured marble floor. The one Mr. Vinnie insisted she keep up with. He took good care of his things, he did. She stared at his body in front of her. From three feet away, he looked as if he could wake up and speak. She froze. Her voice trembled. "Mr. Vinnie, Mr. Vinnie." Maybe he was alive. There was no response.

He was dead, of course. But so alive, just minutes ago. How could it be, one minute here, and one minute gone? Head above the water, head below the water. One minute here. Next minute with Jesus. Like the thief on the cross, Mr. Vinnie's last words counted. What if he hadn't prayed? She shuddered. What if she hadn't been home? What if she hadn't seen him out the window? A sob burst from her lips.

The whole thing was more than she could comprehend. In one swift move, she reached for the paper. Yes, it was part of a crime scene, like on TV shows. but Lusmila didn't care now, she had to read it. Then she would put it back where she found it. But what about fingerprints? On TV they said fingerprints stay on papers.

She would tell them what she had done. Admit the truth. That she had read it.

Opening the paper, she flattened it against her thigh.

"Dear Vinnie..." The handwriting, very much like her ex-husband's—the one who had run off with her sister and died—appeared to be a man's.

She read the first line. "It's taken me many years to be able to say this. I do forgive you for the train accident so long ago."

Lusmila frowned. Her own son had died in a train accident.

"What you did to me was wrong. But you were just a kid, and I know in my heart that you didn't mean for it to get out of hand.

"I did nearly die. But you did not kill me. You have to know that, and I am sorry to wait this long to tell you. But I had to deal with my own unforgiveness first."

Lusmila could read no more. Who wrote this? What had Vinnie done to need forgiveness? Lusmila turned the letter over. "I would like to visit you and explain how my life has been blessed because of this accident. Sincerely, Robert Cavasos."

She gasped. Her heart leaped to her throat. Robert Cavasos? Her son? The one who had died? This could not be true. Her son alive? Surely, many people shared that name. But a train accident, too? Too many coincidences.

Her legs weakened. Folded. She sank to the floor and read the letter again. Rocking back and forth, she pressed its words against her heart. Was the man at the door her Robert?

How could she not know him, her own son? She had to find him.

Chapter 46

Thursday, 9:30 PM

At the ice cream shop Tony dragged out the opening of his violin case just to tease everyone.

Emily's feet danced up and down under the table. "Tony! How could you be so mean? You're killing us with suspense!"

"Just give me a minute, guys." He scooped the last drops of melted ice cream into his mouth and wiped his lips.

His mother and Emily had long-since finished. "Ah, that was so good. Thanks, Mom." He looked around at everyone's face. "What?"

"Tony, quit torturing us!" Emily squealed.

Mom drummed her fingers. "Come on, son."

"Okay." He lifted the case onto the table and unsnapped the latches. Actually, he was dying to see what it held, but petrified at the same time. The papers lay just inside, under the instrument. Very gently, he lifted the violin so he could pull them out.

Just then, Mom's cell phone rang. "I'll get this. Go ahead, Tony. I'm watching."

Emily's eyes bored into him. "Come on, Tony, please."

Time to get serious, now. "You know, I hardly even noticed these at first. All I remember is shoving them aside that first night to get the bow out. He held the papers. "What could be so...?" He unfolded the first one.

"No!" Mom lurched forward with the phone against her ear. Her other hand shook over her mouth. "No!"

Tony stared at her.

Mom's eyes filled with tears. "A shooting? Vinnie? At our house? Are you sure? Hang up. I need to call 9-1-1 right now."

Tony threw the papers back in the case and snapped it shut as Mom, choking and sobbing, dialed. He grabbed Mom's purse and fished out her keys. "Get her out to the car, Emily. I'll drive."

What could have happened? It would only take five minutes to get to the house.

Chapter 47

At The Rock, it only took Robert a couple of minutes to toss his belongings together. It took another 10 to fold and stack the rest of the chairs. Behind The Rock he tossed a few shovels full of sand over the smoking fire-pit. It was only five or six blocks to the train station, and he could make it by 9:45 with no worries.

Tossing the backpack over his shoulder, he lifted the violin, turned the lock on the door, and made his way around the side of the house. He slipped the key onto its secret nail under the floorboard and said a quick blessing for the man who kept the place up.

He spoke to God as he walked away. "If only Vinnie had come to one of the meetings. If he'd only let me in the house, or read my letter." It was too much to think about. The whole trip had boiled down to the three kids getting saved. And that was worth so much. But the main person he'd worried about, the main one he'd fasted for, the one he'd walked the sidewalks and prayed for, had rejected it.

Maybe there'd be another time. Maybe he could try again. *I'm sorry, Lord. I know I let You down, but I don't know what else I could have done.*

He stepped through the muggy air along Tuscawilla Pond and made fast progress toward the train station. The loud bleeping of the frogs pierced the air, but he tuned it out.

He rounded the corner by Timucuan Feed Store. *Uh-oh.* Lights ahead. Blue ones. Up there by Vinnie's house. It had to be the police. He picked up his pace. Jogged. "Lord, please, don't let it be bad. Don't let it be Vinnie."

His feet drew him closer. Closer. The blue lights were definitely coming from Vinnie's place.

Outside of Vinnie's iron fence he pulled to a stop. He extended his arm through the hedges for a better view. "God, no, please. No." He shook his head at the police tape, CRIME SCENE, DO NOT CROSS. On the opposite side, a forensics van sat with its back doors hanging open. After such a good week, why had it come to this? Beside the bright aqua waters of Vinnie's well-lit pool a woman talked to the detective. It might even be the lady he had talked to at Vinnie's door. The maid, maybe. A nervous little dog wandered back and forth around her feet.

The covered body lay on the ground. He swallowed hard. "Father, how could this happen?" He sighed and stepped away. With this bad event, the family would certainly be needing all they'd gotten from his two meetings.

Not far away the train's horn blared several times—long, loud, and multi-toned, insistent. The rumble of Robert's Amtrak approached the Gaskille station. He turned his back on the crime scene. Time to go. The next blast of the train's horn filled the quiet street around him. "God, what have I done? Forgive me. Forgive me. I've messed everything up." Nearby the train whistle sounded. It wouldn't stay at the station for long. He took long strides, replaying the scene in his head. His lungs sucked in a ragged breath. And then he could almost hear the words, "You did your part, my son."

He picked up his step. Jogged again. Black shadows lay across the sidewalk, contrasting sharply with the yellow-gold cast by the street lamps above.

Once again he took out the card Eve had handed him. He read her number and then pressed it against his palm, carving it into his memory, like he'd engraved her name on that orange tree so long ago. It would stick forever.

Reaching the platform, he pulled the list of names from his pocket again. Turning his back to the train's windows for privacy, he sniffed back his tears, wiped his nose on his sleeve, and pulled out a pencil. The penciled checkmarks were there by each name, Dougie, Freckles, Pony Tail. That was all good. But there wasn't one by Vinnie's name. With trembling fingers, he tried to cross out Vinnie's name, but the pencil was not dark enough. "I'm sorry, Father. I don't know what else I could have done." Taking a seat on the bench, he laid the paper on the hard wood where he could cross the name off. But sorrow thundered between his ears, and he lowered his head. A sob escaped his throat. His shoulders heaved. "I'm so, so sorry, Father, I failed. Forgive me."

After a minute he lifted his head and wiped his face. He glanced at the clock that dangled between the roof joists as passengers walked around his bench to board the train. A couple scowled at him, most likely for his apparent drunken state. But he didn't care.

Just a few minutes to go.

Robert needed to get control of himself.

He stood. Walking away from Tony's family felt wrong. But his ticket said 9:45 and here was the train. Time to go.

Two steps to the train's door.

He placed his foot on the step. It would be a long ride to New York, and he'd have plenty of time to pray for the family. They would certainly need it.

Chapter 48

Tony swerved the car into his backyard and slammed on the brakes behind the line of police cars. A gaping Medical Examiner's van was parked beyond the pool. He turned off the key and shoved open the car door. Mom had been in no shape to drive, and the way his hands and knees shook, Tony hardy felt up to it either.

Dad *couldn't* be shot.

Tony's feet hit the ground with Mom and Emily stumbling and tripping along behind him through the flashing blue lights.

Dad's body lay under a sheet right where Tony had left him sitting beside the pool a few hours ago. Crime scene tape and a cop with his arm stretched out brought them to a halt. Tony gaped at the surreal scene.

It seemed like minutes ago Dad had been alive, right there. Breathing. Talking. He couldn't be gone.

Prevented from crossing the line, Mom and Emily clung to Tony's arms and sobbed. The officer stepped up and told them all how very sorry he was at the family's loss. He explained what the police had found. They had no suspects yet.

Tony wiped tears against his shoulders.

Beside the pool on the other side of the tape, Lusmila gestured as she talked with a policeman. She turned and Tony gasped. Dark blood covered her skirt. Dad's blood.

She gestured toward her window then the hedges. Nearby,

Teresita circled then flopped down on the concrete and rested her chin on Vinnie's body.

One of the officers bent over, picked up the dog, and brought her over to the small group. Tony took the trembling dog and freed her inside the house where she'd probably wet on the floor and whine herself into a tizzy.

After the questions an officer walked a weeping Lusmila over to them.

She pulled a wadded paper out of her pocket and handed it to Nancy. "It's what Mr. Vinnie was looking at when he…" A sob burst through her lips.

Mom took the paper, and Lusmila grabbed her arm.

"Please read it."

Mom stared at the paper without reading it. She seemed to be in a daze.

"What am I going to do, Miss Nancy? Tell me how am I going to find my son."

What was she talking about? All three of them stared at Lusmila.

Her eyes grew wide. "Don't you understand? My son Robert is alive!"

"What son?" Mom said.

Lusmila covered her face and hung her head. "Oh, Dios mio, I have to explain."

Tony guided her to a chaise while the others dragged chairs close. "What's going on?" he said.

Lusmila had never acted like this. And she certainly had no children. The stress must be confusing her.

"First, I am Amalia. Not Lusmila."

Everyone looked at everyone else.

"Go on," Tony said as three pairs of eyes returned to Lusmila.

"It's all so long ago. My husband, he take up with my sister, Lusmila."

Tony stole a peek at Mom, whose frown revealed her own shock and confusion. This seemed to be news to her.

"Lusmila and I, we look alike. So I say Lusmila can keep him if he want to be unfaithful. If that is who he is, he is no good. She can have him. So I take her job as a waitress. She can go sleep in the fields with him."

Lusmila raised her hands as if in disbelief. "Why would my sister trade a life like that for a life in the fields? For so long I hate my husband for doing this to me."

She leaned against the arm of the chair. "So I keep my sister's identity. I am now Lusmila. A better life for me, for sure. Nobody know the difference."

"The next day, my husband he going to a new farm and he die in a migrant bus crash. My sister die too. Both gone. My husband, my sister. Others. Dead. What can I do? I cannot tell the truth. They send me back to the old country. I refuse to work in the fields again. I have to pretend, and pretend, and pretend, forever."

"So you have a son?"

"I hide him. Keep him home. Nobody going to take him away. But the next day, my son die in a bad accident. Under a train."

"What happened?" Emily asked.

"Here I am, Lusmila now. All alone."

"Lusmila, Amalia," said Nancy, touching her arm. "We never knew. I'm so sorry."

"I so tired of pretending. One day, many years later, Mr. Vinnie come to the bar. He hire me to work here, at the house. He is a good man. He save me from that place. He say

291

he remember me from the camp by the trailer park. He the only one who know who I really am. He don't say nothing. He just help me." She broke down and wept into her hands.

Nancy closed her eyes and blew out a deep breath.

Lusmila wiped her face. "Read it. Please, Miss Nancy. Help me find my son. He is still alive."

Tony stared at Mom. It would be a huge coincidence if what he was thinking was correct. "Read it, Mom."

Emily and Tony gathered behind Mom to read the letter over her shoulder. When she turned the letter over, Tony's eyes darted to the signature. No way!

"Quick, Mom, tell her."

A train's horn blew in the distance. The Amtrak was on the way.

"Lusmila. Your son! He's on the way to catch that train."

Lusmila stumbled out of the chaise and clambered toward the steps to the back door. The quickest way to the station was through the house and out the front door.

Chapter 49

Thursday, 9:45 PM

Robert's foot touched the bottom step of the train. "*¡Roberto! ¡Hijo mío!*" Twenty yards behind him, from the direction in which he'd just come, a woman's voice called out. Before he could turn to see who it was, the voice called out again, only closer.

With his hand on the edge of the door, he twisted around.

The maid from Tony's, breathless and disheveled, stumbled toward the platform. This didn't make any sense. Chasing Robert down couldn't help Tony's family.

Poor frantic thing. Truth was, hysteria could make people a little nuts.

He waved good-bye to her and continued up the steps. He could do nothing to help her.

The pitch of her cries reached a desperate wail as she crossed the platform.

He turned again to find her hands stretched up to him. Imploring. "*¡Roberto! ¡Mijo!* Stop, please."

He gave her a kind smile and waved again. If he could bring Vinnie back to life for her, he would. But it was too late.

"Come off the train. Please. I'm your mother!"

His mother? A mudslide broke loose inside Robert's head, his heart.

Impossible. *Mamá* had died.

In a migrant bus accident. Like the nuns told him.

The train groaned and lurched. Robert's knees buckled

momentarily, along with the loud metallic clank. "Sir," the porter said, with his hand around Robert's bicep. "Sir, you need to get on the train. On or off. We can't wait."

Robert stayed where he was. "But, ma'am. You can't be her. My mother's gone."

The porter tugged at Robert's arm. "Safety, sir. Time to move."

"*¡Roberto!*" the woman wailed between sobs as he moved away. She stepped along with the departing train. A pole stood in her way, and she sidestepped around it. Tears bathed her face. "Don't you know me? *Soy Amalia. ¡Soy Amalia, tu mamá!*"

Robert's eyes widened.

There was no mistaking his little mother's face now.

"*¿Amalia? ¿Mamá?*" He tossed his backpack onto the platform. Then, holding the doorway, he stepped off the moving train. Unable to stand, he dropped and rolled. The violin remained in his arms. He winced as his prosthetic hardware clattered over the concrete, missing the train's wheels by inches. The porter, his mouth agape, leaned out of the doorway and stared. Shocked passengers pressed their faces against the window glass and gawked at the prosthetic legs sticking out from under Robert's pants.

Robert tried to sit up, but Amalia knelt, cradled his head, and plastered her kisses over his cheeks and forehead.

He wrapped his arms around his mama and buried his face in the soft crook of her neck.

"*¡Mamá, mamá!* I thought you were dead!"

How could she be alive after all these years? If he'd only known.

He hugged her tighter. "*¡Mamá! Mamá!*"

Chapter 50

Thursday, 10:00 PM

Tony stared at the lit-up insides of the Medical Examiner's truck where Dad's body lay under the sheet. Workers prepared to close its doors and exit the gate. Tony couldn't take his eyes off the scene. In a minute the truck would dip and turn into the street, and Dad would disappear. Forever. To a morgue. Or a funeral home. Tony could only imagine what cold, sterile place Dad would spend his night. Tony wiped his eyes. There would be no cozy bed or favorite pajamas.

It hardly seemed real, but this day had changed his entire world.

Tony slammed the palm of his hand against the iron gate post. If only he'd been here, Dad might still be alive. Tony might have seen it coming, might have noticed a suspicious character, might have given Dad a warning. Or scared the shooter away.

And Lusmila. She'd seen nothing.

Over by the pool she stood with Robert, of all people her son, explaining things to whoever would or could listen. Like him, they were probably all in a daze.

Numb, he returned to the group and stood beside them. His eyes felt swollen, and burned from all the tears.

Lusmila, blowing her nose into a lace handkerchief, clung to Robert's arm, half crying, half laughing. Tony stared at them. He'd sort things out later. For now he just had to get a grip on what happened to Dad.

Thank goodness he'd told Dad he loved him. And Dad had said the same. Thank goodness. It helped so much to know that.

Tony scraped more tears out of his eyes.

On the inside and outside of the fenced area, the forensics team, in their white rubber gloves, continued their search and bagging of evidence around the broken statue. A photographer snapped pictures of their little numbered markers. An investigator scribbled notes on a clipboard as he questioned Mom.

Eventually, he pocketed his pen, gave Mom his condolences again, and stepped away.

Tony met her halfway and wrapped his arm around her. He guided her to a chair with her back to the crime scene. "I know you're exhausted. It's all so unreal."

She unrolled a wadded tissue from her palm and dabbed it against her red nose. "I'm so sorry, son, about your dad. I can't believe he's gone. Just gone. I can't wrap my head around that." She bowed her head.

Lusmila let go of her son's arm. "Just a minute, *mijo.*" She reached for Mom's arm. "Miss Nancy. I forget to tell you. Mr. Vinnie have some last words."

Mom gave her a bleary-eyed, worn-out stare. "What?"

Lusmila grabbed Mom's hands. "Miss Nancy. Listen to me."

Mom took one hand away and wiped her eyes again.

"He say, 'Jesus forgive me.'"

Robert stepped closer, listening.

Mom frowned. "I don't…"

"He say, 'Jesus forgive me.' He say it before he die."

Tony gasped. Dad was saved? What a shock.

Mom doubled over and started bawling again. Tony knelt beside her and wrapped his arm around her shoulders. What a sad but great day.

Emily clutched his Mom's hand.

Finally, Mom sat up. She pulled herself together. Then she reached for Tony's face. "The letter. Please. I want to hear your letter, honey. We've done everything else tonight but hear about you and whatever secret is inside that violin case."

Emily stood and headed toward the driveway. "It's still in the car. I'll get it."

Robert reached over with the bloody, scraped up hand he'd acquired at the train station and patted Tony's shoulder. "Tony, I want you to know, I wasn't trying to pry when I read your papers. I thought they might have something to do with the maker or history of your instrument."

"Don't worry about that. But I've been meaning to ask you about that day at Tweedle's. Aren't you the "orchestra connection," the one who fixed the violin? Gave it that tune-up? Mr. Tweedle said he needed some help."

"The same day you followed me down the back alley."

"No way. You knew?"

Robert smiled. "I know a lot of things. Just because my limbs are missing doesn't mean I don't have two eyes and a working brain. Does it?"

"The strings you donated. Those were sixty bucks a set in the catalogue. Thank you."

"Mr. Tweedle had none. And I had spares."

Tony offered his hand. "That's very generous. Thank you."

Emily returned with Tony's violin case and laid it on the chaise. She popped it open."

Tony dug the letter out from under the instrument and held it out with trembling hands. "Look at me shaking like an idiot." He thrust the paper toward Emily. "I can't. You do it."

"Really? Me read it? I'd be glad to." She took it from him

and cleared her throat, a serious expression sweeping her face. She dropped the note to her side. "I'm not sure I can, either," she said, her voice cracking.

"Come on now," Tony said.

Emily adjusted her shoulders. "Okay. Here goes, then. Dear Grandson, your grandmother and I are getting older now. But we want to make sure you get this instrument. With you being the older of the…" Emily's mouth dropped open, "*twins?*" A smile crept over her lips. "I felt you should have this one."

Tony took the letter. "You're kidding. Give me that."

He read it silently. Slowly. Read it again.

Emily studied the letter over his shoulder then summarized for the others. "He saved the money for a long time, and finally found this 'fine Italian instrument in Europe' when he was 60."

Emily offered the paper to Mom then jumped up and down, clapping. She grabbed Tony by the shoulders. "Tony, you're a twin! You're a twin!"

Then she slapped her hand over her mouth with a horrified expression. "Oh, I'm so sorry, Miss Nancy. I'm so embarrassed. I don't even know how to act right now. I'm so sorry."

"It's okay, Emily." Nancy stood and wrapped Tony in a bear hug. "This is so exciting, son."

Emily latched on to them both. "A twin, Tony, a twin! Oh, my gosh, two of you!" she said. "I can't believe you're a twin!"

Lusmila raised her hands in the air, and walked around in a circle. "*¡Qué día de milagros! ¡Dios mío, Dios mío! ¡O, Jesús!* I just can't take any more."

Robert smiled and pulled her close. He pressed his lips against her hair. Tears glimmered on his face.

Dizzy, Tony shook his head, trying to absorb it all. Now he'd have a whole bunch more questions.

Rocky patted his shoulder. "Congratulations, Tony."

"So I'm a twin? A *twin?*"

Just then the urgent voice of a female EMT yelled out from the back of the forensics van. "Medic! Medic! We've got a *heartbeat* in here! This man's *alive!*"

Epilogue

Emily's mom stood over the stove in the kitchen. The coffee pot percolated beside the sink. Emily had just finished her bowl of cereal.

"Come on, Mom. Please. Say yes. After all we've been through."

Mom raised an eyebrow and flipped over the eggs in her skillet. She placed her hands on her hips and looked square at Emily.

"Lower your voice, young lady." She turned back to the pan. "And stop bringing it up."

Emily's cell phone vibrated in her hand. *Tony.* Her boyfriend. She'd have to call him back in a minute. She pushed her cereal bowl away. "It's just this one time, Mom. Let Dad come over. He can sit on the swing. You don't even need to come outside."

"Emily!" Mom renewed her glare.

"Like Grandma said, Dad's my family, even if you *are* divorced."

Mom turned off the stove and pointed the spatula at Emily. "Grandma doesn't know everything. You remember that."

Emily clutched her head and rolled her eyes. Mom was so unforgiving. Couldn't she understand?

Mom said nothing.

Emily lowered her hands. "Grandma's right most of the time."

Mom arched an eyebrow.

"You never listen to her."

"Never listen to who?" Grandma appeared in the doorway with a half-open newspaper. She yawned.

Mom ignored Grandma. "He's a drunk, Emily. A no good stinking drunk. We will not encourage him to come visit."

"I'm not asking you to entertain him," Emily yelled. "But people can change. And I want to see him."

Grandma crossed to the sink where she poured herself a cup of coffee. She unrolled her newspaper and glanced at the headlines.

"Oh, y'all are going to be love *this*. Listen to this. *Vinnie Vinetti's Shooter Caught.*" She studied the article. "They've arrested a Mr. Esposito and his wife, for the attempted murder of Tony's father. Says clear evidence, the footprints, the shell casings and the cigarette butt DNA all led to him."

"We've got to call Tony," Emily said.

"I'm sure he already knows, honey," Grandma mumbled as she read a little further. "But there's more than just that one thing about Esposito and his wife. They've got them for money laundering, illegal importing of gems, and so on and so forth. I'll have to read the whole article, but that's the gist of it." She shut the paper and poured some cream into her coffee.

"Well, they won't be bothering the good citizens of Gaskille for a while, I guess," Mom said.

Emily waited a beat before getting back to her and Mom's conversation. She didn't intend to let that drop. "Tell her, Grandma. Tell her about Dad, how I should be able to see my own father."

"I'm staying out of this."

Mom scooped the egg onto her plate and snatched it up. "He couldn't change while we were married. So why would you think he's really changed now? It's a waste of time." Mom thunked her plate onto the table.

"Stop yelling, Mom."

"You're setting yourself up for disappointment. Whether Grandma Rene agrees or not."

Grandma turned. "I haven't even expressed my opinion."

"Don't talk back to me." Mom paused and turned to Grandma. "Not you, Mother. Emily."

"I'm not asking you to go outside or visit with him. You don't even have to speak."

"Emily! Didn't you hear a word I said? We're not going through this again."

Emily thumped her spoon on the table. "I'm only asking for you to let him visit. Please?"

Grandma finally spoke. "A visit? Could it hurt? It's just a visit."

"Come on, Mom," Emily pleaded. "Dad won't bother you. We'll just talk outside."

"He'll think I'm still interested, Emily. And I'm not. I don't want him coming around."

"He's *my* dad. Don't you think I have the right to see him?" Emily stood and threw her wadded napkin in the trash. "Think how I feel, Mom. For once." She marched out of the room and left Grandma staring at Mom and Mom staring at the table.

"All right. All right." Mom's voice followed Emily through the dining room. "But not today. And not right away. All I'm saying is I'll think about it."

Emily smiled and pushed open the screen door. She headed for the porch swing to return Tony's call.

Out by the pool Tony placed his phone on top of the bar.

He didn't want to miss Emily's call as he scooped up another dustpan of broken concrete.

Tony, after several days at the hospital with Dad, he'd finally gotten around to sweeping up the mess by the pool. What a disaster. Mom was still up at the hospital with Dad. He sure missed Lusmila, off in New York with her son Robert. But she deserved time with him.

He glanced over at the seven garbage bags of stuff. Packed light of course to keep from tearing the bags.

The broom trembled in his hands. A debate raged in his mind. Should he tell Emily about the phone call just now? It would probably scare her. Should he tell Mom? She had enough on her mind.

He sure couldn't tell Dad.

It was Dad's caller again. This time he'd heard the guy for himself. Right there on the answering machine.

"I heard about your little accident. That wasn't me. And I'm still comin' after ya."

About the Author

Jennifer Odom, 2003 Teacher of the Year, is a 40-year veteran teacher of elementary education. She has taught kindergarten through fifth grades in all subjects. For the last ten years she has incorporated video-production for her magnet school students at Dr. N.H. Jones Elementary, leading them to win many local, state and international video awards, as well as those in writing, and technology.

Jennifer writes human interest stories for her local newspaper, *The Ocala Star Banner*, and has also been published in such national magazines as *Splickety* and *Clubhouse Jr.* In 2015 she was honored to be named the Florida Christian Writers Conference's Writer of the Year.

Her award-winning Young Adult series, Black, began with *Summer on the Black Suwannee* and continues with *Stranger with a Black Case.*

Connect with Jennifer online at:

www.jenniferodom.com

Also Available From

WORDCRAFTS PRESS

Believe
  by Abby Rosser

Furious
  by Aaron Shaver

Tears of Min Brock
  by J.E. Lowder

The Awakening of Leeowyn Blake
  by Mary Garner

You've Got It, Baby!
  By Mike Carmichael

www.WordCrafts.net

Made in the USA
Columbia, SC
14 November 2021

48801475R00188